A
Holiday Romance
in
Ferry Lane Market

by
Nicola May

First published in the UK in 2023 by Nowell Publishing
Copyright © Nicola May 2023
Print Edition

Cover design by Ifan Bates
Cover illustration by John Meech

British Library Cataloguing in Publication Data
A catalogue record for this book is available from the British
Library

ISBN: 978-0-9568323-9-9

The quieter you become, the more you are able to hear.
RUMI

Prologue

Sabrina Swift violently ripped off her diamond-encrusted satin veil and threw it on to the four-poster bed of the smart Soho Farmhouse cabin.

'And here endeth the fucking fairytale.'

'Do you have to be so bloody dramatic?'

'Dramatic! You shagged someone half your age and she's turned up on *our* wedding day... all the way from Paris, might I add, to share this life changing mic drop, with not only me but all of *our* wedding guests. So yes, I think on this occasion, I do, Dominic.'

'It was a stupid mistake, a one-night stand.'

'Just the once. That's alright, then.' Sabrina laughed coldly. 'Let's get those vows done and dusted, sing hosanna and run off into the sunset together, then, shall we?'

'It honestly meant nothing to me.' The man's face twitched.

'Well, it clearly meant something to Little Miss Frenchie downstairs, didn't it.' Sabrina's face, a mixture of anger and hurt contorted as the tears started to fall. 'The only blessing in this mess is that I hadn't yet said "I do".' She dragged her Vuitton suitcase up on to the bed and started to haphazardly fill it with anything in sight.

Dominic's voice took on an edge of panic. 'Sabrina, please. I love you. We can work this out. There's too much between us to throw it all away.'

'Well, you should have thought of that before you pulled your cheating dick out of your trousers, shouldn't you.' She slammed the case shut. 'Now, please get out of my way. I'm leaving.'

'Shall I meet you back at home?'

Sabrina shook her head in disbelief. 'You are something else.'

'But where are you going?'

Sabrina blew out a long breath of despair. 'I don't know yet – but what I do know is that I need some time away from everything and everyone to think.'

Chapter One

Sabrina Swift yanked *The Newlyweds* label off the welcome pack, cast it to the floor and twisted at it viciously with the heel of her Louis Vuitton boot as if stubbing out a cigarette. As the lights in the old Cornish cottage flickered wildly, the brunette looked up at the ceiling with a pained expression. 'Don't you flipping dare go off. Not now it's dark. Please, no!'

Arm held aloft and waving her phone around in the air, she made her way to the bathroom and stood shakily on the toilet seat. With her right hand almost touching the bathroom skylight, the familiar dialing tone gave way to the even more familiar Essex twang of her oldest friend and confidante, Delilah Dickinson. Sabrina breathed out a huge sigh of relief.

'Dee, thank God! The signal here is SO shite.'

A careworn voice greeted her relieved one. 'Rini, you do realise it's midnight, don't you?'

But Sabrina hadn't called to listen. 'I told him *The Scarlet* might be a better option, but no, he had to go all Bear bloody Grylls on me and book off grid.'

'Darling, wait until it's light. You've had a long drive. And from the photos you showed me before you went, it looks like a stunning location.' Dee was whispering now. 'Give me a sec, I don't want to wake Stu.'

As Dee crept out of her cosy bed and on to the

landing, Sabrina's sorrowful diatribe was unrelenting. 'I'm stood in the smallest bathroom in history, on an effing toilet seat, reaching up as far as I can for signal, in the middle of effing nowhere. There is no coffee machine. No full-length mirror. And the TV isn't even a smart one.' Sabrina let out an exaggerated breath. 'I could be raped, pillaged, or worse still, murdered, and nobody would even know.'

Dee yawned. 'Anyone would think you were an actress, the way you're going on.'

'Ha bloody ha.'

'I hate to say it, Rini, but it was you who made the final decision to escape to the depths of Cornwall, for this...this... noneymoon. And to be frank, the mood you're in, I think even the most determined of intruders would run a mile.'

'Noneymoon? You're such a smart arse!'

'Well, that makes up for the TV then.'

Sabrina managed to laugh.

'Get some sleep, sweetheart,' Dee soothed. 'And in the morning, I'm sure you'll feel and think differently.'

'You reckon?'

'I know.'

'I love you, Dee.'

'I love you, too, mate.'

'It will be OK, won't it?'

'Your life, or not having a full-length mirror?'

'I hate you.' Sabrina shook her arm to relieve the numbness.

'Make your mind up.' Dee chuckled. 'And if you're still alive in the morning, call me.'

Chapter Two

S abrina awoke with a start to a light tapping at the cottage door. She had been so exhausted from the drive and her own dramatics that, to her amazement, she had dropped straight off to sleep. In fact, she had slept so soundly that she felt like she had to prise open each eye with a finger and even when she had managed that, it took her a good minute to jiggle her brain to fathom exactly where she was and where the noise was coming from. Sitting up and sneaking a peek between the duck-egg-blue shutter slats, she could see a willowy blonde woman patiently waiting for her to answer, a wicker trug basket in hand.

A swearing Sabrina put on her best fake smile, waved, and hurriedly pulled on the jeans and jumper she had worn for the six-hour drive down from London.

'Hey.' Sabrina opened the door, sounding as lack-lustre as she felt. However, with her hair dragged into a messy bun and huge Gucci sunglasses hiding half of her face, she could certainly pass as a woman who should have just consummated her honeymoon.

'Hey, I'm Belle. Welcome to Kevrinek Cottage.' The blonde smiled warmly. Her shoulder-length hair was naturally light, Sabrina noticed. Plaited neatly each side. Her lips rosebud and untouched. Her complexion pale. Her blue eyes as soulful as her demeanour. Her cut-off jeans and plain t-shirt effortlessly worn. She was one of those women, Sabrina thought, who really didn't realise just how beautiful she was and whose skin was so perfect that she was very difficult to age. 'And huge Congratulations!' Belle enthused to an awkward smile from the new house guest.

Sabrina found the young woman's Cornish accent endearing. It was also refreshing to be chatting to somebody who clearly didn't know her business, despite it having being splashed all over the newspapers and socials for the past week and the main reason that she had wanted to run away. To escape the embarrassment. To recentre herself from the madness that had ensued and that no doubt was continuing to do so.

'You rented this place off us – well off Isaac, really. My partner. The cottage is on his land, you see. I didn't want to knock too early since it is your honeymoon and everything, but we both wanted to see you have got everything you need. He rarely has guests staying here, so there must have been a special reason you made the grade.' Belle's smile lit up her face. 'I'm not really used to this hospitality business, to be honest.'

Feeling like she didn't have the energy or inclination to ask why they were the chosen ones or explain that she had just been jilted at the altar for a French Stick, a quiet 'Oh,' was all Sabrina could manage.

Then, as if on spectacular cue to save her embarrassment, a brown-and-white sheepdog came running up to the front door and barked at them both.

'Aw, there you are.' Belle rubbed her hands through the friendly hound's ears.

'Meet Beethoven, our beloved deaf-as-a-post sheepdog.'

Sabrina perked up. 'A deaf sheepdog? that's funny.'

'Yes, Isaac informs me that they communicate via their own form of BCL.'

Sabrina frowned, puzzled. 'I thought it was British SIGN language.'

The pretty blonde let out an infectious giggle. 'It is. But they use British CANINE Language instead.' She tittered again. 'They sure broke the mould with my fiancé.'

Sabrina thought for a fleeting moment that maybe now *would* be the ideal time to confess that there was no mould breaking, just heart breaking where her own ex-fiancé was concerned, but then Belle held out the basket for her to take, and the moment passed. Instead, she did her best to appear interested in the contents.

'This is great.'

'Fresh milk in there.' The soft Cornish accent conveyed. Plus, there's artisan bread, eggs, butter and local honey. There's also coffee and tea in the cupboard above the sink, so help yourself.'

'Sounds amazing, thank you.'

Belle rubbed her nose. 'Hmm. What else did Isaac remind me to say. Oh, yes. If you do want to venture out, Penrigan is only a couple of miles back down the main drive and over the cliffs. It's signposted and really is a stunning walk if you fancy some fresh air.' She noticed Sabrina's grey Audi convertible parked to the side of the cottage. 'Or you can drive it, of course, in ten minutes. There's a Co-op for supplies and – err – and a pier and beach there, it's genuinely nice. Ooh, and of course you have the estuary town of Hartmouth around a twenty-minute drive from here, forty minutes on the bus, where you will find Ferry Lane Market. It's so quaint and quirky there – definitely worth a visit.'

'Perfect.' Sabrina was now itching to get back inside and hide away from civilisation again.

'We always keep the gate up to the estate locked. We have access to open it 24/7, though, so do come and go as you please. You just have to press the buzzer to get in, just like you did last night.'

'OK, thank you.'

Belle pointed to the basket. 'There's plenty in there for the pair of you, when your husband wakes up.' Belle continued. 'Lovebirds and the fresh Cornish sea air, enough to knock anyone out.' Sabrina noticed the woman's cheeks redden slightly. 'I really am so sorry if I disturbed you.'

At the mention of lovebirds Sabrina felt herself dying inside. 'Not at all. Right, well it's lovely to meet you, Belle and, umm, thanks for all this. I didn't realise breakfast was included.'

'Oh, it's not, but I knew that you had arrived late and there's no fresh stuff in the welcome pack.'

'I appreciate it... We appreciate it.'

Belle gently squeezed Sabrina's arm and smiled warmly.

'My number is on the back of the welcome pack label, so please do message me if you need anything. *Anything* at all. Oh, I don't think we have your name. Just your husband's.'

Sabrina took a deep breath.

Jilly 'Erm. Jilly. My name's Jilly.'

Back inside, Sabrina filled and flicked on the kettle. Then, noticing the sun streaming through the many windows, she opened the back door to let some fresh air through the old cottage. She switched on the television and listened to the south-west weather presenter stating that after a chilly start to September, it was at last going to be a beautiful day, with highs of nineteen degrees and a light westerly wind. She made herself a cup of instant coffee, slathered real butter and honey on to a thick slice of white bread, then sat at the weathered pine kitchen table and realised what she had just done without thought. Not only had she lied through her teeth, but she was also ready to uncharac-teristically shove into her mouth a huge portion of carbohydrates and fat.

Her usual morning routine, in the luxury Blooms-bury apartment she had shared with Dominic Best, her wayward fiancé for the past two years, was to grab an Espresso from their all-singing, all-dancing coffee machine. Eat a small bowl of porridge with half a banana and chai seeds. Then dash out of the door to work.

She'd had a big storyline going on the past few months so had been in the TV studio five days a week, usually from eight in the morning, sometimes not getting home until after seven at night. Not ideal with a wedding to plan, and very draining as she'd had to channel her inner villain every day, but she had managed. Just like she'd managed all her life, growing up as a sister to a brother with a brain injury, a depressed mother and a workaholic father. She would be hungry by mid-morning so would have one of those yoghurts that were so small they would be lucky to feed a grasshopper. Lunch would be some kind of salad grabbed from the studio catering van and either a no-carb dinner or just a few vodka and slimline tonics. She put her hand to her now rumbling stomach and began to eat hungrily.

Maintaining a size ten at five-foot-seven wasn't easy. And now that she was only a year and a bit away from the big four-oh, she felt like she had to be on a permanent diet. But the feeling of slipping on a hired Alexander McQueen frock to walk down the red carpet at the Soap Awards and being featured on every woman's magazine cover the next day had been worth it, for her. For the most part.

It had never been easy for her, especially living with newspaper editor Dominic Best, who despite being slightly overweight himself and ten years older than her, felt it was his 'job' to keep her trim. So even if he found the smallest squidge of a muffin top, he would squeeze it and say something like, 'Ignore this pathetic, woke "let's all pretend we're happy being fat and embrace each other" business. Hollywood still wants bread sticks, not baguettes, and that's a fact."

Thinking on it now, Sabrina wondered why on earth she hadn't dumped him the first time he had dared to squidge. But the game of love had already commenced – and pretty swiftly, at that. The pawns had been played. The blindness had set in. The charismatic Dominic Best overrode all her sense or sensibility with his intelligence, wit, chat and charm. She'd also loved the fact that he edited one of the top newspapers in the country. His status turned her on. He was as famous as she was in his own right. Probably more so. They were, in fact, quite the power couple.

But it turned out it wasn't just Hollywood that was fickle. A twenty-one-year-old French stick going by the name of Françoise Bardot had served him champagne in a corporate box during an international rugby match at the Stade de France. Her errant fiancé had generous-ly given the young waitress two tips. Just the one in Euros though, *merci beaucoup*!

But what he hadn't bargained for, during this sor-did pre-marital bonk, was the girl dramatically travelling over from Paris on their wedding day. And during the speak now or forever hold your peace bit, daring to spill her guts and naively confess her undying love for him. Thank God they had turned down the

Heya Magazine offer for their nuptials, settling – oh, how ironically – for a day of calm and privacy with close friends and family instead.

Her wedding day had been like one of the Hollywood movies that Sabrina had forever aspired to star in, playing out right in front of her eyes. But this time she was the star clown, for it had been far more of *meet puke* than a *meet cute*, and a scene that not even with the most enthusiastic begs for forgiveness from her cheating fiancé, could ever be turned into a happy ending.

But despite the man's pathetic pleas of woe, Sabrina Swift was not for turning. Mademoiselle Baddy could forever hold Monsieur Pest's penis and they could both fuck off down the Seine without a paddle as far as she was concerned.

Taking another glug of strong coffee, Sabrina groaned. Just thinking about her long-awaited wedding day made her feel slightly sick. The gleeful look from Dom's grown-up daughter, Mercedes; the glance of sadness from her father, who she knew wanted to say *I told you so*, but never ever would. Her disabled brother, Simon shouting "Cunt" and throwing a shoe at the French stick and just missing her head. The ever-faithful Dee and her husband Stu, scooping her up in her tailor-made mauve Vivienne Westwood-inspired gown and driving her straight back to their place in Chigwell. Where they allowed her to rant and sob and drink vodka until she fell asleep, then carried her to the spare room still in her wedding dress. And where she had awoken to Thea, eight, and Phoebe, twelve, asleep either side of her. Oh, how Sabrina loved those girls. And how they loved their Auntie Rini back.

'Wanker!' she said aloud, turning off the television and shoving in another huge bite of the soft white bread and tasty heather-infused honey. She ate it smacking her mouth wide open on purpose because she could. And because she wanted to.

Taking another glug of her coffee, Sabrina sat back in the old, spindled pine chair and took in her surroundings. Yes, the holiday cottage may be basic, but it was charming and homely. Rustic, some might say. Huge grey flagstones lined the kitchen/living area, at one end of which a deep brick fireplace encased a log burner. A deep sheepskin rug lay in front of the fire, just asking for a dog or cat to contentedly lie there snoozing. The thick stone walls were painted white inside and out. Every window boasted old-fashioned shutters in a duck-egg blue.

Facing the fireplace was a slouchy, faded red two-seater sofa with three plain white cushions sporting a tiny butterfly motif in each corner. The hand-carved pine table with four chairs sat in the kitchen area, where units with wooden worktops housed an electric aga and a deep Belfast sink. A small fridge freezer stood alongside a small yellow dustbin. On the hand-carved wooden mantlepiece above the fireplace, a dragonfly-embossed vase was home to freshly picked wildflowers. And above it hung a beautiful painting of a rainbow over a sparkling estuary with a ferry boat making its merry way to shore. She could make out the artist's name, *Glanna*, in swirly paint at the base of the picture.

Feeling a sudden urge to explore her surroundings – and, more importantly, seek out some more signal hot spots – Sabrina drained her cup, put her phone in her jeans pocket and made her way from the kitchen down the short hall, the walls of which were covered in gorgeous coastal inspired prints. Most of them, she noticed, included dolphins. To the back of the cottage, passing her now messy bedroom on the left and the functional bathroom on the right, was the open stable door, also painted duck-egg blue.

On stepping through it and at last taking in her surroundings, she gasped loudly. It was as if she had walked through the wardrobe into the magical world of Narnia!

So full of her own sorrow at the front door earlier she hadn't even heard the crash of waves, the sound of gulls or even imagined the beauty that had been surrounding her. For stretching out in front of her, wasn't a back garden, more like a heaven on earth. The few images that Dominic had shared with her when booking the place had been undoubtedly stunning, but it was a more breath-taking vista than she could ever have imagined.

In the distance to the right and down a hill, she noticed a fort-like, granite-built farmhouse with a high-ceilinged glass extension and outbuildings. In front of her, luscious green fields rolled down towards a cliff's edge, the drop of which must have been at least thirty metres. And beyond, the autumn sunshine touched the huge expanse of blue-green water, causing millions of shimmering sparkles to skim across its surface. Throngs of seabirds were soaking up the rays and bobbing on the tiny bumps of waves forming as they splashed on the rocks. Sabrina felt surrounded by Mother Nature at her beautiful best. Even the distant horizon was currently free of any boats. It was so quiet up here that literally all she could hear was the heavenly sound of birds singing, rustling leaves and the distant motion of the sea. She tilted her head to the sky. This was all she needed to give her the clarity and confirmation that her decision to get out of noisy, smelly London had been the right one. To realise that this place *was* the perfect escape. That this place *was* paradise. And that this place was to be her home for the next couple of weeks.

Forgetting her hair was styled *à la* bird's nest and that she was wearing yesterday's knickers and no bra, Sabrina began wandering towards the cliff top. It brought back a happy memory of playing Catherine Earnshaw in a theatre production of Wuthering Heights.

It wasn't until she was nearing the edge that she was jolted from her mindfulness by the sound of a series of texts all coming through in one go. She was reaching for her phone when she was startled by a sudden creak from a branch of a tree swaying and rustling in the light morning breeze. As she drew closer to the edge of the old oak's impressive roots, she could make out a wooden cross with an engraved plaque in the dappled shade. A bunch of sweet peas sat in a metal jug in front of it, moving gently with the light coastal breeze.

She walked towards the makeshift grave and, putting her hand to her chest, read aloud: '*Lizzie & Sweet P, a girl and her horse, together forever.*'

Another memory flew to the front of her mind. She had loved riding as a child. But her brother's accident had put paid to that, with her mother forbidding her to do anything that might be dangerous thereafter. The anxiety that had been instilled in her then had travelled with her through her life – with regards to horse riding at least. Feeling sad at this sombre discovery and a sudden nostalgia for her childhood, the unclouded vision of both her brother and mother pre-accident caused tears to sting her periwinkle blue eyes: Simon with his beautiful clever mind and her forthright, opinionated but fiercely loving mother without the crippling depression she had suffered ever since.

Checking first to see if the ground was dry, Sabrina sat down with her legs out in front of her, sighed deeply and set about the task of seeing who had messaged her. A text from her dad simply stated, *You know where I am, love* with a red heart. She put the handset on speaker to allow a voicemail to kick in. On hearing the deep, sexy voice of silver-fox Dominic Best, she omitted a little sound between a laugh and a cry. *Darling, it's me. Out of anyone I know, you must know that whatever you're reading about us in the papers and online… about… her…and me… well, it's not true. Where are you? I'm missing you. I told you I'm sorry. I know I've been a fool. I love you. Come home.*

'Don't even go there, you twat!' Sabrina shouted out, the pain of just hearing his voice searing through her heart and right out of her back, like a rusty cupid's arrow. And what exactly was in the papers? Why were people so happy to read of other people's misfortune, especially if those people happened to be successful? She didn't dare Google anything, would rather not know. The less she knew, the less there was to torture herself with. Dominic had told her himself that there was rarely smoke without fire and if the pictures desk had a photo, the newspaper usually had it on the front page.

Sabrina said 'Fuck' as the next message clicked in. *Rini, please ring me. I know the signal is shite there so I'm not worrying, but I am your best friend and have a right to know if something has happened to you. Hmm, but I guess if you have been murdered, you won't be able to. If the worst has happened, I'd like your Stella McCartney swimsuit, please; it will fit over one breast, at least. CALL ME, you tart!* Sabrina laughed.

She was just about to dial her mate's number when the words 'Caroline Smart' flashed up on the screen. Blowing out a huge breath and screwing up her face in readiness for the tornado that was to follow, she answered.

'Sabrina Swift, where the *hell* are you?' the Mancunian accent bellowed.

'Hi, how nice to hear your voice. How are you? Isn't that how most agents address their clients?'

The woman carried on without taking one single breath. 'Not the ones who've gone AWOL with big career decisions to make, no. And don't be smart with me, Sabrina. I've had the producer from *Prancing on Ice* hounding to see if you are still considering the gig, because if you are, I must give them an answer by Friday latest. Training starts in November and the money they're offering you is massive.'

'As is the risk of breaking every bone in my body.'

'You'll be insured.'

'Oh great. I'm more interested in fixing my broken heart, to be honest. If you hadn't noticed, I was due to get married last week.'

Caroline softened momentarily. 'Look, I'm sorry for what happened. But you just don't know what it's like from my end.' Sabrina could hear Caroline nearly sucking the end out of her vape. 'The pressure is immense. Can't you just forgive him? It was just a shag, after all.'

'Bloody hell, Caroline. Just because you don't set one single boundary where women are concerned, doesn't mean I'm the same with men. I'm going.'

'No, no, I'm sorry, Sabrina, I'm just frustrated at

you and *for* you.'

'OK, so give me a little respect. I'm going through one of the most difficult personal weeks of my life. I've not only been publicly jilted, but my huge storyline has also just ended. I'm theoretically in prison until February and have no idea if the biggest soap in the UK wants me back.'

'Just calm down. It'll be OK. I'm working on that. And to be fair, you wanted this break.'

But Sabrina was now in full rant. 'Yes, I did. I needed this time off for my honeymoon and a little sabbatical, so you shouldn't be ringing me anyway as I would have been on holiday and not answering my phone!' She blew out a noisy breath. 'And as for *Prancing on Ice*, I really don't think I can do it.' Tears started to stream down the actress's face.

'What do you mean, you don't think you can do it?'

'I can barely stand on my own two feet at the moment, let alone throw myself around on fricking ice in front of a pitying audience.'

'But you just said yourself we haven't even got the guarantee of a new contract yet. And with you being all over the socials, I can probably get you another twenty grand, at least. You're a hot topic, lady.'

Sabrina attempted to level herself by taking in the calming motion of the twinkling sea yonder. 'I don't give a shit about the money. My own sanity is what I'm trying to keep hold of that moment. And what is every small-minded twat saying, Caroline? Just tell me because I don't want to look.'

'You mean you haven't seen anything?'

'It seems one can only get signal here at one o'clock on a February 29th, so clearly not.'

'Where are you, anyway? Is that seagulls I can hear?' Another long drag on the vape.

'It doesn't matter where I am. And I know you're

going to tell me what's being said, so just hit me.'

'It's nothing that bad. There are a few photos of him in Paris with *her*, though.'

'Well, I guess that was inevitable. The French stick clearly was out for his money and five minutes of fame when she pitched up at *Soho Farmhouse*.'

'I'm sorry Sab, but they are saying he was with her just two days ago, too.'

'Oh.' Sabrina felt her whole face crumpling. Her voice began to crack. 'Look, let me think about prancing about on bloody ice. I can't deal with anything now. It's too much. Everything is too much. I'll call you next week.'

Caroline's voice softened. 'I'm sorry I was so hard on you. I'm worried about you. You know what I'm like. When the empathy gene was being handed out, it skipped me and went straight to Mother Theresa.'

Through her anguish, Sabrina mirrored her agent's familiar mantra: 'And who wants a soft agent anyway.'

'You've got it, girlfriend! Catch up soon, and wherever you are, try and find some peace. He was too fucking old and fat for you anyway.'

Chapter Three

Standing up clumsily from the grassy slope, Sabrina wiped her eyes with her sleeve, brushed her jeans down and, deep in thought, started to make her way back up to Kevrinek Cottage. Caroline Smart was usually right, but her acerbic delivery was never easy to swallow. Maybe, Sabrina thought, the fact that her feisty agent was so like her mother was the reason she had put up with her for so long.

Despite a stiffening breeze, the sun still shone brightly. But neither the glorious day nor the sound of sea birds and happy children playing on the beach far below could lift her mood. Sabrina sighed heavily. Her life had been turned on its head through one sheer moment of madness from her duplicitous ex. It seemed unfathomable that only a brief time ago, the pair of them were getting excited about coming here together, as a couple. As Mr and Mrs Dominic Best.

How could he have been SO stupid? He really had ruined everything. Now she would have to completely rethink her future. Marriage had seemed like the obvious and perfect next step for her. The security she had needed, her chance to step off the fickle carousal of showbiz for a moment, whilst she took stock of what she really wanted to do. Fortunately, children had never been on her wish list and with Dom already having a daughter from his first marriage and with no desire to carry on the Best name, there had been no pressure on her in that regard. But she was getting older, Hollywood hadn't called and unlike others who wanted to just keep going in the same old soap, the thought of that brought her out in hives. The pair of them had discussed her running an acting school when she got older, but the capital required to set one up in London was hefty and she wasn't sure if she was prepared to risk all her savings on something like that – especially now she wouldn't have the back up of a wealthy and well-connected husband.

It wasn't until Sabrina approached the cottage and saw the back door swinging in the breeze that she realised what she'd done. 'Shit,' she said aloud. If she'd been in London, she would have religiously set the alarm and double locked every time. It was fine, she convinced herself as she picked up the pace. She was in the middle of nowhere here, and the cottage lay within the locked gates of Kevrinek that had to be opened electronically by the owners. Belle had even made a point of saying how safe it was.

Then she heard a dog barking from inside the property, and she realised that maybe that wasn't the case after all. She froze at the stable door. A second later, she let out a sudden, blood-curdling scream. Walking towards her down the hallway was a six-foot-six hunk of a man, sporting a mop of tangled mahogany curly hair, a matching unkempt beard, and the hugest hands she had ever seen in her life.

She turned to run but his soft voice stopped her. 'Jilly, I take it? I don't believe you were born in a barn, so please don't treat my cottage like one.'

Her heart was beating at one hundred miles an hour, but on sudden realisation that this man had just called her Jilly and at the familiar sight of the deaf sheepdog at his side, she nearly fainted with relief.

'I'm assuming you must be Isaac,' Sabrina stuttered. The friendly hound began to sniff around her legs.

'You got that right, at least.' The giant of a man smiled warmly.

'I'm so sorry. I...err. I wasn't thinking straight earlier. I should have locked up, and...' She suddenly remembered what a complete fright she must look, with her unkept hair dragged up in a bun, swollen eyes, and a coffee stain down her cream cashmere sweater. Her breath could probably sink a battleship from ten paces, too. If she'd been in London, she wouldn't have even considered putting the bins out without first putting on a full face of makeup and false lashes. 'I'm so sorry, I look such a mess.' She began patting her hair down and folded her arms across her chest to hide her braless nipples.

The giant of a man sat down on the ornate wrought-iron bench that rested against the back of the cottage wall. 'Here.' He signalled for her to join him. Beethoven flopped down underneath, panting heavily.

'I'm not concerned about what you look like, Jilly. Whether you're standing in front of me in a shell suit or your birthday suit, it's the bit between those ears of yours that matters to me.' He huffed. 'Belle tells me about all this looks-obsessed behaviour these days. I don't even own a mobile phone. Drives everybody mad, but I don't care. We used to manage, so why can't we now?'

Sabrina's jaw dropped. 'No phone? Oh my god. That's crazy.'

'Is it?'

Sabrina's bottom lip suddenly wobbled. After feeling a fleeting peace on the cliffside, she really wasn't ready for an odd confrontation of this sort.

Isaac's expression softened.

'Listen to me. I had a right old rant going on there,

didn't I? I'm sorry. I'm a private man, see. I rarely let this place out to strangers, and it made me angry you weren't respecting it, it set me off, that's all.'

'It won't happen again, I promise.' She felt tears welling up like acid raindrops. In a bid to hide them, Sabrina leant down to stroke Beethoven's redundant silky ears.'

'Be your own kind of beautiful, Jilly.'

She replied quietly. 'What a wonderful thing to say.'

'It's the age-old adage: if you don't love yourself, who the bugger's gonna love you back? But sadly, through time I've realised that's true of many people.'

Sabrina stood up. 'You've got some decent lines there Isaac, I'll give you that. And who says I don't love myself?'

The man remained silent.

Sabrina cocked her head to the side and took in the stranger. He was slightly eccentric and maybe a bit patronising with his bold assumptions. But despite knowing him for a matter of moments, she had also picked up on a kind and intriguing energy from him, which was weirdly captivating.

He was the opposite of her Dominic, who was brash and showy for most of the time, only revealing his softer side when they were alone at home, without a constant audience. The side of him she had fallen in love with. The bear hugs when she was tired or stressed from work. The flowers that would be delivered to the studio if she was having a particularly bad time. And despite him finding it difficult to spend time with her ailing brother, he had got together a team from his office to run the London Marathon a couple of years previously where all monies raised were for Headway, the brain injury charity.

Isaac shrugged. 'It was more the principle of you leaving the cottage open. We're remote up here on

Penrigan Head and there was an incident before.'

Sabrina's eye widened. 'What kind of incident?'

'Nothing to worry about now. I've fenced us in as far as I can. Aside from someone trying to get in from the public footpath along the cliffs, that is. But I have cameras around you see. Not inside the cottage might I add – I'm a purveyor of peace, not a pervert.' Sabrina managed a smile as he pointed to a small device above the back door. 'As I said, I like to keep myself and my grounds as private as can possibly be. I saw you head out earlier and leave the door open, so I just came up to lock up and check if the key was in the key safe. If not, I'd have left you one and a message on the door. He smiled sympathetically. 'So… you are alone here?'

'Yes.' Sabrina whispered.

'I saw you arrive on your own last night, too.'

Sabrina wasn't sure if she was comfortable with this level of personal intrusion, but at this point she was too sad to care.

'Is everything OK… Jilly?'

Her voice trembled. 'No, no, it's not OK.' She then started to sob so uncontrollably that Beethoven, picking up on her vibrations of distress, began to lick her hand gently as if to kiss her better.

Not fazed at all by this outpouring of emotion, Isaac stood up, took her hand, and guided her to the table with a bench seat either side at the bottom of the back garden. She was sure she could feel her blood pressure lower at just the sight of the impressive views over the headland. Beethoven made a little whimpering sound, then lay down on top of her feet.

There was a battered old flask on the table.

'Here.' He sat down opposite her, his back to the extraordinary view, and handed her an old orange towel from his rucksack. 'Wipe your face.'

'Thank you.' Sabrina, not daring to question

whether it was clean or not, did as she was told, her whole body shaking in an uncontrollable explosive blubber as she did so. Once she had levelled herself, Isaac spoke.

'I take it you drink normal tea? We don't pander to any pretentious alternatives on my watch.' He pulled two plastic cups off the top of the flask and poured the steaming liquid in each. 'Is black alright?'

Sabrina nodded furiously, took a tentative sip from the comforting liquid, and then grimaced as she realised the big man had laced it with sugar.

'If you tell me you're sweet enough, I won't believe you.' Isaac acknowledged Sabrina's watery smile with one of his own infectious ones.

Placing one of his huge hands on top of her tiny manicured one, his enigmatic green eyes looked right into her almond shaped watery blue ones.

'You can have this place for as long as you like...if that would help?'

Isaac was hypnotic in his delivery. His soothing west country accent and tender touch enveloped her like a soft warm dressing gown after a relaxing bath.

'Thank you. That's so truly kind when you don't even know anything about me.' Sabrina replied as he moved his hand away gently.

Isaac stretched his long arms out in front of him and let out a contented sigh. He was dressed very simply, Sabrina noticed. Dark, not particularly well-fitted jeans, a plain green t-shirt and old walking boots that had certainly seen better days. He looked directly at her as though he was looking right through her soul. 'The thing is... Jilly. It's knowing who to trust in this world. I think people are like music, you see. Some let out a meaningful tune, and others are just noise.'

'I haven't quite mastered *Requiem* yet but give me time.' Isaac smirked and Sabrina's voice lilted. 'I can't believe you brought tea for us. My mum always dished out brandy for shock. Thinking on it, she dished out brandy for everything, since...' her voice tailed off. Isaac waited for her to fill the gap with words that never came.

'I didn't really make it for us, as such,' he said eventually. 'I always carry a flask of something. And honestly, my intention wasn't to scare you.'

'I know. My bad. I should have locked the door.' She blew her nose. 'I really am sorry.'

'Let's forget that now.' Isaac waved his hand nonchalantly in front of his face, then with softened voice, asked. 'Does your mother know that you're here?'

'Isaac, I'm thirty-eight years old.'

'And...?'

Sabrina still wasn't sure what to make of this man in front of her, a man in his mid-fifties, she guessed, with the looks of a Viking and his odd, opinionated air.

'I guess I'm not up on what *normal mums*' – she outlined the words in the air with her fingers – 'might do. She died, you see,' Sabrina said matter-of-factly. Then she put a hand over her eyes as if to block out the memory of finding her flamboyant mother motionless, an empty litre bottle of vodka and tablet packets strewn around the side of the bed.

'I'm so sorry.'

'Yes.' Sabrina's voice was almost inaudible. 'So am I.'

There was a moment of silence, which allowed the heavenly sound of birdsong to filter down from the fruit-loaded apple tree next to them.

'Five years ago, now.'

'You were young.'

'So was she.' Sabrina managed to control the wobble in her voice. 'It was the shock of Simon's accident that caused her downward spiral. She blamed herself, you see. Saying, that she was always depressed as far back as I can remember. No wonder dad threw himself into work. She called herself an appalling mother and a failed actress, despite the fact that she had some decent roles in the seventies.' She stopped speaking suddenly. What was in this tea – a truth drug? She never usually gave away so much on a first meeting. In fact, she never usually gave this much away, period.

'Simon?'

'He was…is my brother… I'm waffling now, sorry.'

'Was or is? I don't understand.'

'He has a brain injury. He thought cliff diving was a great idea as a teenager, showing off in front of some girls he had met on the beach. We used to always holiday down here, actually…' Sabrina looked up to the cloud dotted turquoise blue sky. 'But it was the one year my mother decided that we only go as far as Dorset…when it happened. Hence her ridiculously blaming herself for his own actions.'

'Ah. So, he still *is* very much your brother.' Isaac removed his hand. 'Did you decide to come here to rekindle some of those pre-tragedy memories, do you think?'

'That's deep.' Sabrina took a sip of her tea, then lifted her face to the sun.

'Have you grieved for them both properly yet?'

'Woah! So many questions. I don't recall booking a therapy session here. And my brother's not dead.'

Isaac visibly inhaled, shut his eyes for a second, coughed and was back in the moment.

'I was in the paper, once. All sorts was printed. It affected me deeply. I didn't care what people thought of me. It was the fact that somebody who I trusted, broke my trust in return.'

'Oh, that's terrible. Should I know who you are then, Isaac?'

'Is anybody, really anybody…Jilly?' He gave her another one of his penetrative looks. 'But the press intruded on my privacy, both mentally and physically, hence this place being like Fort Knox.'

'The incident?' Sabrina confirmed.

'The incident.' He nodded.

Skilfully extricating his long legs from between the table and the bench, Isaac stretched his arms up to the sky with a loud noise of release. Then he tapped his foot three times on the ground sharply, and Beethoven ran to his side.

'Good boy.' He stroked the old dog's head. 'Right. I must go. Belle will be home from work soon, and I like to greet her at the gate.'

'She's very lucky.'

'And so am I.' Isaac shook the liquid from each cup, put his flask in his rucksack, then reached over to squeeze Sabrina's arm exactly as his girlfriend had done that morning. 'You know where we are,' he said.

He'd gone a few metres down the hill towards his stunning *Kevrinek* home when he turned around to see Sabrina staring blankly towards the breath-taking seascape. Demonstrating his own kind of beautiful, the indomitable Isaac Benson called up to her,

'Sometimes…Sabrina Swift…the quieter you become, the more you are able to hear.'

Chapter Four

'So, he didn't ask you any probing questions at all.'

'No, nothing.'

'Phoebe!' Dee shouted at the top of her voice. 'Get off that iPad now and start your Maths homework'.

Used to her friends' unsubtle parenting skills, Sabrina held the mobile away from her ear and took a bite from a thick slice of toast dripping with butter and honey.

'Sorry, chick, I'm back. What are you scoffing?'

'White toast, real butter and honey.'

'Shit, you must be feeling sad.'

'To be fair, it's the only food I've got, aside eggs. Oh, and crisps and biscuits from the welcome pack. I must go out and get some healthy stuff.'

'Just eat what you want. You've got enough going on without having to worry about your weight. Is that the sea I can hear?'

'Your ears are good. Yes. I'm sitting on the bench seat at the top of the back garden. Apparently I can get guaranteed signal up here.'

'I know you're hurting, but just try and look at this as a proper holiday, Rini. You need to relax. You've not only been working flat out but getting ready for the wedding has been like a military operation.'

Sabrina harrumphed. 'And what a waste of effort all of that was.' She sighed. 'I'll have to go back to work, you know. If they want me back, that is. I'm not sure I can face it, though.'

'It's OK, you've got time. And, well, maybe it's time to have a rethink about changing from a pointy faced soap villain to a soft middle-aged woman with curves. We all need to take a leaf out of Kate Winslet's healthy body image book in my opinion. Plus, we could then borrow each other's clothes.'

Sabrina tutted. 'Middle aged! You cheeky mare.'

'You know what I mean – and I'm the same age as you if you remember.'

'And as you know, I want to be a Disney princess forever.' The women laughed. 'And it's alright for you to say, "just get another job", but a soap is guaranteed money and, joking aside, we're not getting any younger.' Sabrina sighed. 'Caroline called.'

'Oh, God.'

'I know.'

'Did you tell her where you were?'

'Definitely not. She'd be straight in the car and driving down here. At least on the phone I can cut her off.' Delilah laughed as her friend continued. 'She's on about me signing up for *Prancing on Ice*. Need to let her know by Friday. Reckons the scandal will up the fee. I can't do it Dee. I'm too fragile.'

'Maybe a whole change of scene and new people would help? There's usually a fit boy band member in it, too.'

'I'm not going on it just for you to live vicariously through a fantasised love affair with some probably gay toy boy.'

They laughed again.

'What Isaac did mention was that he had been in the newspapers for the wrong reasons, too.'

'Aw, sounds like you've got a real man there. He was clearly being emotionally vulnerable to make you feel better.'

'You're such a softie, but yeah, I guess you're right. One moment he was telling me how private he was, then the next he let all of that out.'

'It sounds like he's one of life's good'uns, Rini. There's not someone out to get you on every street corner you know.'

'You've confirmed my gut feeling about him.'

'And that is the one feeling you must trust.'

Sabrina dragged her finger around the buttery plate and licked it.

'He's a well-known artist from down here, apparently. Exhibits at the Tate in London and everything. Proper famous, so it seems.

'You've lost me, Rini.'

'Isaac is. I don't know why Dom wouldn't have mentioned that.'

'Because nothing impresses that man, much. You know that.'

'I wanted to be nosey to see what he had been in the papers for.'

'And?'

I found some press coverage about a disgruntled ex, outing him as asexual and then him having a fling with Glanna Pascoe, a local artist to prove otherwise. Anyway, of all people, who am I to believe what we read?' Sabrina tutted.

'Just another press circus by the sound of it.' Dee yawned.

'Yes – and what was I thinking of, wanting to marry a ringmaster?'

'Ha! You may be sad but you're still sharp as a tack, missus.'

'It's miss, actually.' Sabrina replied deadpan. 'Forevermore.'

'Shit, sorry, love.'

Sabrina laughed a little sadly. 'It's fine. I've got to

get used to being the spinster of the parish, haven't I? Anyway, back to Isaac – another one of the articles said that his sister, Elizabeth, had a mystery illness. Fuck!'

'What's wrong?'

'I just realised she must have died. I came across a grave, with the words 'Fly Free, Lizzie' on it.'

'Aw, Rini. That's sad,' Dee said.

'Yes, isn't it? Sad, and a tad weird as she's buried in his garden, so to speak. I say garden, but he has acres of land and it's such a beautiful spot where she is, under an oak tree looking out to sea.'

'Aw, bless him.'

'Yes. Despite him appearing to be on his high horse, he does seem to be a good guy, too. His girlfriend is so sweet too… Belle. She bought me the breakfast supplies earlier. I feel such a fool as I told her my name was Jilly and now they both know that I'm a complete charlatan.'

'Rini, are you on something? Why did you tell her that?'

'Because she played along that my new husband was sleeping inside and then asked me my name as she said they hadn't been given it. I just figured it might add a layer of anonymity just in case she wasn't aware of who we were. I mean, not everybody watches the soaps.'

'But most people can't miss the headlines these days. Maybe she didn't know then or just realised that you didn't want to talk about it. Made it easy for you.'

'Yes, You're right. She's so lovely. What a flipping mess!' Sabrina sighed. 'She told me that Isaac only allows a select few to stay here so the plot kind of thickens as there must have been some sort of connection with him and Dom.'

'Calm your drama-twisted mind, sweetheart. There probably isn't a plot at all. You know what that ex of yours is like, he knows everyone and plays everyone like a fiddle when he wants something.'

'I know it sounds mad, but I actually miss his belligerence. I miss… God, I miss him.' Her voice became that of a whining teenager. 'Stupid tosser!'

'OK. So, why not take this time to realise exactly what you miss about him? And, more importantly, what you don't. I think sometimes we get so wrapped up in our busy lives we don't sit back and think about our relationships, what works and what doesn't. We just let it all flow and then moan without even confronting the issues.'

'Are *you* OK, Dee?'

Dee faltered for a second. 'This is about you two, not me.'

'You've never liked Dom, have you? You can tell me now.'

Dee broke the far too long silence. 'Do you think you'll take him back?'

'My head is screaming "NO" in every language. My heart is still gently saying "maybe". How is someone supposed to deal with something like this? How can love just turn to hate in a nanosecond? I mean, I haven't fallen out of love with the man, and as much as I am calling him every swear word under the sun, I'm still quite clearly very much fanny-deep in.'

'You're gross. And you're right – that's why we grieve and hurt at the loss of a relationship. Saying that, if Stu did what Dom did, I'd be talking to you from a prison phone.'

Sabrina, taking a breath to contain her sob, made a gasping sound. 'Oh, Dee, what the fuck am I going to do?'

'Oh, darling. I'm so sorry you're having to go through this. I am here for you, you know that. 'The loyal Essex woman's voice started to wobble as well.

'It's going to be alright, mate.'

'I don't want to face anybody. I don't want anyone to talk to me. I can't bear it.'

'That's just how you're feeling now.'

'Maybe, but I especially don't want Dom to know I'm here. I just hope he hasn't contacted Isaac already to see if I am.'

'From what you've told me about Isaac, I doubt if he would tell him.'

'You're probably right.'

'How are you getting on being somewhere so remote? I think it would freak me out.'

'I did think I might feel a bit anxious. The silence is deafening, until the birds wake up that is and then the dawn chorus is something else. And as for darkness, I can't even see my hand waving in front of me. But I feel completely safe, Dee. The peace is so soothing. I haven't even taken a sleeping pill. Getting off the mad treadmill that I was on has been like a natural sedative.'

'That's bird song to *my* ears if that's the case. You needed to slow down, mate. I guess the only reason that Dom may call Isaac is that he'll want his money back on the cottage,' Dee mused.

'No. Dom may be some things, but he's not mean financially, and it was such short notice.'

'OK, so just tell Isaac and Belle that you don't want him to know where you are. Anyway, what are you going to do? Are you going to stay down there?'

'I certainly don't want to come back yet. I mean, where would I go? I'm essentially homeless. The Bloomsbury flat is Dom's. He said I could stay there until I found somewhere else, and he would get a hotel. But being there would remind me of us. Plus, I figure that if I stay out of the way for a couple of weeks, everything will calm down and the news cycle will move on.'

'Yes. The next big hashtag trend will be fuelling the fingers of the tormented trolls by then. Well, as soon as you're ready, whether it be a day or a month, you know our spare room has your name on it. The girls would love having you around, you know that. They adore their Auntie Rini.'

'I appreciate that. I just don't want Dom *or* Caroline knowing where I am. I'm surprised they haven't been on to you already to try and sniff me out. I don't want anyone to recognise me. No pointing fingers or people feeling sorry for me in the street. Oh, to *not* be famous – just for a year, at least.'

'I feel I should tell you that *Daily Swine Online* has a thread asking, *Where is Polly Malone? Maybe it's really Sabrina Swift who has gone to jail!* With a hashtag of *#FindPollyMalone*, and they're offering a real-life reward if anyone spots you in public.'

Sabrina grimaced. 'I braved a look earlier and saw it, along with the photos of him in Paris with her. They're recent, too. I know exactly what clothes he took when he went for the rugby trip, as I blooming well ironed them and put them in his case. He's such a cock!'

Dee tutted 'And he's surely not that silly to not try and make it up with you whilst carrying on with her, as he knows damn well that you are going to find out about these photos.'

'Oh, Dee. It makes me feel sick that she's half his age, it's so bloody cliched. Knowing him and his already inflated ego, he'll love the fact they could be the next Bogart and Bacall.'

'Maybe it'll do you good to stay for the full two weeks in Cornwall then.'

'I agree, and Isaac did say I could stay as long as I like.' Sabrina became animated. 'Oh, come down and play with me, Dee. It's magical down here and that's without even exploring.'

'I'd jump at the chance, but the girls are only just back at school and Stu's got some work event in Munich next week. I'm sorry, Rini.'

'No, of course. I forget these practicalities.'

'Yes. You have a lot to be grateful for. The day I don't have to do a school run again will be the best day of my life!'

'Maybe I'll feel that way again, one day. Free and happy. Isaac came out with something earlier. He said, "the quieter you become, the more you are able to hear."'

'Oh, to have just one moment of peace. You need to keep listening to that man, he sounds wise. I've gotta go mate. Thea is at a play date and is phoning me. Catch up soon. Love you.'

Before Sabrina had a chance to reply, Delilah Dickinson had hung up.

Chapter Five

S abrina awoke to brilliant sunshine streaming through the shutters, spotlighting a million dancing dust particles that twirled frivolously against the walls. After two years of co-habiting, it felt strange sleeping alone. Strange but pleasantly liberating not having to share a space and being able to stretch her legs across both sides of the bed. She wondered fleetingly where Dom was and what he was doing, but she was adamant that she was going to let him suffer. Not call him back. Let him do the worrying, after hurting her so badly. Or maybe he didn't give a shit. His inflated ego was why he was leaving his daily message on her voicemail, telling her he wanted her back. Just thinking of him with the French stick suddenly made her shiver. Her face contorted and she made a little groaning noise as she threw off the covers.

Pulling on the sexy cream silk dressing gown she had bought especially for the wedding night, she made her way to the bathroom. The one and only mirror in the place caused her to double take. Who was this woman looking back at her? Just days ago, when she had been getting ready in the stunningly decorated Soho Farmhouse bedroom, she had looked like the film star she had always aspired to be. Her pre-wedding preparation had been immense. Personal gym and yoga sessions to fit around her tight work schedule. A course of non-surgical facial treatments to make sure there was not a drooping jowl in sight. Dyed and curled lashes and micro-bladed brows. A tiny bit of lip filler. Perfectly styled hair. She'd even had Donna, the make-up artist from the show, travel to the wedding with her to ensure that every step of the way she would look amazing. The vintage mauve Vivienne Westwood inspired gown she had had specially made by Vera in wardrobe, in homage to the great lady, was one that dreams were made of. It really had been set to be a fairy-tale wedding.

'Stupid bastard,' Sabrina said aloud. Far from her now being 'simply the Mrs Best' (Dom's words!), looking back at her was a shadow of that woman. A sombre Swift. Her long, wavy brown hair was greasy and all over the place. There were shadows under her extraordinary periwinkle-blue eyes. And aside from yesterday's bread binge, she had been eating like a sparrow, so her chiselled features now fashioned an unattractive gauntness. For a split second she could see her mother's face within her own. A mother who had taken her own life due to blaming herself for the accident of her beloved son. Then, as if her forthright mother was suddenly inhabiting her, a bright shard of sunlight hit the mirror and with a lone tear falling down her cheek, Gillian Swift's beloved daughter whispered. 'Swifty, you've got this girl.'

Chapter Six

During the Summer holidays, Penrigan Pier was alive with amusement arcades, fortune tellers, ice cream carts and cheeky gulls hoping to catch an unsuspecting tourist off guard and steal their fish and chips from a newspaper-printed cone. With the kids now back at school and it being a Monday, there was just a mobile coffee and snack van at the entrance and one other coffee and ice cream port to the middle of the pier. All other stall holders had stayed closed for a well-earned post-weekend break. Pensioners, reliving their youth and glad of the lack of crowds, could be seen taking a leisurely stroll along the boardwalk or sitting with a newspaper on their knees on a bench in one of the alcoves that ran down the middle of the pier, some with flasks of tea and tinfoil wrapped goodies. At weekends, teenagers would hang out after hours in these alcoves smoking, drinking, shouting, and play-fighting.

Sabrina found herself an empty bench and smiled at the engraved plaque before sitting down, which read, "To my Molly. There's never an end to the sea, so why for you and me? Your Ronnie."

Plonking herself down on the white-painted wooden seat and wondering who else might have sat here before her, she took in the salty, fishy aroma of seaside coming from the seaweed-covered struts on the old

Victorian structure. To her right someone had left a copy of the *Hartmouth Echo*. The area's local paper, she assumed. Intrigued at exactly what the news might be in a sleepy area such as this, she popped it in her bag for a nosy later. Resting her head back, she closed her eyes for a second and breathed a huge sigh of relief. Behind her huge dark glasses and with cap pulled down and hair dragged back in a scruffy ponytail, for once she felt truly anonymous. Not one person in the world knew she was on this bench, on this pier, in this coastal town, and it felt strangely cathartic. It gave her a sense of peace that she hadn't experienced for such a long time. Being in the public eye was a privilege, yes, and her pay cheques were certainly higher than the average salary, but the downside of this was that everyone wanted a little piece of her – the public *and* the press. This was great when things were going well, but now she realised how ugly things could get when they weren't.

To be by the sea had always given her free spirit such a lift. The holidays she had had down here as a child, pre-Simon's accident held, such great memories of both freedom and joy for her. Sadly, she had never managed to fully replicate either of these in her adult life.

When her own busy filming schedule allowed her and Dom to make it away for a weekend or, if lucky, a week's holiday, he would be forever on his laptop or phone. And as much as she enjoyed his company, it hadn't taken her long to realise that she was not only marrying a very charismatic and at times beautiful man, but she was also marrying his job.

She laughed to herself as she imagined ever having a bench inscribed with Sabrina and Dominic. He would think it trite. She found it really endearing. "Sabrina and Dominic, the actress, the editor, the ex-wife and his

French lover", she said to the sky with a dramatically Shakespearean air. The most romantic thing he'd ever done was to propose to her at the top of the London Eye, as he'd thought it would just be them alone up there in the sky with no prying eyes. That was until he admitted it was his PA Jessica's idea, and that by the time they'd got all the way round, the paparazzi had been called and she had been jostled relentlessly for selfies by people waiting in the queue to get on the big wheel. Thinking about it now, she realised how ridiculous it had been. Who picks a huge glass bubble in the middle of central London for a discreet proposal?!

Just as she was having these thoughts, and much to the disdain of an old couple who were walking by hand in hand the arrival of a voicemail caused her phone to ping loudly.

Smiling apologetically, she put the handset to her ear.

Darling. It's me. You know how sorry I am. Dominic Best's daily plea floated on the breeze. *See sense and come home. Or at least have the decency to return my calls. I miss you.* Like you had the decency to shag someone just weeks before our wedding day, Sabrina thought, the feelings of hurt suddenly cutting through her like the noise of the jet ski about to whizz under the ornate Victorian structure of the pier. Granted, she was finding the strength from somewhere not to talk to him, but not listening to his messages– she wasn't ready for that yet. She had also thankfully managed to bat off any form of rational thought as to what she might feel or do if the wounded pleas from the man *were* to stop coming.

Fancying some caffeine, she wandered up the pier to the coffee kiosk and as she opened her purse, said 'Shit!' rather too loudly. Without thinking, she took off her sunglasses and shook her head. 'We take cash and cards, if that's what's the bother.' The middle-aged server interjected with a strong Cornish accent. Sabrina nodded and handed over a five-pound note.

'Keep the change.'

'Thanks love.' The woman began staring at her in quizzical fashion. 'That's very kind. Oh...My...God!... It's Polly Malone, isn't it? You're a wanted woman. Can I have a selfie? I've never met anyone famous before.'

Sabrina whacked on her sunglasses and in an atrocious Scottish accent replied. 'Nay, I get that all the time.' Before she had a chance to turn around, the woman had reached for her phone. Composing herself, the actress managed a flimsy smile and shouted back. 'No fun being a doppelganger to a villain, I can tell ya, that lassie. Have a wonderful day.'

Coffee in hand, she walked back as fast as she could to the pier entrance and called Dee.

'Thank God, you answered.'

'Oh no, what's up?'

'One, I've just been recognised and not sure if the woman got a photo or not and two, in all the kerfuffle of leaving London, I changed bags and I've only got my joint account debit card with me.'

'That's alright isn't it. There must be money in there?'

'Of course, there is, but you're not getting it. Dom will know exactly where I am. For fuck's sake!'

'Can't you get a new personal debit card sent there – say you've lost it?'

Sabrina groaned. 'Oh, I don't know. I'll work it out when I get back to the cottage.'

Dee laughed. 'You'll have to get a real job down there and work for a living like everybody else does.'

Sabrina scowled. 'You're not remotely funny.'

'I'm actually surprised anyone recognised you with those saucer-sized sunnies you wear.'

'I'm surprised anyone recognised me, period, as I look so God darn awful. I took them off for a split second. I hope I got away with it, though, pretended I was Scottish and that it was always happening to me.'

'Good that you ventured out, anyway. Where are you?'

'Penrigan Pier. It's gorgeous here. I walked along the clifftops from my little cottage and thought I'd sit quietly and just be for a change. I have to say I didn't realise I needed to do nothing until I came here. I'm tired, Dee.'

'I know you are, darling. Have you called Caroline yet?'

'No, I'm still weighing up loot over limbs.'

Dee laughed out loud. 'Don't ever change, mate, will you. I better go, meeting a couple of mums in the pub for lunch today.'

'I didn't ask how *you* were. As much as I think it is, sometimes, it's not all about me.'

'Let me know how you get on with Caroline and the bank. Gotta go.'

'What's up, Dee? As soon as you can, come and see me, OK?'

'I'm good… good as gold.' The phone went dead.

But after thirty-three years of friendship, Sabrina knew she wasn't.

A weary Sabrina walked down the long drive to Kevrinek and, on reaching the security gate, pressed the intercom. After realising she'd destroyed not only the welcome note but Belle's mobile number that was on the back of it into a thousand pieces with her boot, she was thankful to hear the woman's voice at the end of it.

'Oh, Belle, just the person, it's Sabrina a.k.a. Jilly. I assume Isaac told you?' She cringed at the admission to her original lie.

'Never mind all that. Are you OK?'

'Yes, yes fine but you know you said if I needed anything, anything at all. Well. The thing is…'

Chapter Seven

A few days later, Sabrina sat at the kitchen table of the cottage, a towel around her shoulders.

'Sabrina, are you one hundred percent sure you want me to do this?' Belle's voice was hesitant.

'Yep, I've never been more certain.'

'I'm far more used to cutting umbilical cords than hair.'

'Ew. OK. But how hard can a pixie cut be? It's just a messy old crop, really. And it will use far less hair dye once it's all cut off. It's just a win, win all round,' Sabrina added unconvincingly as Belle took the one mirror down from the bathroom wall and propped it up with the iron on the table in front of them. She turned the old TV to an angle and pushed a DVD into the side of it.

Sabrina shut her eyes as big swathes of her lovely, shiny dark locks began falling to the stone floor of the cottage. She could even sense Beethoven wondering if the pair of them had gone completely mad.

'There!' Belle looked exhausted as she ruffled the now extremely short hair of the pretty woman in front of her an hour later. 'Now to put the bleach on – I know how to do that at least.'

Sabrina looked at herself fully in the mirror and blew out an exaggerated breath. 'It kind of suits me.'

'It *really* suits you.' Belle started painting on the

blonde hair colour. 'And I can't believe we got there by following a step-by-step hair cutting DVD.'

'Yes, what an eBay find that was! Vidal Sassoon eat your heart out.' They both laughed.

'And thank God for you having antique technology.' Sabrina fiddled with the remote.

'I know! Dreadful, isn't it? When we kitted this place out, I said to Isaac no one has DVD's anymore, but he didn't care. He didn't even want me to put a TV in here. We rarely watch TV at home, you see. This one was in my old bedroom at my parents' house. When he's not painting, he's reading, and I have to say I do watch stuff on my iPad. If he knew I never missed an episode of *Love Island*, I'm sure he'd leave me.'

They laughed again.

'OK. To finish the look.' Belle pulled out a pair of huge tortoiseshell spectacles from her bag and gently placed them over Sabrina's ears. 'They're just a plain lens, I used to wear them for effect.'

'Wow! I look almost intelligent.'

'And...' She handed Sabrina a little silver ring. 'For your nose.'

Sabrina regarded it dubiously. 'Not sure about that.'

'I think you should. It'll give you a kind of preppy, trendy look, rather than your usual Hollywood glamour. And we need to make sure we've done the job properly.'

Sabrina put the faux ring in place. 'Ha! Look at me! I look boyish.'

'A very pretty boy at that.' Belle smiled. 'And if I do say so myself, we've done a pretty good job of disguising you, my friend.'

'Thank you, thank you so much.' Sabrina bit her lip. 'You could be a stylist at this rate. But you're a midwife, I guess, from your earlier comment? What an amazing profession.'

'I used to be a baby bringer, but I'm more of a general nurse and carer now. I do agency work as I prefer the flexibility. That's how I met Isaac, actually.'

'Good for you – and that sounds intriguing.' Sabrina pursed her lips in the mirror. They looked fuller now she was nigh on bald.

'It was very sad actually, and he won't mind me telling you as it is public knowledge, but I was helping him nurse his sister.'

'Lizzie? I saw the grave.'

'Yes, she had learning disabilities but then had a horrific accident. She fell down the cliff and her brain was injured. She died in her sleep a while after. A happy release, really.'

Tears started to roll down Sabrina's cheeks. 'Poor Isaac.'

'Don't cry. It was incredibly sad, but he's good now. He put his life into making her happy and we wouldn't have met if it wasn't for her, so we look at it as Lizzie's final act of love. Putting us two together.'

'Aw, that's so lovely. And I'm selfishly crying for me, Belle.' Sabrina started to ramble. 'I know why my ex and your Isaac bonded about the cottage now, and it shows he cares and I kind of don't want to know that he cares or cared for me as it makes it even harder to leave him.'

Sabrina burst into sobs.

'Oh, darling. You mean that he cared about your brother and what he did for Headway?'

Sabrina nodded and whimpered. 'Do you know everything?'

'I do now.' Belle put her arm gently on Sabrina's. 'Isaac pieced everything together and told me. And I don't blame you wanting to change your look and identity. I can't think of anything worse than being in a goldfish bowl in this mad world. How do you do it?' She tore off a piece of kitchen roll and handed it to Sabrina.

'I used to like the fame. But being here on my own, even for such a short time, has made me think, do I really?'

'You're going through a lot. Let things settle and hopefully you'll see things more clearly.'

Even though they had just met, Sabrina felt the same comfort in Belle's presence as in that of Dee's. 'It was something Isaac said the other day, and he's right, that maybe it's because I don't love myself that I want everyone else to love me.'

Belle tutted. 'He doesn't mince his words, that man of mine.'

'He didn't direct it at me.'

Belle smiled. 'He never does. So, are you going to talk to him? Dominic, I mean?'

'I'll have to at some stage. There's some stuff of mine still in our... his flat. We had a joint account for bills and holidays and, well, it does seem so unfinished the way it ended. But I don't think I can forgive him. What would you do?'

'It doesn't matter what I'd do, Sabrina. Because whatever anyone advises, you'll follow your heart anyway and in my humble opinion, if you don't do that, then you're a fool.'

'My mother used to say, "Follow your heart and you won't get lost".

'Your mother sounds very wise.'

'She was... sometimes.'

'What would she say about the Dominic situation, do you think?'

'She'd say, whatever you do, do it for you.' Sabrina sniffed. 'Life is tough, sometimes, isn't it, Belle?'

'Yes, it is. But think how boring it would be if the

road we call life was just straight, if the weather never changed, there were no crossroads. If the lights were always green, people didn't come and go and if we as travellers on it didn't expand our knowledge or broaden our horizons.'

'I can see why you and Isaac get on now.' Sabrina smiled and put her hand on top of her new friend's. 'I'm sorry I lied to you, Belle.'

'I trust actions, not words. Now, come on, let's crack open the bottle of champagne that was in the welcome pack if you haven't already, and toast this fresh look of yours, shall we?'

Chapter Eight

The next morning, showered, with hair scrunched into its new messy style and doused in her favourite *Jo Malone* fragrance, Sabrina made her way to the kitchen with a huge yawn. Noticing a piece of paper sticking through the letterbox, she read it and opened the front door. Belle's note made her smile. *Happy Friday, Sabrina Valentine. Enjoy market day. You'll be one of the locals soon xx.* On the stone step was pint of milk and loaf of fresh bread. Sabrina looked around for her phone to thank her new friend. But she couldn't find it.

Still stuffed from the fish and chips Belle had brought up for her last night, Sabrina decided to opt for just a coffee for breakfast. As she was putting the milk away, a sense of relief rushed over her as she saw her handset on the top of the fridge. Relief and also realisation that this was the first night in around ten years that she had not taken it to the bedroom. Granted there was no signal in there, so it was pointless anyway, but in her eyes it was still an achievement. At home, her endless scrolling of Instagram had become a ridiculous habit before bed. So much so that she sometimes she felt her hand getting a weird pain in the side of it, purely from it being in an abnormal position whilst she got her fix of everybody else's seemingly perfect lives. Hers included. Sabrina began to text.

Sabrina Valentine?

We're not quite on a Greek island but you are doing a bit of a Shirley Valentine, aren't you?

Sabrina laughed to herself at Belle's response.

My mum loved that film – and hardly! Thanks for the goodies, you're an angel.

I try. Have an amazing day. I think you'll love Hartmouth and especially the market. Pop over the estuary on the ferry if you can, too. There's a Cornwall Trust property the other side, and the gardens there are beautiful.

OK… thank you… have an enjoyable day too xx

The ten a.m. Penrigan to Hartmouth trundled its way noisily around the windy Cornish roads. It had been a while since Sabrina had been on a double decker bus and it brought back feelings of being a teenager again. Of when she used to hop on and off the iconic red city buses with her North London mates, without a care in the world. Her impulsivity and spontaneity were at a high, back then. Without fear, she would say yes to the risky and no to conformity, both of which had got her into trouble many times. It constantly surprised her that she had kept working on the same soap role for five years. Her butterfly mind rarely settled in one place for that long.

Belle had talked her out of driving to the busy estuary town on a market day; said it would take as long to find a parking space as it would be to sit on the bus, and that it really was a lovely route where she could take in the stunning elevated coastal views along the way. Like the old days, she had headed upstairs and sat right at the front in the goldfish bowl-like window. A woman in her late forties, who was in a seat at the top of the stairs, had smiled at her and Sabrina was relieved that there was not a sniff of recognition. That could be because the woman wasn't a fan, of course, as she wasn't so up herself as to think that everyone watched the biggest soap in the UK. But still, it was a good sign. She had thought about maybe changing her accent too, but as her alter-ego Polly Malone was Liverpudlian and she clearly found Scottish difficult, she thought that keeping her North London twang would be alright.

With the bus stopping every five minutes, Sabrina realised she could be on here for a while, so she opened the local newspaper she had found on Penrigan Pier. Pushing up her glasses (which she was just about getting used to), she laughed to herself at the '*Off their trolley*' headline. The story explained that trolleys from the local *Fresco* supermarket had been going missing daily. The *mystery trolley nicker* had eventually been discovered in neighbouring Penhaven, lining them with bin bags and growing cannabis plants in them in a greenhouse packed full of heat lamps. Then under cover of darkness he would wheel them around the streets selling his wares, fresh from the vine, so to speak. She wondered what Dominic would think of this headline, and even more how he would cope with being faced with such regular slow news days. She put the paper down next to her and reached for her phone, which showed an icon for a new voice message. On hearing his aggravated tones, she sighed deeply. *This is getting ridiculous now. Just pick up the phone. Let me know you're safe, at least. I haven't got time for all this mucking about. Sorry, sorry. I love you Swifty. Just come home, will you? Or text me at least.*

Her dad's mantra of "Treat others as you would have them treat you", sprung to mind, and she felt chastened. She would give it until tomorrow and then message him. Yes, he had been a complete arse, but two wrongs didn't make a right. He needn't know where she was, but he could at least rest assured she hadn't done a Lord Lucan on him. Today was for making her decision about *Prancing on Ice* and enjoying a little mosey around an old market town, something she had so enjoyed doing before she had met Dominic three years previously. And something now she found she rarely had time for. In fact, her life had become so busy recently, she rarely had time for anything that made her happy. She thought back to what Dee had said. She had been on such a constant treadmill of working, wedding planning, eating, sleeping and repeating that her focus on reality and what her relationship stood for *had* been lost.

Sabrina looked out of the huge upper deck front window of the trundling double decker. To her right a long stretch of sand dunes was being licked by an inviting looking turquoise blue sea. The decent weather was holding and there was not a cloud in the sky. This place really was a taste of heaven. She was suddenly catapulted back into reality as they rounded a corner and the left side of the bus scraped the tops of trees, causing a few branches to break off and poke through the tiny push open windows. She gave a small, gleeful laugh.

The view from their Bloomsbury flat was as far from this as one could imagine. Just rooftops after more rooftops. Grey, noisy, pollution-ridden London seemed a million miles away right now and if she was honest with herself, at this moment in time she wasn't missing it or everything it held for her one bit. Having time away from Dominic had made her realise just how little time she did spend with him anyway. They were like ships that pass in the night on a working week, and at the weekends, he would play golf, she would go to the gym and if they did do something together, they were rarely alone, it was usually a dinner party with one of his cronies or a weekend at his ageing parents in Dorset. She had hoped that marriage would change this, that they could do more just as Mr and Mrs Best. The reality of leaving him suddenly hit her. However much they didn't see each other. He was still a heartbeat in her home and in her life. For all his faults, she did love him but the butterflies he used to ignite in her tummy, even up until their wedding day, now felt dead inside of her. She felt a physical pain of both hurt and regret for ever getting involved with a cheater. Dee had untactfully intimated that maybe this hadn't been the first time. Maybe it wasn't. But she didn't need to know that, for she genuinely believed a leopard did not change his spots and that once was enough for Dominic Best to have blotted his own copybook.

The top of the bus was filling now, with the chitter chatter of families and a handful of lonesome individuals of various ages, all heading to the market, she assumed. Thankfully nobody had joined her at the front. Maybe they could smell her wish that they would keep away from her. On noticing a 'two miles to Hartmouth' sign, she stuck her head back into the paper to get as much of a sense of the place as possible before she arrived. There was an advertorial page covering Ferry Lane Market, and Sabrina read with interest. It explained that the market consisted of indoor shop units but on the outdoor market days – every Friday and Saturday, whatever the weather – the owners would sell their wares in front of their shops.

There was a story covering Star's Crystal and Jewellery stall. Telling how Steren (which meant Star in Cornish), a teenage single mother at the time, had started by selling jewellery along Penrigan beach and after receiving a small inheritance had set up her own shop in the market where she made bespoke jewellery as well as selling individual crystals. She had found love and now had two small boys as well as a teenage daughter, Skye, who worked for her half-sister, Kara, in Passion Flowers, the florist next door. It all sounded a bit incestuous, Sabrina thought, but then rationalised that if people stayed in their hometowns, there was no avoiding it. Not like anonymous old London town, where you were lucky if your neighbour so much as raised an eyebrow at you, and where your family was most likely to be spread around the globe.

Sabrina read on to discover that Monique's Café, formerly Tasty Pasties, while not a market stall as such, sold delicious pasties and pastries with outside seating. It was owned by Big Frank Brady who also owned Frank's, the American-style diner-café next to the ferry crossing, where the article claimed you could buy the best breakfast in Hartmouth. Sabrina also learnt with interest that there was an eclectic mix of stalls to keep both the tourists and the locals happy, given that it was a year-round market. On Star's side of the street, you could not only find Passion Flowers, but also the Hartmouth Gallery & Art School run by Glanna Pascoe and her fiancé, Oliver Trueman.

'Ah, I see,' Sabrina said far too loudly as she put the facts in her head together. Glanna Pascoe – that was the name of the artist of the rainbow painting above the cottage fireplace and the woman Isaac had been associated with in the newspaper article, wasn't it? With head fully down into the magazine after her outburst, she read that there was the artisan bakery Holly and Glover, where Belle got her goodies from, and Clarke's the butchers made up that row. On the other side, the units were made up of the Dillon family's fruit and veg stall. Nigel's Catch the fishmonger, The Sweet Spot belonging to Alicia, selling home-made fudge and local honey including the Honeysuckle Honey made at Bee Cottage by the old ferryman Joe Moon and another stall that was loaded with antiques and run by, in the article's words, an 'eccentric Welsh gentleman named Gideon Jones'. At the bottom of the article, it stated that Brian Todd, who had run the second-hand books and records stall for the past fifteen years, was taking a sabbatical. Rather than somebody take over running his unit, he had stored his stock in a lock up and an empty market unit was to be available for a three-month let from October to December. Interested parties were to contact Lowen Kellow, Market Inspector for further information. A mobile number followed.

The bus stopped with a jolt, and everyone started gathering their belongings and making their way to the stairs. Assuming this must be the last stop, Ferry Lane Market, Sabrina donned her huge sunglasses, stood up and joined the queue.

Chapter Nine

'Bet they're lining up like hot cakes to get their hands on this one before Christmas, ain't they?' Charlie Dillon shouted across from his already heaving fruit and veg stall. 'They so rarely come up, I'd take it myself, but I've not got enough hands on deck.'

The brooding market inspector gave the greengrocer a reluctant thumbs up and made his way inside the empty unit.

'Good morning, madam.' Charlie Dillon directed straight at Sabrina as she began to make her way down the hill and through the middle of the bustling market. 'Fancy getting your north and south around one of my ripe and juicy Cox's. Rich and aromatic, they are – not unlike myself.' Sabrina laughed and walked on as the bald man gave her a huge wink. The straggly-haired woman next to him shook her head and shouted after her. 'Don't mind him, love, he thinks he's bleeding Casanova.'

Opposite, Sabrina noticed a heavily pregnant woman putting bunches of mixed coloured dahlias into buckets outside the florists. Feeling a sense of recognition on spotting Star's Crystal and Jewellery stall next door to the bloom-laden one of Passion Flowers, she walked over to it and started perusing the decorative array of handmade jewellery laid out neatly in front of her.

'Hi.' The petite, long-haired blonde greeted her. Sabrina recognised her as Star from the newspaper. A tiny baby was nestled close to her chest in a papoose. 'Love your nose ring.'

Sabrina put her hand to her face to touch it. 'Err, yes. Thanks. I was just reading about you in the *Hartmouth Echo*. Well done on following your dreams.'

'Aw, that's kind. It was hard work, but I got there in the end. Good to see selling my soul to an *Echo* journalist got me one customer, at least.' Star stroked her baby's downy head softly. 'Welcome to my humble market stall.'

'Aw, it's lovely and bloody journalists, eh.' Sabrina felt a pain in her tummy again at the mention of a journalist. 'How old is your little one?'

'Two months today. Thankfully, he sleeps a lot. He luckily seems to like the hustle and bustle noises of the market already. His name is Storm but he's more like a gentle breeze – so far, anyway.' The stallholder gave a tinkling laugh.

'Great name!'

'Yes, my husband is not so keen, but I compromised on Matthew for our first born, so he's coming around to it.'

Star looked to Sabrina's left hand. 'Your engagement ring is stunning, by the way.'

Sabrina felt a dart of panic. She knew she should have taken the huge sparkling diamond off as other questions would surely follow. But it just felt so final doing that.

The pain again. 'So, umm, do you sell nose rings, Star?' Sabrina diverted.

'Yep, studs too, in every birthstone. I'll show you. When's your birthday?'

'November the fifth.' Sabrina hoped the woman

didn't offer to try and put anything in the non-existent hole in her nose.

'Ah. That's cool. A passionate Scorpio, and you get fireworks displays laid on for you every year without ever having to pay for them.'

'Whoopee!' Sabrina said with flat sarcasm, putting her hands in the air in mock celebration.

Star handed Sabrina a black card containing a mixture of earrings, nose studs and rings predominantly carrying a yellow stone. 'Have a look. Your birthstone is a lovely one. They all have meanings, did you know that?'

'I've never been really into that crystal or stone malarkey to be honest.'

'Well, in brief, just so you know: Yellow Topaz is a stone of luck.'

'I could do with some of that,' Sabrina said solemnly.

'Ah, sorry to hear that. Maybe we can remedy that now, then, because it's also a stone of destiny and fate. It helps you bond with the people who are good for you and keeps you away from those who are a harm to you. It strengthens your belief in yourself and enhances your confidence level.'

'Wow. That's hard to believe, but I'll take it as you clearly know your stuff.'

'Oh, God, I don't mean to sound like I'm doing some full-on sales pitch here – although that is my job, I guess.' Star's tinkling laugh rang out again. 'I tell you what.' She put her hand to a bag hanging from under the purple gauzed covered table. 'Have this piece for free. Stick it in your pocket.'

'No... No. I can't do that. You've got a business to run.'

'You can. Please, take it.'

'Well, to go with it, I'm going to buy this ring for

my little finger, then.' Sabrina pointed to a simple silver ring that encased a small round yellow topaz stone. 'I shall surely have double luck, then.' She laughed. 'Thank you, so much, Star, I love it!'

Sabrina walked back up to Monique's, grabbed herself a take-out coffee, then began ambling her way down the cobbled lane toward the ferry quay. The sights of people haggling for a bargain, the sounds of the market cries and delicious smells of fresh bread and scented candles that engulfed her were a joy to the senses. In her ocean of sadness, it seemed she had momentarily found a small life raft of happiness, and she smiled.

In the far distance she could see the blue of the sea and the dot of the red and yellow ferry going across to where she had learnt was Crowsbridge, where the historic Crowsbridge Hall could be found.

She had been relieved to find that her bank had a satellite branch in the village hall over there, and even more delighted that she was able to pick up a new debit card for her personal account later that day.

Now she had seen how lovely all the stalls were, Sabrina's plan was to buy local meat and veg and some treats from the bakery for herself and to make up a food hamper for Isaac and Belle as they had been so generous to her. As she now only had fifty pounds cash left, after buying the ring, she thought it made sense to get to the bank first and come back over to Hartmouth to buy the goodies. Plus, it would also ensure they were kept fresh as it was a warmish seventeen degrees today.

As she carried on her merry way down Ferry Lane, Sabrina began looking up for a sign for Glanna's gallery. She loved the painting over the fireplace in the cottage and thought it would be interesting to meet the artist.

Then, CRASH!

'For God's sake!' The man shouted, wiping drips of coffee from his lapel with his bare hand. 'Blinking tourists. Doesn't anyone look where they are going in this place.'

'Oh, shit. I'm so sorry.' With the coffee cup now rolling along the pavement, Sabrina whipped a tissue from her bag and began dabbing at the man's jacket. 'Only a little bit, got you, thank goodness.'

'Maybe if you took those fly-like sunglasses off.' The man tutted and pushed her hand away. 'And that will just put white marks on it.' He then softened. 'I'm sorry. So sorry, I've been here for what seems like hours waiting for someone to view this place. Was just popping my head out the door to see if I could see them coming and some crazy woman walks right into me.'

Sabrina bristled. 'Less of the crazy, thanks. And I guess I could say that some rude man walked into me.'

Then, suddenly, they both burst out laughing. And as they did, Sabrina looked at him properly for the first time – then looked again. For standing in front of her was a tall and attractive square-jawed man. From his chestnut brown hair, which was styled with an endearing quiff, to his interesting odd-coloured eyes, he had what her and Dee would call 'the allure'. His navy suit and white shirt fitted his fit frame perfectly. And despite looking at men being so far down on Sabrina's to-do list, he was, in her humble opinion, the epitome of sex on a stick.

'So, are you going show me around then?'

He frowned. 'Are you Jemima, my ten o' clock?'

'No, but if it will stop you shouting at me, I can be anyone you want me to be.' It took Sabrina a second to realise she was flirting! What on earth had happened to her? Maybe it was the shock of the impact when she bumped into him.

The man gave her a side glance that almost brought

the dead butterflies in her stomach back to life. He pushed the open door. 'Come on in, then. It will take seconds to give you the grand tour.' He held the door open, and his hand brushed hers as she past him. The tingle of lust hit her. He smelt so good. Her mouth spoke before her brain engaged. 'Is that Tom Ford I can smell?'

'If it is, I'll leave you to him, shall I?' The man smiled to reveal a perfect set of far too white veneers. But good nose: it's Black Orchid by the very man.'

'Oh, the moody bastard does have a sense of humour then.'

With that one smirk, Sabrina could tell that he liked her too.

Sabrina hurriedly swapped her shades for her tortoiseshell specs and stood next to him in the vacant space. It was empty aside a small counter, a high stool and one battered hardcover book that was spread out, cover up, on the dusty wooden floor. There were empty shelves dotted everywhere and an archway that led to a small kitchenette, with a room that led to a storeroom and small toilet. A through door led to a small courtyard via the back door. A No Entry sign attached to a rope blocked the stairs leading to the flat above.

'Does the flat come with this place then?'

'Sorry to disappoint, but no. Brian, the guy whose space this is, is coming back in the new year so he just wanted to make the extra cash on the empty unit but to save sorting all his personal possessions, just lock up and leave his flat. So, I'm just doing the deal for downstairs. He said it'll pay for his trip to Australia, and who am I to argue with a man on a mission?'

'You're going to tell me it's cash only in a minute, aren't you?'

He looked to his left and coughed. 'Umm, yes, it is.'

'I see. So, what's the deal then?'

'Well, it's available for three months from beginning of October – or earlier, if you want it – and we can sort a pro-rata amount for any extra weeks. Rent is £1150 a month which includes utilities, which in my eyes is extremely cheap considering the state of the economy at the moment. You get one key. And need to leave the place exactly as you find it by midnight on December the thirty first.

'How very Cinderella,' Sabrina said wryly.

'Anyway, you're clearly not a tourist if you're considering this. What's your name and where do you come from?'

'What is this, the TV show *Blind Date?*' Sabrina smirked. 'But it's Jilly and I'm staying in Penrigan.'

He screwed up his face, clearly not knowing what she was on about, then held out his hand and shook hers tightly. A firm handshake was a must for Sabrina. Another tick – not that she was keeping count...

'Lowen Kellow, your friendly market inspector, pleased to meet you Jilly...' He paused. 'I take it you do have a last name?'

Sabrina grimaced, then catching sight of a stray book on the floor added. 'Yes, it's Dickens. Jilly Dickens.'

'And what's the nature of your business, Jilly Dickens.' He slowed his words on her name and then, as if reaching for her soul, stared directly at her with his one green and one bluey-green eye. 'You do know what you are going to be selling surely?'

The book title came up trumps this time. 'Gifts. Mainly... erm, Christmas gifts. That's it! That's what I am going to be selling. All your festive frivolities, from novelty crackers to seven-foot trees.'

'Wow, that sounds perfect – and you won't be upsetting any of the other sellers as it's a unique sales proposition to here. So, I take it you're interested?'

Sabrina gulped. What was she doing? Here was that impulsive side of her that hadn't reared its head for a while. She didn't need the money, she was supposed to be taking some time out for herself and even though she had worked in her mate's interior design shop, she had never actually run a shop in her life, but suddenly she felt a sense of excitement that she had never felt before. The cheeky chimp of doubt on her shoulder began its process of justification. After all, it was only for three months and things would have most certainly settled down for her publicly by then when she returned to London. She had always adored Christmas. And as a child, she'd loved playing shops with her brother, when he could be bothered. She'd had one of those press tills, where a price shot up and the drawer sprung open to reveal plastic coins and paper money. And what was the worst that could happen?

'Do you have a lot of interested parties?' Sabrina noticed his lips were a decent shape, not too big, not too small. She couldn't be doing with a man with a non-existent top lip. Not that she was considering doing anything with them – or him…

He glanced down at his phone. 'Looks like blinking Jemima Puddle-Duck was just wasting my time, so you're my first today. But tomorrow I have a couple of early viewings, then Monday I'm flat out. If you don't take it pronto, I guarantee it will be gone by Tuesday. It's a prime space here and if you play it right you could make yourself a pretty penny. Anyway, Jilly, what's your story? Because I would have sure remembered seeing a beautiful woman like you in these parts.'

'Said the salesman to the buyer.' Sabrina winked. 'Look, I'm in a hurry, I have an appointment at the bank.'

'To get the cash for me, I hope?'

Sabrina laughed. 'You're unbelievable.'

'Yes, I am – and I also can be whatever you want *me* to be.'

'Touché, Mr Kellow. Now, do you have a card? I left the newspaper with your number in it on the bus.

'Here.' He handed her a simple black and white card, then held his hand flat out to her and grinned. 'Yours?'

Sabrina smirked. 'I've gotta run.'

'I'm afraid sales doesn't work like that. What if I have to urgently contact you to let you know there's a bidding war or to …' He stopped himself.

'Or to what, Mr Kellow?' Sabrina seductively looked over the top of her glasses at him. She was sure she could see him redden. She pulled a pen from her bag, scribbled on the edge of the card he had given her, ripped it off and handed it over.

'I must go. Sorry again about the coffee. And let me take this book, it's cluttering up the place. She quickly shoved the battered copy of *A Christmas Carol* into her handbag.

And with that Sabrina Swift, aka Sabrina Valentine and now Jilly Dickens, hotfooted it down the hill, leaving the usually cocksure Lowen Kellow with a somewhat bemused smile on his face and a slight stirring in his nether regions.

The sun was about to set over Penrigan Head when Sabrina eventually got back to Kevrinek Cottage. Seabirds on the wing made tiny black silhouettes against the stunning hues of red, pink and orange striping through the evening sky. The hypnotic sound of the sea gently rushing up against the rocks was one that she would never tire of.

Sabrina started to run a bath, then turning on the television for background noise, put her food shopping away and decided that she would make up the hamper for Isaac and Belle tomorrow and take it down to the main house in the morning.

Lying on her bed, she first called Simon to see how he was doing and checked with his carers that he wasn't in need of anything, then began to draft and re-draft a message to Dominic. After five minutes, she jumped up to turn her now full bath off and came back to lie on the soft white duvet. Shutting her eyes for inspiration, a vision of her wayward partner ran through her mind. He was handsome in a classic way. Silver white, perfectly cut hair. Hazel eyes with lashes far longer than hers. Big features that suited his big personality and six-foot frame. And at forty-nine, although slightly soft bellied due to the amount of drinks receptions and dinners he went to, he was still extremely attractive for his age. He also knew that he had 'the allure'. Men of the worst kind, with egos as big as their dicks.

More fool her to think she had tamed Dominic Best's wild ways. And now she was back in the quiet cottage with just her thoughts for company, and despite knowing all this, she still felt the dreadful pang of missing him. And when she felt low like this, there was usually only one person she would go to who would understand. Throwing the handset to the end of the bed, she went to her suitcase. Tucked in the front pocket was a blue envelope containing a well fingered piece of paper which she took out, lay back on the bed and started to read it for the five hundredth time since the day she had found it five years ago, the day that she had screamed until she had no breath left in her lungs.

The day she realised that her life was never going to be the same again.

My darling daughter,

I have to go. The pain I feel for ruining your brother's life is too much to bear. I should have stopped him from jumping… but I didn't. I always heard that losing a child was the worst thing that could ever happen to anyone, and it is. It really is. I know he's not dead, but he is really, in my mind anyway. The home he is in is outstanding and the trust your father and I have set up for him will free you from worry about making sure he's safe for your whole life. You don't have to worry about me now, either. Your dad is a good man. He will be there for you. I know he will. You gave me such joy. Even in my darkest moments, that smile of yours lit up a room. You are a shining star and an amazing actress. I am so proud of you and what you've achieved, and I hope you find a true love that is deserving of you. A few things before I go:

- *Always have something to do, something to love and something to hope for*
- *If a man shows you he's a loser, believe it*
- *Follow your heart and you won't get lost*
- *Take chances!*
- *Be your beautiful unique self*
- *Some people are going to reject you because you shine too bright for them, but you ignore them and just keep shining, my girl.*

Please don't cry for me, darling girl, for wherever I am going frees me from the terrible pain I feel every day. I'm no fun to be around. I'm a burden and this black dog of depression is too hard to bear now.

Love forever.
Your mum X

Sabrina folded the letter and replaced it carefully in her suitcase, then stripped naked and walked through to the bathroom. Stepping into the old-fashioned free-standing bath, she lay back and shut her eyes. As the hot bubbles began to ease her whirring mind and tired legs, she began to mull over the three very important and life changing decisions she was about to make.

Chapter Ten

Belle knocked loudly on the door of Kevrinek Cottage. She saw the shutter twitch in Sabrina's bedroom. She knocked again. No reply. Then with a concerned face, she turned the key in the door. She walked slowly through to the bedroom to find a pyjama wearing Sabrina, curled up in the foetal position, her face tear-stained and sorrow ridden.

'Oh, my darling girl. I know the key I have is just for emergencies, but this felt like one. I also don't want you to think I've been stalking you, but late last night the camera alerted us that someone was outside the cottage in the darkness. Then I made out it was you sat outside at the end of the garden, head in hands. What's happened, Sabrina?' The nurse's voice was soft and gentle.

Sabrina started to sob. Belle put down the box she was carrying, took off her shoes and lay down behind her new friend holding her tightly like a big spoon. When her crying eventually subsided, Sabrina sat up, reached for the tissues by her bed and rested her head on the headboard. Belle sat up next to her and held her hand.

'I just made some cherry scones.' Belle nodded to the box she had brought in with her. 'I can't eat the whole lot alone.' Sabrina managed a watery smile as her friend got off the bed. 'Let me make some coffee and you can tell me what's going on.'

Still in bed with hot drink in hand, Sabrina sniffed loudly. 'I messaged Dominic and told him it was definitely over.'

'Woah. You did it over text?'

'Oh Belle, please don't judge me – not today, anyway.'

'Sorry, sorry, I have a habit of not thinking before I speak. Are you sure this is what you want, Sabrina?'

'No, I'm not sure at all but I can't talk to him. I know it would end up in a screaming match – on my side, anyway. It's all too raw.'

'What did he reply?'

'That's the thing: he hasn't. He clearly doesn't care.'

'That's your assumption. Maybe he's working out in his head what to say. Being brutally honest, love and lust do sit in a different stable and I'm sure he's feeling as wretched as you. I mean, look at you. You're a lot to give up, Sabrina Swift.'

Sabrina sighed. 'Yes, but if you love someone, surely you don't even think about getting intimate with someone else.' Sabrina waved her hand in dismissal. 'No, Belle. I won't get over this. Trust is so important to me. The number of indecent proposals I used to get and could have taken... Even when I was a bit tipsy, well, I managed to say no. And I said no because I loved and respected that man.' She made a groaning noise, and her face contorted. 'I'm so confused!'

'I'm not defending him, Sabrina. But three years is a long time to be with someone, and maybe if you had a conversation with him and heard all the facts from the horse's mouth, it might be easier to move on whether you took him back or not.'

'The facts are that he shagged someone whilst engaged to somebody else. I think it would be a unanimous guilty verdict from the jury, don't you?'

Sabrina bashed down an imaginary gavel. 'Extenuating circumstances, your honour, too much Guinness and a huge fucking ego.' She blew her nose loudly. 'I've also told my agent that I don't want to do *Prancing on Ice*.'

'OK.' Belle nodded. 'How did they take that?'

'She, Caroline...went ape shit, which I knew she would as it was a big deal for her – literally. But she's not the one who was going to be catapulted around the ice wearing sharp blades on her feet and no helmet.' Sabrina paused. 'Actually, that sounds like an exact description of my life at the moment.' Belle stuck her bottom lip out in sympathy. 'She also thinks its career suicide me taking too much time out of the public eye.' Sabrina sighed. 'I'll talk to her when she calms down. Which, knowing Caroline, could take a while.'

'I understand your logic, but do you not maybe think throwing yourself into something else might take your mind off everything else that's going on?'

'With throwing being the operative word, there.'

'Ha! Yes, sorry, I didn't think.'

'Well, there is actually something else...'

Belle looked quizzical. 'Go on.'

'I had a wonderful time in Hartmouth yesterday. You said I'd love the vibe of it, and I really did. What a beautiful place, so full of life and history and the backdrop of the sea, and the whole community around the ferry and the market was captivating. I was only there hours, and I could feel something that I couldn't really put my finger on. Maybe it was because I felt a sense of belonging, even though I know no one. Anyway, Star, one of the stallholders, was just a delight and well... I ended up viewing a market unit that had become free.'

'Oh, my goodness. Why on earth...?'

'I had no intention of doing it, but I literally bumped into the guy doing the show around as he stepped outside looking for the intended lessee, and threw coffee all down him.'

'Oh, shit!'

'Yes, he was a moody bastard, but a handsome moody bastard. Talking of lust, I do have to say that despite all the feelings of distress whirring around in me, he did stir up some sort of carnal desire. Anyway, the unit is as cute as he is and it's only up for a three-month rent.'

'Don't tell me you're going for it? How exciting!'

'I told him the Jilly lie. I mean, I couldn't tell him who I really was and you're going to laugh but I didn't say my last name was Valentine but Dickens.' Sabrina pointed to her chest and laughed. 'Meet Jilly Dickens, Ferry Lane Market stall holder extraordinaire – or soon to be, maybe.'

'Dickens? Where did that come from?'

'A random copy of *A Christmas Carol* that was lying on the floor. It used to be a second-hand books and records stall. Here!' she lifted the worn book from her bedside table.

Belle laughed out loud. 'That's hilarious.'

'Even more funny is when he asked what I would be selling, I clocked the book again and said, "everything Christmas". I'll sell general gifts too, but he seemed happy with that.'

'I love everything about this, Sabrina. Oh my God, a Christmas gift store in the market, I already can't wait to see what you are going to fill it with.'

Sabrina laughed at her new friend's enthusiasm. 'Ooh, whilst I remember, I got you and Isaac some goodies from the market. Remind me to pack them up before you go.'

'Aw, you didn't need to do that.'

'I really did. You two have been so amazing and so generous since the minute I arrived.'

'That's very kind, but come on, spill the tea: are you taking it – the market unit, I mean? Please say you are – then I have three more months of you. But what about your soap role?'

'I am in prison until next year, so that's OK.'

Belle goggled at her. 'Your life is extraordinary.'

'Not really. I'm just a normal woman like anyone else. I just choose to role play for a living. So, dear Belle, should I take the market stall unit or not?'

'Sabrina, you know my answer on that one. The same as when you asked me about your relationship: whatever I say, you will make your own decision.'

'It'll be a whole clean start, and it will be hard work for not so much reward, I know that. But it's not about the money. It's about me and getting off the all-consuming treadmill of fame and meeting real people, with real lives. Who take me at face value, for who I am, not who they imagine I am.'

'Wow, I can see why you are an actress. I feel like I want to stand up and cheer you after that little soliloquy! But for now, how about we just go to the bottom of the garden, sit on the bench overlooking the sea and eat cherry scones and clotted cream?'

The two women sat munching the gorgeous fresh bakes, then – PING – a message alert sounded from Sabrina's phone.

Expecting it to be Dominic, Sabrina took a deep breath, but on reading the message a glimpse of a smile, and then her mouth fell open.

'What's up?' Belle enquired.

'Mr Market Inspector only wants to meet me for a drink... tonight!'

Chapter Eleven

Sabrina sat in the window seat of the *Penrigan Arms* at the appointed hour feeling slightly sick. Was this what the first stages of betrayal felt like? Was this how Dominic felt before he had decided to do the dirty on her with the French stick? But this was different, surely: she was technically single now, so she could do what she bloody well wanted. Couldn't she?

Twisting the yellow topaz ring around her little finger, she thought back to what Star had said about the meaning of the stone. Maybe it was fate that she had bumped into Lowen Kellow and been given the chance at a new opportunity, just when she needed it. She wasn't stupid: he clearly wanted to seal the deal on the unit. Or maybe he took all his prospective clients for a pre-deal-signing drink. And as for betrayal – well, if her no-good ex-fiancé didn't even have the decency to acknowledge her heartfelt message from last night, he could Foxtrot Oscar! And she was only having a drink with the man, wasn't she?

The dark-haired man gave her a brooding smile and waved as he walked past the window. He greeted her with a kiss on the cheek. 'So sorry I'm late, I had to drop my...um...my sister at the train station, she's off on holiday.'

'Lucky her. Anywhere decent?' A noisy group of five adults bowled through the door causing Lowen to raise his voice.

'Ibiza.'

'Nice! Best time of year to go, I went last year with my... with my ex.'

Lowen looked to her left hand and noticed the huge diamond ring he had clocked at the market. 'I see.'

'Right, what are we drinking?' Sabrina put her bag on the table.

'I'll get them.' Lowen pulled a wallet out the back pocket of his dark, well-fitted jeans.

'I'm driving, but I will have a white wine to kick off with please. A French Sauvignon if they've got it.' Just saying the word French made her think again to Dominic's fuck up. She blew out a deep breath.

Whilst Lowen went to the bar, Sabrina took in the old pub that was beginning to fill up with Friday night revellers. It certainly wasn't the kind of chichi joint she and Dominic would usually frequent. Low beams that looked like a woodworm's paradise, and amongst framed, yellowing black-and-white photos of days gone by in the Penrigan area, there were some modern canvases containing quotes. One caught her eye – *Don't worry about failures, worry about the chances you miss when you don't even try* – and she smiled. She fiddled with her *new* ring again.

Lowen put down a glass of wine in front of her and held up his pint of cloudy cider. 'Cheers to you becoming a Ferry Lane Market stall holder.'

Sabrina grinned. 'You reckon?'

'I know you want it.'

Sabrina ignored his seductive tone. 'I like it in here. Not so many old traditional boozers left around my neck of the woods, now.'

'So, you're not from around here originally then?'

'No. I used to live in North London.'

'Gotcha.'

'How about you?'

'I was actually born and bred in Exeter but moved down to Penrigan… hmm let me think… I'd just celebrated my fortieth, so must be three years ago now.'

Sabrina clocked the black polo shirt he was wearing. Well, it was more the muscly brown arms on show that caught her attention. He had good hands, too. Another important tick for her. His skin was smooth, and his well-cut hair and Tintin-like quiff made him look far younger than his years. Now she was sat opposite him, she took a good look at his one green eye and one bluey-green one.

'Heterochromia.' Sabrina announced.

'You what?'

'You have different coloured irises – that's what it's called.'

'Clever and beautiful, a wicked combination.' Lowen bit his lip as he looked at her. She looked away, feeling her cheeks redden. She couldn't recall feeling anything like this even when she had first met Dominic at a soap awards after-party. It was as if some sort of electric current was running between them. She felt compelled to smile. She went to fiddle with her long hair, then realised there wasn't any there to fiddle with. Pushing her glasses up on her nose, she took a huge gulp of wine, then another for good measure.

'You should have got a taxi.' Lowen took a drink.

She laughed. 'I'm a terrible drunk and I wouldn't want you taking advantage of me.'

'Are you sure?' He laughed back. 'Anyway, obviously I'm here not for pleasantries but to ensure you sign the contract for the unit.'

She stuck her tongue out at him. 'Well, you need to do better than just buying me a white wine, then, don't you.'

'Oh, really?' Lowen pushed his tongue into the side

of his mouth.

'Lowen Kellow! I meant buy me dinner. I saw a tasty steak and kidney pie on the blackboard.'

'Then your wish is my command, Jilly Dickens.'

With food on order, Lowen returned to the table and lifted her hand to get a better look at the huge diamond sat on it. 'He must have loved you?'

'Not enough, clearly.' Sabrina sighed.

'Then he was a fool.' He squeezed her hand.

With a huge slug of wine, a visible deep breath and a defiant, 'Yes, he was a bloody fool wasn't he!' Sabrina Swift ripped off her engagement ring and shoved it in the zipped pocket of her handbag.

Five large wines, six cloudy ciders and a whole lot of flirty talk later, the pair stood in the car park next to Sabrina's convertible.

'Well, you clearly can't drive home,' Lowen said, stating the obvious, his Devonian accent far more evident with a drink on board.

'I know that, you know that, the police know that and oh shit how am I going to get back?'

'Where do you live? If it's not far I can try and get you a cab or as that's not easy down here, I could always walk you.'

Sabrina had enough sense about her to know that she couldn't face being on foot and pressing the Kevrinek gate intercom in this state. Then she remembered Isaac saying that she could cut through from the public footpath that ran alongside the cliff, without the gate having to be opened.

'I'm gonna walk myself it's fine.'

'I get it, you don't trust yourself with me.' Lowen said in a dead-pan voice, grabbing her hand as he did so and kissing it. 'It's OK, Miss Dickens, I shall ring a cab for you. Where to?'

'Kevrinek please.'

'Ah, you're staying with the great Isaac Benson himself, are you? How do you know him?'

'Umm. It's a long story.'

Lowen held the handset to his ear for a minute. 'Nah. Just ringing out. I guessed we'd have trouble getting a car on a Friday night.'

'We'll have to walk along the cliff path. It's going to be so dark. Are you sure you don't mind walking with me?'

'I've got a torch on my phone, it's fine.' He put his arm around her shoulders. 'Come on, it'll be fun.'

By the time the pair of them had finished the remainder of the bottle of champagne in the fridge as well as every snack that she had left in the welcome basket, they were properly smashed.

'Did you call the engagement off, then?' Lowen asked out of nowhere.

Sabrina hiccupped. 'I don't want to talk about it.'

Breaking into Rod Stewart's bestselling hit of the same name, Lowen mirrored her words and without thought added the *"how you broke my heart"* bit.'

'Very funny. But what happened *wasn't* funny.'

Lowen looked genuinely upset. 'I'm sorry. I really am.'

'Don't be. It's fine, and what was it that Maya Angelou said? "When you know better, do better."' She clumsily stood up and did a funny little dance. 'The only way is up baby!' She grabbed him by the hand and led him into the bedroom. Without losing eye contact, she slowly slipped off her silk cream shirt to reveal a sexy white lace *Victoria's Secret* bra, then undoing his belt slowly, she purred, 'You know I said earlier that you could do better.'

A captivated Lowen nodded.

'Then fuck me like you mean it.'

Chapter Twelve

The dawn chorus was not quite so appealing at seven a.m. with a thumping headache and a mouth as dry as a nun's chuff. Sabrina groaned as she remembered what had happened the night before. She swept her hand over to the other side of the bed and with a rush of relief found it empty. She shouted out a shaky 'hello', and thankfully the only reply was a high pitched 'kiou-ki-ki-ki' from a Red Kite hovering above the cottage. Not wanting to be spotted by either Isaac or Belle in this state and for fear of them being angry at her for inviting a near stranger to their land, rather than head up the garden like she usually did for her morning coffee, she opened the back door, flicked on the kettle, then stood on the toilet seat and called Dee.

'Rini, it's seven a.m.'

'But you're always up for the school run by now.'

'Not on a Saturday, I'm not,' her long-suffering friend continued.

'Oh, mate, I'm so sorry, shall I call back?'

'I'm awake now. Hang on, I'm going downstairs to make a cuppa.'

'What's up?'

'I've done something really terrible.'

'Oh, Rini, what now?'

'I've shagged someone else.'

'Good for you, I say.'

'Really?'

'Yes. Who was it – and more importantly, how was it?'

'From what I can remember, it was hot. Lowen – you know, the market inspector bloke I told you about the other day? – it was him. He's got a great body and did make me laugh.'

'Well, as long as you were safe and nobody got hurt, then what's the bother?' Dee underplayed.

'I just spotted an open condom wrapper on the sink, so all good.'

'I guess that means the contract for the market stall was sealed with far more than a kiss, then.'

'Very funny, but yes. I want to do this, Dee. I'm certain. And it was you who said I would have to be getting a proper job.'

Dee laughed. 'In jest, I did, yes. I didn't think for one minute you'd take it literally. But, joking aside are you OK about last night?'

'To be honest, I feel fine about it, although that might still be the drink talking. Drunken sex with a nigh-on stranger has made me feel young again. I instigated it, like a proper harlot. And I know an eye for an eye is not the answer, but stupidly it doesn't make me feel such a fool, now. And we had fun, he seems like a nice guy.'

'Well, that's a good thing.' A short pause. 'Rini, I need to talk you about something, too.'

'Oh dol, I knew something was up.'

Suddenly, the bathroom door opened and a familiar voice said, 'What doesn't make you feel such a fool now, eh, Sabrina Swift?' She jumped a foot in the air, dropped the handset and nearly fell off the toilet seat.

The man walked back through to the kitchen and sat at the table. Sabrina furtively pushed the condom wrapper into her dressing gown pocket.

'Rini, Rini, are you OK?' Dee shouted through the phone.

A breathless Sabrina retrieved her handset. 'I've gotta go, Dee. It's Dominic. He's here! Promise to call you later.'

Pulling her newly named 'noneymoon dressing gown' tightly around her, she went through to the kitchen and hurriedly removed the champagne bottle and flutes from the table and threw the various food wrappers in the bin.

'Quite a party, it seems. Good to see you're not missing me too much – and what the fuck have done to yourself? Your beautiful hair!'

The past pain of a plethora of nasty comments rose up and stung Sabrina worse than any bee. And as the feelings of hurt began to fuel her pent up her anger, Sabrina's voice became growl like.

'It's not all about what's on the outside, Dominic Best. And do you know what, I'm very happily munching my way to my very own muffin top, too. Fuck you and fuck the shallow world of show business!'

'Wow.' Dominic replied, eyes wide.

'What are you doing here anyway, Dom? I quite clearly stated in my message that I wanted some time away from you, away from work, away from everyone and that I'd be in touch when I was ready to sort out my stuff in the flat.' Dom stared at her, mute. Her eyes were wild. 'That's not too unreasonable, now, is it?'

'Actually, Sabrina, I think it is. We've been together three years and you disregard me with a simple text telling me all this.'

Sabrina felt her blood beginning to boil. Her face contorted in anger. 'I tell you what's unreasonable, Dominic Best. What's unreasonable is that seconds before we were to sign our lives away to matrimonial bliss, your young French breadstick of a girlfriend arrived, joyfully telling me and all our guests that you'd fornicated with her after a rugby game. In the toilets, was it? Or did you take her back to your fancy hotel?'

'I've driven through the night to be here, for you.' Dominic's voice was slow and steady. 'I need to tell you something.'

'It's not quite with the Cindy Lauper intention, though, is it? I mean, you weren't exactly going to follow her lyrics and creep in my room to make love to me, or maybe you were? Whoopee, every hole's a goal for Dominic Best.'

'I mean, if I could have got away with it.' The charismatic editor smirked, causing Sabrina to reluctantly smile and wish that a couple of the dead butterflies hadn't come back to life in her tummy. Then she felt her face crumple and another surge of anger rose to the fore.

'I hate you. I fucking hate you! You've ruined my life. Now, please go back to the stone you crawled out under from and just FUCK OFF!'

'We're not at Kindergarten, Sabrina. We are grown adults. I made a mistake, I was drunk. I'm human. I don't love her. It was just sex. A stupid… drunken… mistake.'

'Well, you clearly made quite the impression for her to show up like she did!'

Dom sighed deeply. 'I'm sorry Sabrina, but what else do you want me to say?'

Sabrina squirmed on her chair. 'But you don't get it, do you? Not every man who gets drunk is unfaithful! The intent was there. How do I know that every time you go away, you're not shagging women across the globe.'

'You're being over dramatic.'

'THAT'S MY JOB!'

'God, I love you, Sabrina Swift.'

'Don't say that.' Sabrina's voice cracked. 'She's gone back to Paris, I take it? I saw the photos of you both. Thanks for that.'

Dominic bit his lip and put his hand to his forehead.'

'Well, this is the thing.'

'For fuck's sake.' A wave of nausea went through Sabrina. Why had she drunk so much wine last night? She went to the tap, filled a pint glass and downed half of it.

'So, she – Françoise – was living with her parents and they are not happy to support her anymore, so I said I'd help her find a place in London. And please don't go crazy, but well she is in the Bloomsbury flat at the moment whilst I help her get a place sorted. But it's not what it looks like.'

'Don't go crazy? It's not what it looks like? What does it look like to ME Dominic Best? It looks like Little Miss Frenchie is sleeping in OUR Bloomsbury flat, in OUR fucking bed!' Sabrina's voice raised another octave.

Dominic's voice remained level. 'Not for long, though. Honestly, trust me on this.'

There was a knock on the front door. Sabrina walked over and half-opened it. Despite his car being outside and Isaac or Belle obviously letting him through the gate, she tried to shield Dominic from view.

'Just checking you're OK.' Belle said lightly.

'Yes. Fine.' Sabrina nodded far too quickly. 'I'll talk to you later if that's OK, Belle.'

'We were so relieved to realise it was Dominic here with you and not a complete stranger. I take it you both went to the pub, and he left his car there. We had to laugh at you both staggering across the field last night.'

'No! That wasn't him!' Sabrina mouthed, a look of horror on her face and cursing the fact that this place was so abnormally monitored.

'Shit,' Belle mouthed back, then her voice returned to its usual volume. 'And then when I realised it... umm... I realised it was old Mr Docherty... the err...ugly potman from the pub, just checking you got back alright, well, that was an even bigger relief...'

Sabrina's face was contorting again, not with anger, but despair at Belle's stupidity. 'Why did you tell him I was here?' Sabrina said in an aggressive half-whisper.

Belle's face dropped and it looked to Sabrina that she was going to cry. Her voice sounded like a high-pitched chorister. 'Talk another time.' And with tears in her eyes, Belle scurried back down to the main house.

'So old Mr Docherty likes a glass of champagne too, does he, the dirty old dog?' Dominic Best was the epitome of not kidding a kidder. 'And before you upset that lovely woman again, she didn't tell me you were here.'

'Who did then?'

'You were spotted on Penrigan Pier, evidently, so I knew immediately where I would find you.'

'Oh.'

'Yes, Sabrina. You need to think before you speak sometimes. But looking at you now, I think you'll be fine. I hardly recognised you. You looked so much prettier with long hair and there's no photo of you on the pier, so I won't be running with the story, don't worry. I just offered the reward as *I* wanted to know where you were.'

Sabrina shook her head in disbelief. Did she even know this man standing in front of her, anymore? Then, not fathoming where or how to place her emotions, she started to cry. On pulling a tissue out of her dressing gown pocket to dry her eyes, the empty condom wrapper fell as if in slow motion to the floor. She moved her bare foot quickly to cover it, but she was too slow.

Dominic looked down at the red wrapper with its torn off corner and then up to her face; a face that had guilt written all over it in huge capital letters.

'I can explain,' Sabrina blew out an exaggerated breath. 'Actually, why should I have to?'

Sabrina steadied herself for an outburst, which surprisingly never came. Instead, a look of pain the likes of which Sabrina had never seen before spread over Dominic's face. She felt that if his heart were outside his body, it would take at least a week to clear up the shards of broken bits that were smashing around the pair of them. He stood up and reached for his car keys. His eyes were full of tears. Without words, he went to the front door and on reaching it he turned around and in an almost inaudible voice, said, 'What happened to us?'

Chapter Thirteen

Sabrina was sat head in hands on the bench seat at the bottom of the garden. The autumn day was as miserable as the actress's face. Even the birds' cheerful chattering had appeared to stop. The wind had started to whip around the apple tree and white clouds were moving across the sky as if trying to escape the huge grey ones that were beginning to loom above the clifftops.

Belle approached quietly and sat down opposite her. 'Hey.'

Sabrina looked up, her face stained with tears. 'Hey.'

'I'm so sorry if I dropped you in it earlier, I just didn't think.' Belle sighed.

Sabrina felt like she was going to cry. 'I was angry with myself, not you. That's usually how it works, isn't it? But when you said I'd been with another man and Dominic overheard, I was like, oh shit!' Sabrina groaned. 'So, I'm sorry I was short with you.' She put her hand to her temple. 'I feel so rough.'

'Bless you. It was Mr Market Inspector, I take it?'

'Yes the very one. Bloody hell, Belle, when the drink is in, the wit is out – another one of my father's favourites. But it's so true.'

'Are you OK, though? I can't even imagine the emotions you're going through, to be honest.'

Sabrina sniffed. 'Last night was fun. Lowen is sexy. I wanted to feel wanted and I got that quick fix. I felt like it wasn't me being played and I was the player, for once.'

'And Dominic?'

Sabrina dropped her sunglasses from her forehead to cover her tired eyes.

'There's no doubt we have a huge connection. We were getting married for god's sake. But – and I can't believe I am actually saying this out loud – the French tart is now living in our flat!'

Belle's mouth fell open. 'What the…?'

'Tell me about it. He says it's not what it looks like, he just feels sorry for her and is finding her a place in London. And beneath the hard exterior of a newspaper editor, he's the softest man, with no clue of how a woman's mind works. Mine included!'

'Clearly.' Belle replied sarcastically. 'And sorry if I'm speaking out of turn here but is that the kind of man you really want, Sabrina? Yes, he's thinking of her but not you in any of this.'

'Exactly, and him doing that just makes me look more of a fool, because this whole debacle isn't just between me and him, is it? When the great British public learn of this through the press, then, well… I can't deal with it.'

'Take the market unit.' Belle suddenly announced, slapping her hand down on the wooden bench seat. 'Take it!'

'Wow. Belle. Where did that come from? And I thought you said you weren't going to give me your opinion on what I should do.'

'I know I did. But if the alternative is walking back into the toxic shitshow that man has created for you, which will undoubtedly affect your mental health, then I see it as a no brainer. Let your heart settle. Let everything settle. What was it your mum said? "Follow your heart and you won't get lost".' Sabrina nodded. 'If you and Dominic are meant to be, then time will not be a barrier. If you love someone, they live inside you. You can block them or say you hate them, but if love is there, then they're here.' The pretty blonde put her hand to her heart. 'And they will live in here until you are either ready to accept that they are going to stay there and you carry them with you even though you'll never see them again, or the love comes alive and you live with them in the real world and not just in your heart.'

'Wow. Talk about me giving the soliloquies, Belle.'

The woman squeezed Sabrina's shoulder, just as she had done on their first day of meeting. 'So, are you going to see Mr Market Inspector again?'

Sabrina laughed. 'Well, I guess I have to now you've made this monumental decision for me.'

They both laughed. A message beeped, and Sabrina immediately showed it to her friend.

Morning sexy. Early viewings done. Say you want me...I mean the unit x

Sabrina took off her shades and looked to Belle, who was clapping her hands together like an excitable sealion.

'Sounds like you've got a new job *and* a new knob. Do it! Just do it!

Chapter Fourteen

Later that morning, Sabrina decided that a bumpy bus ride was not a viable option when she was likely to be sick all over the other passengers. And despite possibly still being slightly over the alcohol limit, a drive through the fields, roof off with the coastal path to her right and the breeze rushing through her hair was the much safer alternative. When she had thankfully managed to find a space in the usually heaving Ferry Lane Market car park straight away, she blew a kiss to the parking angels and tried to call Dee for the second time, but to no avail.

Star Murray beckoned to Sabrina as she walked by her stall. 'Good morning. Did the ring work its magic yet?' The long-haired blonde jiggled her tiny body from side to side as baby Storm began to stir in the papoose.

'Well, I guess it could have, as I've decided to take the spare unit across the street.'

'Oh my god, that's amazing. We'll be neighbours. As long as you're not going to be selling jewellery, that is. Or I will never speak to you again.' Star grinned.

'No, of course not. I can already sense that some people might have my guts for garters if I dare step on their toes.' Sabrina put her hand to her temples. 'Oh, my head.'

'Are you OK?' The baby let out a big shriek, then settled down again just as quickly.

Sabrina groaned. 'Just a tad hungover. I'd have been in bed if it wasn't for signing for the unit.'

'Chance would be a fine thing for me. I'm so tired with getting up in the night to feed this little man, a hangover would be a breeze. So, are you going to be staying above the shop?'

'No, the guy has kept all his stuff there as he's only having an extended holiday. I'm staying in Penrigan at the moment.'

'Oh, that'll be a bit of a trek in the winter, then.'

'Hmm. I was wondering that. I bet those windy track roads get icy, too.'

'Yes, my mum lives up that way.' Star offered. 'It's not pleasant as it has to be real blizzard conditions before the gritters come down as far as us. Actually...would you ever consider moving here? To Hartmouth, I mean'

'I haven't thought about anything other than the unit, to be honest.'

'Well. I only say that as Kara – you may have seen her the other day, pregnant, long auburn hair, my half-sister and beautiful person inside and out, but I am clearly biased.'

'Aw, that's nice.' Sabrina laughed. 'And yes, the flower shop lady.'

'That's her. Well, she has a flat down the front she wants to rent out, and the timing would be perfect for both of you. It's a lovely place, looks right out over the estuary. She's sorting a wedding over at Crowsbridge Hall at the moment. Would you like her number?'

'Yes, that sounds like a great idea. No harm in getting the details and having a look maybe?'

'Exactly. What's your name? Sorry, I didn't think to ask yesterday. I'll tell her you're interested and to expect a call.'

'Wow, maybe this lucky crystal lark is a thing.'

Sabrina grinned. 'I'm Jilly, and yes please.'

'Oh, it's a thing alright.' Just as Star finished reciting Kara's number for Sabrina to put straight into her phone, Storm started to wail from the confines of his cosy papoose as a strong odour began to fill the air. 'Bugger. I better go in and change him. Oh, and Big Frank does the best fry up in town, perfect hangover fodder. Good luck with it all!'

Lowen had his back to her filling out details on a clipboard when Sabrina walked into the unit and shut the door behind her. She walked quietly up to him, put her hands over his eyes and whispered in his ear. 'I didn't recognise you with your clothes on.'

He whipped around. 'You scared the bloody life out of me.' He grinned. 'Well, that was fun, wasn't it? I blame you, of course, for my thumping headache this morning.'

'Of course.' Sabrina grinned. 'It's called a casting couch in my profession. What is it in yours? A leasing couch, maybe? 'Cos it certainly worked.'

'I don't think anyone has EVER made you do anything you didn't want to do in your life before, Jilly Dickens.'

She laughed. 'You're right there, and no, I want this, just like I wanted you last night.' She squeezed his bum.

'You are a very naughty girl.'

'Don't tell Santa or he won't be coming to visit my Christmas shop. Actually, what a good idea that is to get the kids in! A real-life grotto at the back of the unit on market days.'

'Don't be looking at me with Santa Claus in your eyes. I'm far too young, even if you throw a white beard on me.'

They both laughed.

'Joking aside. I'm excited, this will be good for me

and to be honest I want access as soon as possible so I can start getting stock in.' Sabrina started to mentally add up how many fixed shelves there were. 'Do you think people will buy stuff for Christmas in October?'

'Yeah, definitely, plus, the stallholders will love it as they decorate all their stalls in November too.'

'Ooh, I hadn't thought about that. Thank you.'

'Also maybe get some Cornish themed bits and pieces for the tourists to take home.'

'Like Father Christmas eating a pastie or a seagull with a Santa's hat with "Hartmouth" written on it?' Sabrina joked.

Lowen was completely serious. 'Exactly that!'

Sabrina rearranged her face to reflect his sincerity. 'Oh. OK. I best get to know my customer demographic, hadn't I?'

'You'll be fine. The footfall up and down Ferry Lane is heavy, you can't go wrong. I've got the paperwork, so shall I put this Monday as a start date?'

'No time like the present.' Sabrina took a glug from her reusable water bottle. 'Actually, can we make it a week Monday please. I need to sort a few things out.'

'As I said, there's a pro-rata amount added on to what I originally quoted. I will need a five-hundred-pound cash deposit today please and the remainder by next Friday latest.'

'Pro-rata? Come on Lowen. You can't really expect me to pay a whole week extra now, can you?' She looked over her glasses at him.

'You are what is known in the trade as a... little minx. OK. OK, just the three months and one week it is then.'

'Thank you, my love.' Sabrina smirked. 'I'm happy to pay Brian or the council directly if that's easier.'

Lowen didn't make eye contact. 'Makes it tidier to do it this way.'

'Actually, to save me carrying all this cash around with me, take this, please. I got it out the other day and it will stop me keep buying bits from the market.' She handed him an envelope full of notes. 'Will that do for the deposit? There's three hundred in there?'

'As it's you and if you're sure. Do you want a receipt?'

'No, don't worry. I think we know each well enough after last night, don't you?' Sabrina gave him a seductive little glance, then shifted back to seriousness. 'I'm surprised you can sublet these units, actually.'

Lowen looked suddenly annoyed. 'So, to clarify, you're OK to pay all the balance in cash, minus this three hundred, by next Friday?'

'Yes, I just said that.' Sabrina looked quizzical. 'What's wrong with you, moody pants?' She ruffled his quiff. 'Get out of someone else's bed the wrong side or something?'

'Anything but the quiff.' He patted it to check it was still in place. 'OK. I'll cancel all other viewings and lets meet here, say, midday a week Monday. And do you know what, just give me the rest of the cash then. I trust you, too, of course.'

'Well, that's good, because you should.' She pushed her index finger gently against his nose and laughed.

'So, in precisely nine days' time, you will have a set of keys in your hand and will officially be a Ferry Lane Market stall holder. Lowen mirrored her nose press. 'As a matter of interest, what did you do for work in London?'

'Let's just say I'm an international woman of mystery.' She gently grazed his groin with her hand and kissed his neck causing him to groan lightly. 'And, sure, a week Monday at midday is great. This is so exciting! I must be mad but I'm hungover and slightly delirious so give me that pen before I change my mind.' Sabrina squiggled on the dotted line. 'I'm heading to Frank's for a fry up – fancy joining me?'

'I'm sorry, Jilly, but I can't. It's best we are not seen together down here. It not really the thing if you're a stallholder to be fraternising with the inspector, got it? And, well, no discussing what a great price I've let you have this for – you know what people get like.'

'Ooh, look at you all serious.'

'Also, the number you've got for me doubles as my work phone, so can we just keep it professional when you text me as I'm sure they monitor stuff, you know.' His voice then softened slightly. 'That's if you fancied a rerun of last night, of course...' He brushed her lips with his. 'In fact, the dreaded hangover horn is upon me right now.' He pulled her hand down to the bulge in his jeans.

'Bloody hell, Lowen Kellow, you're insatiable.' A vision of Dominic's broken face this morning flashed through her mind. But it was soon counteracted by thoughts of the French stick sleeping in their bed, and how vile Dominic had been to her about her fresh look. Sabrina Swift was angry and hurting, and like an addict, her emptiness needed a high to make her feel at least normal again.

As Lowen led her to the stairs that went up to the private flat. Sabrina giggled. 'It says "No Entry".'

The horny inspector gently rubbed a finger under the crotch of her jeans. 'I don't recall you saying anything like that last night.' He locked the front door and led her upstairs.

Frank's was a stand-alone oblong brick building located right on the edge of the estuary wall. It had a black-and-white striped awning and a pink neon sign saying plainly, Frank's Café. In the summer months, to the right of the building there was a roped-off concrete area housing fixed wooden table benches with red and white sunshades, where market stallholders and visitors alike would companionably unwind and watch the sun go down over the sea as boats of all shapes and sizes negotiated the busy waterway.

A slightly flushed and tousle-haired Sabrina pushed open the door to be greeted with the interior of an old-school American diner, sporting red leather booths, white Formica tables and a jazzy tiled floor. There were six high metal stools where you could prop yourself up at the counter and, if you didn't fancy some of Big Frank's infamous hooky booze, you could choose one of the milkshakes, hot drinks or plentiful juices on offer. Sabrina felt a sense of happiness on spotting the All-Day Breakfast sign propped up next to the till. She also loved that the walls were jam packed with black-and-white prints of the Hollywood stars of yesteryear. Sabrina smiled as she clocked Audrey Hepburn in *Breakfast at Tiffany's*, the famous photo in which she is wearing a gorgeous tight black dress and seductively holding a cigarette holder.

'Now there's a girl who looks like she's in need of an all-day breakfast, if ever I saw one.' Frank Brady put a menu down in front of Sabrina, who was now sat at a table overlooking the water.

'Is it that obvious?' She smiled. She had always had a bit of thing for an Irish accent. Dominic had Irish roots but sadly that was as far as it went.

The sight of the imposing and heavily tattooed Frank Brady made her wonder what was in the water down here, for this man took up a lot of space. Six feet four of it, in fact. What with Isaac and Lowen, it was like a battle of the giants. But the café owner would most certainly win on both looks and charm, with his wild Romany look, black collar-length hair and eyes so dark they were impossible to read.

With a full English breakfast, Americano and a full-fat Coke on order, Sabrina felt a little tingle go through her as she thought back to the fast and furious sex she had just had with Lowen Kellow. He was confirmation that bad-boy blood definitely made the heart beat faster. Her lust had counteracted the guilt she had felt in having sex on another man's bed, and she wasn't even put off by the thought that any man who carried a condom in his wallet probably wasn't the type you'd want to take home to your mother. If you had one, that was. But she was savvy enough to realise that he wasn't anywhere near her Mr Right. He was her Mr Right Now, a sticking plaster over the knife wound that Dominic Best had firstly driven in and then turned at the announcement of crumbs now being left in her bed by the French stick.

But what *was* she doing with him? And how could she be doing it so soon after supposedly wanting to marry the man she had once fallen deeply in love with? Maybe the relationship hadn't been what she thought it was with Dominic. That when the first honeymoon period had ended and they'd gone into frenetic everyday life, she assumed that was what her relationship with him was destined to be like. But now she had been away from it for a while, she was already beginning to question its substance. They rarely spent time together and she couldn't remember having sex like she had just had with Lowen with him. Not since the early days anyway. But sex like that was just a snack, a McDonald's cheeseburger, a momentary fix of a primal urge and not a fulfilling and tasty roast dinner of intimacy and enjoyment. And yes, to a degree, she had had roast beef and all the trimmings with Dominic. But she was now beginning to realise that perhaps the custard on the apple pie had been missing all along.

Maybe Belle was right in saying that by removing herself from her hectic and sometimes false lifestyle, she could now concentrate on herself as a person, not as an actress, and focus on what she really was feeling. She had also ruminated a lot on what Dee had said about it being a good chance to realise what she did actually miss about Dominic. She looked to her phone to see if her dear Essex girlfriend had replied to her messages. Nothing. Sabrina felt a stirring of disquiet. She hoped that she was OK. It was hard to be so far away from her mate, where there was normally nothing they couldn't sort out over a cup of tea and biscuits at the Dickinson family's kitchen table.

She thought back to their last conversation, where Dee had conveyed an almost over-the-top reaction of joy at her sleeping with Lowen. At the time it had seemed like her friend was just being supportive, but now... She brought her overthinking mind back to the moment, gave herself a mental shake. Trust was the word. And she trusted her lifelong friend with her life.

'So, two eggs, two bacon, two sausage, black pudding, two toast, mushrooms, tomato, baked beans and a little special hair of the dog to welcome you to my establishment, as I don't believe you've been in before.' Big Frank placed a huge oval plate full of food down in front of her, along with a shot glass of a purple liquid. He winked. 'Sloe gin, but if anyone asks, it's blackcurrant cordial.'

Sabrina knocked the sharp elixir back in one and felt her face contort like a bulldog chewing a wasp. 'Slow is the operative word this morning,' she gasped, 'but thanks so much – that would get a sloth going!'

'Just visiting for the day, are you?' Frank enquired, removing the empty tray from her table.

'Actually, no. I'm going to be selling in the market very soon.'

'Oh. Are you now? You took Brian's place, I take it. Well, I'm so glad you've come in today, then. I'm open to suit the stallholders' needs and you'll be very welcome here. You also get a ten percent discount on food. And...' – he did a little drum roll on the side of her table with his free hand – 'you also get an invite to the exclusive Frank's end of season party for stallholders and their families.'

'That sounds like the hottest ticket in town.' Sabrina grinned and for a second felt like her old warm and witty self. 'When is this extravaganza?'

'Look at you, giving out the cheek already, so you are. You'll be giving Charlie Dillon a run for his money at this rate.'

A guy wearing shorts and a bum bag around his waist had just come charging in the back door adjacent to her table. 'Charlie Dillon? The most un-PC man in town, you mean.'

Sabrina took a gulp of her iced cold coke. 'I take it that's the bald man who runs the fruit and veg stall?'

'The very person...and my dad.' The ferryman added and laughed. 'Of course, you two have met already. He never misses a pretty lady.' Sabrina felt herself blushing to her dyed-blonde roots. 'Billy Dillon. Son of Charlie and Pat, husband to Kerry – or Kara, as you may know her – and your charming ferryman, at your service.' He doffed a pretend cap.

'Hi... I'm Jilly... and I'm sorry to be rude about your dad.'

'Well, a big hello Jilly, from Billy.' They both laughed. 'And please don't apologise – my old man, well he taught me everything I know. And you're right, he does need to rein in that tongue of his, sometimes.'

He looked from Sabrina to Frank. 'Sorry to interrupt, mate, but can you do me a couple of coffees pronto, please? Extra shot in one of them.' He yawned noisily. 'Both my little angels were up at four thirty!'

Sabrina took in the ferryman who was only a couple of inches taller than her, his tight black t-shirt highlighting his toned chest, back and arms. He looked noticeably young to be a father of two. But was there ever a right time for anything, especially where babies were concerned? She often got frustrated with workaholic Dom's constant mantra of 'when I retire, this will all change'. After him refusing another holiday with her due to work commitments, a lightbulb moment of an old drama teacher telling her, "You think you're being selective in your search for a partner, but everyone ends up marrying their father anyway", had sprung to mind. And that was exactly what she had done. Nearly married a man who for whatever reason didn't want to ever sit long in his own reality. Would rarely enjoy 'the now' and like a lot of people who didn't stop working, thought that when they did, that would be the answer to all happiness. When in fact, the reason they were workaholics was so that they never had to sit down and face life's realities, which usually equated to facing their demons.

A smiling Billy waved his goodbyes and hurried back to the *Happy Hart* and its attached car ferry. Taking in his tanned, hairy legs and cheeky face, she made a mental note to tell Dee that for some reason the "allure" percentage in this town was off the scale.

At home, the circles she mixed in were hardly full of 'real' people. Instead, they were full of preening men and 'plastic fantastic' women, with designer clothes and *Turkey teeth* –the expression for someone whose teeth were as perfect and white as fresh snow following a trip overseas to get them fixed for a whole lot cheaper than in the UK. People, whose social media profiles were

more important to them than them sitting in the now
and experiencing life with their loved ones. Where they
felt like they had to share everything, even what they
were having for breakfast, with the world. She could
slate Dom for not being present, but she knew that
sadly she had fallen into the trap of social media
acceptance, too. Before the wedding, her selfie-taking
had been off the scale. As an actress, she loved to be
adored. Until she had been faced with this scandal, that
was. Being photographed was the price you paid for
fame and on a night out she was so used to what she
called the PPR cycle – Pout, Pose, Repeat – that she
quite often would whisper it to herself as she continued
it. She often wondered what the public expected her life
to be like behind the scenes. Did they imagine that her
hair was always beautifully blow dried and that she
wore a full face of make up to bed?

In reality, five days out of the six that she was on
set, she would come home absolutely shattered. She
would immediately take her bra off, cleanse herself of
makeup, put on a tracksuit and throw herself on the
sofa. If Dom wasn't at one of his fat cat dinners, they
would have food delivered. Lights would be off by ten
or sometimes before, as quite often Dom headed off
before the sun was up. He would never leave without
kissing her goodbye – a selfish as much as sweet act, as
it always woke her.

Yes, she did a job where millions saw her as a character in their homes and yes, she was on the odd TV
show to promote her storyline, but other than that and
the Soap Awards once a year, in essence, she felt that
her life was pretty ordinary.

And the more time she spent in this beautiful setting, the more she realised that ordinary was OK. More
than OK, in fact. She was finding it joyous not to be
recognised. That she could sit here and stuff her
breakfast in, knowing that someone wasn't going to

take a sly photo of her with egg on her face. And more importantly, that Lowen's attraction towards her was more for her fanny than her fame! And that was alright, because in this instance, shallow was a good thing. No complication. Plain old-fashioned sex with a fun, handsome man who had made her smile again; what wasn't there to like, really?

She also loved the friendliness of everyone in the community. It was so refreshing that everyone seemed to talk to each other. It was as if an invisible line of respect and kindness to fellow man was the norm.

'So, where were we?' Frank picked up the empty shot glass, and Sabrina shook herself from her thoughts. 'Next Friday, from six, outside on the deck area.'

Sabrina stuffed in her last bit of toast. 'Sorry?'

'My extravaganza, of course!'

Sabrina hurriedly finished her last mouthful and laughed. 'I'm so not with it. But I do have to say, after that feast, my hangover will soon be running for the hills. And, yes, of course I would love to come. It'll be good for me to meet everyone before I get up and running.'

'Or not.' Frank winked. 'It's a mixed bag of folk down here I tell you.'

'And there's nought stranger than folk,' they said in unison, then laughed. He wiped his right hand on his apron and held it out to her. A huge smile lit up the gentle giant's face, a face that looked like it had seen more criminality and violence in the past than most good cop dramas. 'I'm Frank Brady, but everyone down here calls me Big Frank.'

She replicated his strong handshake. 'Jilly Dickens. Pleased to meet you, Big Frank.'

'Grand, grand. And I hope that both Hartmouth and Ferry Lane Market bring you great happiness and good fortune.'

Chapter Fifteen

The quayside was buzzing with an electric atmosphere when Sabrina arrived at Frank's end-of-season party. Music was blasting out from the two big speakers set up by the outside seating area and the murmur of celebratory chatter hung on the evening air like a light fog. Strings of warm white fairy lights lit up the gloaming and the mid-September evening chill and heady smell of Autumn felt refreshing after the recent humid days.

Belle had kindly dropped Sabrina off at the top car park and had handed her a card with a taxi number on it, and reminded her that the last bus was at nine p.m.

Sabrina reached the edge of Ferry Lane and viewing the party from across the street, took a deep breath and centred herself. Here she was, for the first time in a long time, in a social situation where she was not hiding behind the façade of Polly Malone. She was not even able to act on the character of Sabrina Swift, well known soap actress. Here she was, just plain old Jilly Dickens, market stall holder. It was going to be an experience that was totally alien to her.

She had asked Lowen if he had been invited, but he had replied that because he was new to the role, he probably wasn't on anyone's radar yet. She had said that maybe it was a good chance to get to know everyone and he could go with her as a guest, but he had politely declined, citing that he had just remembered his sister was coming back from Ibiza and he said that he'd pick her up from the station.

At first, she had been a bit annoyed at his dismissal of her invitation, but she guessed that maybe a market inspector wasn't everyone's friend and it wasn't really her place to invite him if Frank hadn't, anyway. She also found it endearing that he clearly had a great relationship with his sibling. Something now, she sadly would never experience in the same way.

Feeling slightly anxious and suddenly alone, she started to walk across the street. Being here as just herself had highlighted the fact that when you're famous, you're never alone, in the physical sense anyway. Someone is always there to talk to, to sit with you, to make you feel wanted, validated. If she were given a pound every time someone had said to her "I recognise you from somewhere, but I don't know where," she would never have to work again. It was also strange that people thought they actually knew her, when they clearly didn't know her at all and as she was so far removed from the tough Liverpudlian character she played, it was quite funny. The only bit of Polly Malone she could relate to was that she too had the heart of a lion, and she would fight for her family and friends and be by their sides whenever they needed her. Fierce matriarch Polly's world had been broken when she was imprisoned for taking the rap for one of her son's crimes. Sabrina's world had not only been broken by the tragedy of her mother and brother, but now by the betrayal of someone whom she loved and thought she could trust.

On hearing Tina Turner's 'Simply the Best' blaring out over the outdoor speakers, a wave of sadness engulfed her. A reminder of another great woman sadly passed, but also the song that had accompanied her on her walk down the makeshift floral aisle at Soho Farmhouse with her lovely, dad. Before the French stick had arrived and blown up her world, that was!

Thinking of her dad reminded Sabrina that she must give him a call to thank him for both putting her in touch with and paying for a designer from one of the many companies he owned. They had made a cracking job of the drawings of how she wanted her outdoor stall to look on market days, and she wanted to show her father the result. Tony Swift had also been really helpful suggesting what he thought might work stock-wise for a small seaside town demographic with just a short selling window.

On the strength of his advice, she had already ordered quite a few pieces, on which she had put an expedited delivery date. There were some gorgeous candles that she had particularly loved the look of. And the sample of the one she had been sent had made the little bathroom at the apartment smell like a Christmas tree forest. Bless her dear dad – despite him being so busy with work since the wedding day debacle, he had made a point of checking in with her once a week. Once she had straightened her head, she really must go and see him. He was living in Twickenham now. Just five miles from Simon. When she last spoke to him, he had sounded animated that she was doing something different for herself and had assured her that he was always at the end of the phone should she have any business questions, however small.

The business questions were easy for them both. This was her father's love language to her and she knew that. They hadn't talked about Dom or her future with him. In the same way that their small family unit had not talked about the death of her mother or about Simon's accident. But that was how the pair of them rolled, muddling on as best as they could, with the strength of their love, somehow diffusing the intensity of the pain that grief, loss and what-could-have-beens had thrown up.

Taking another deep breath and holding her head high, Sabrina steadied herself ready to make an entrance. She'd got this. No doubt it would be a challenge, but she was an actress, after all and she could be whoever she wanted to be.

She had dressed simply in cut-off jeans, white pumps and a blue jumper that highlighted her extraordinary periwinkle eyes. The jumper was shaped to slip off one side to reveal a toned and tanned right shoulder. She had shoved a light hooded rain jacket in her bag, just in case. Sexy but relaxed chic had been her intention. And with her blonde crop, big spectacles and nose ring, she felt that she had achieved that look with aplomb. She had also noticed whilst getting ready that despite not having had her weekly facial, her skin was looking dewy and clear. She put it down to the fresh sea air but also to the fact that she was no longer caking foundation on her face for her job or otherwise. Rather than taking a good forty minutes to highlight, accentuate and create a youthful glow, her makeup routine now consisted of a five-minute splodge of her favourite paraben-free moisturiser, a smudge of mascara and a smear of clear lip gloss. She chose not to touch her eyebrows at all, as being naturally dark, she didn't want the difference to be even greater against her new blonde locks. Polly Malone would wear a bright red lipstick, even in prison, and Sabrina would often wear the same shade when she was out herself. She had put it on tonight, then swiftly rubbed it off as if there was anything that would give her away that was it – after all, she still had the same face! However, it was amazing what a geeky-looking spectacle and change of hair colour could do. Also, a plain unmade-up face made her look so different. Even better, amazingly, she felt comfortable in her stripped back natural look. Who'd have thought that it was easier to hide behind a bare face than a face full of make-up?

She was also relieved that her face was starting to fill out again and was surprised at how much she liked that her belly was slightly soft at the bottom and her bottom was slightly soft at the top. It gave her a shape; she was no longer an ironing board. And it was just such a feeling of freedom being able to eat what she fancied when she wanted. It made her realise what a restriction she had placed on her life by being made to feel that she had to look a certain way. She knew it would make her unhappy to become overweight but to be a normal healthy weight for a woman of her height – and dare she admit, her age – well, that was beginning to feel rather liberating. She had realised that she had been trying to look the way she did for other people, not for herself, and that was both sad and also very difficult to maintain without sacrifice.

She would just ignore Dominic being such an arse about her hair. He was at times so cruel. She thought back to Dee reminding her to think about what she did miss about him. Him being derogatory about her looks was one thing she definitely didn't. How dare he mask his own insecurities by projecting them on to her.

She hadn't heard from him since he had turned up at the cottage. Her anger and his hurt at realising she had slept with someone else had put paid to them having any kind of resolutory conversation, at the moment anyway, she knew that.

Dominic had at least had the decency to tell her what was going on with the French Stick. And he had driven a hell of a lot of miles to do just that! So, maybe it was all innocent now and he was just being the kind Dominic Best, the part of him, she had fallen in love with. And maybe he did want her back but had to work through sorting out his misdemeanour first. What a bloody mess the intricacy of relationship and blurred communication caused!

Sabrina walked slowly towards the frivolity of Big Frank's extravaganza. Enjoying the change in tempo to *As it Was* by Harry Styles, she took another deep breath. It could never be *as it was* ever again, it was *how it was* now, and she'd just have to get on with it.

There was a makeshift bar set up outside with Frank using the private party excuse to be able to legally serve booze on the premises for once.

'Bonjour and welcome.' A woman in her mid-fifties with platinum-blond shoulder-length hair styled in a 1940s chignon greeted her. She was one of those women, Sabrina thought, who had such effortless style that she could easily get away with making a cloth sack look good on her.

'Can I get you a drink?'

'Umm, a vodka and tonic if you have it, please.'

'*Oui, oui*, sure. I'm Monique, by the way. Frank's better half.' She smiled. 'I didn't see you here before. Are you a guest or one of the market stall holders? I love your hair and those glasses, *trés chic*.'

'Thank you. No, not a guest. I've just signed up for a unit, actually. Just for a short time.' Monique's comment had made her feel warm inside but also made her wonder if this was also another strange coincidence, that a beautiful French woman was being placed in front of her face to remind her of what she had lost. And it was a big loss. She had loved the errant newspaper editor. He had been her future, but he had broken her trust and she wasn't sure if she could ever forgive anyone for that.

'Ah, I see.' Taking a scarlet lipstick from her pocket, Monique reapplied it expertly to her slightly filler-enhanced lips without a mirror, causing Sabrina to feel a slight tinge of mourning for one of her preferred shades and also a distinct envy at such application skills.

'What are you going to be selling?'

'Umm. Christmas stuff. A full-on festive bonanza.' Sabrina smiled.

'A whole shop for Christmas? *Mon Dieu*! I am so happy for this. I need some new baubles for the big tree I put in our hallway and please no tat, just luxury. How about expensive crackers, too? I love pulling crackers.' She handed Sabrina her drink in a plastic cup. 'And here comes my favourite one.'

Frank walked over singing a very out of tune, *As it was*. 'I wouldn't have put you as a Harry Styles fan.' Sabrina took a sip of the extraordinarily strong hand poured measure of vodka and grimaced slightly.

'He eez, what you say, the darkest of horses.' Monique blew the big man an exaggerated kiss.

Sabrina laughed and held her cup up. 'Cheers to you both.'

'Cheers to you, Jilly and grand you could come down tonight.' Big Frank had put on a crisp white shirt and a blue bow tie for the occasion. 'And I see you've met the gorgeous Monique. Isn't she just the most beautiful woman you've ever seen?'

Sabrina nodded. 'You're a lucky man.'

Monique shook her head. 'A lucky man who kissed zee blarney stone a million times.'

They all laughed.

'Are you OK?' Monique directed at the big man.

'Yes, all good. Just heard from Conor. His train's been delayed, so he'll be missing out on the craic.'

'That naughty nephew of yours – he was late when he showed up here last year, do you remember?' The French woman continued to enthuse. 'I cannot wait for him to arrive and catch up with him. It's been so long.'

'And I can't wait to see young Billy's face when he does!' Frank grinned, then on noticing Sabrina looking a little lost, saw Kara and took her by the hand.

'Jilly, meet Kara. Kara, Jilly. The new girl in town. I need to refresh the bar.' He hurried back inside the café.

Sabrina smiled at the voluptuous pregnant woman in front of her. Her long, wild auburn hair enhanced her look of Boho summer dress, white denim jacket and flat gold sandals perfectly. 'Ah, so are you the Jilly who may be interested in my apartment?'

'Yes, potentially. Sorry, I meant to message you before and time ran away with me.'

'That's OK. It's lovely to meet you. Star mentioned you may be needing a place for a while, not just a short stay.'

'Well, if you consider three months a while, then yes. I'm staying up at Kevrinek Cottage at the moment. Just as a holiday let.'

'Lucky you. You must be special to Isaac Benson then. Quite the recluse, he is.'

'I'm hearing that a lot.' Sabrina smiled.

'It's not easy to get a unit when it comes up and from what I've heard about the new market inspector, he's not the most accommodating of characters, so you must have done something to impress him.'

'Look at me feeling all special.' Sabrina suddenly felt slightly uncomfortable in knowing why she had clearly been put at the top of the list.

'Look at me, assuming. You may well be local to us for all I know; I just haven't seen you down here.'

'I'm from London.'

'What brings you all the way to Hartmouth, then, to run a market stall on your own. That's brave.'

'It's a long story.' Sabrina's emotions began to get

the better of her acting skills. She gulped in anticipation of the next interrogatory question.

The intuitive Kara Dillon noticed and replied kindly. 'Well, good for you, I say, girl. After a slow start, I became a much freer spirit and I'm open to anyone wanting to try a new venture, but ready for a bit of backlash, I'm afraid. It's like second-homers down here. It does get annoying when local homes are purchased and never lived in. It's priced a lot of us out of the market.'

'I hear you on that. Can't be easy.' Sabrina began to doubt if she had made the right decision. 'So, about your place?'

'Yes, I usually Airbnb it on a night-by-night basis, so for someone to take it for the full three months is music to my ears, especially with this precious cargo on board.' She put her hand to her huge stomach. 'I'm cooking twins and have another set not long out of the oven at home!'

'Oh, my goodness.' Sabrina's eyes widened. 'You must be exhausted.'

'Oh, yes. I'm only here to be social for a little bit, then Billy – my husband – will do the second shift. It's how we roll these days.'

'Where exactly is the place you rent out?'

'It's literally just along the quay down there. Look.' Sabrina followed Kara to the railings overlooking the estuary. The pregnant woman pointed over to the water facing apartment block to the left of Frank's. 'It's nothing special inside, but it's special to me. Two bedrooms, one bathroom and a view that's worth a million of anything.'

'Well, the location is perfect, that's for sure.'

'When were you thinking of moving out of where you are? I'll need to work out a rate as it'll be cheaper for you than doing it per night. And I want to get it occupied as soon as possible.'

'Sure, I understand. To be honest, I hadn't thought further about it until this minute. And I really do appreciate that on the cost.'

Billy Dillon appeared and kissed his wife on the cheek. 'Kerry Anne, shall we dance?'

She kissed him back. 'What are you doing here, husband? I thought we were tag teaming?'

'Mum wasn't up for socialising, bless her, and told me she was happy to babysit as we need to enjoy ourselves before the next Dillon duo arrives. Have you seen Dad?'

'You probably just passed him, he was going back to join your mum – he won't be expecting her to be with the kids.' Kara put both her hands to her back and stretched.

'Oh, hello.' Billy gave Sabrina a weird look. 'Don't I know you from somewhere?' *Oh no, here we go*, Sabrina thought. 'Erm...' Out of anyone she didn't expect a twenty-something ferryman to recognise her. He was quite clearly not the soap's usual demographic. 'Got it!' He grinned. 'You were stuffing down one of Frank's finest full English breakfasts here the other day.'

A rush of relief. 'That's right. It's your dad who has less filter than the bionic coffee shots you get at Monique's.'

'You're learning fast, lady. Right, quick.' He grabbed Kara's hand. 'I know you love this tune.' And with a grin and a shout of 'happy wifey, happy lifey', Billy whisked – or rather waddled – Kara off to the dancefloor.

'Bugger! Sabrina muttered after being told by the taxi company that of course they were fully booked due to a party in Hartmouth, and they weren't aware anyone else was travelling out to Penrigan or she could have maybe hopped in with them. Why did she never learn! The party itself had been fantastic. It had given her the chance to see the kind of people she would be working alongside in the market. Real people, who said it how it was. She was under no illusion that running a market stall was going to be easy but she knew she was more than capable. Having worked on and off in her friend's interior design shop between acting jobs, she had been accustomed to both stock managing and ordering and certainly wouldn't be shy in dealing with customers. And with her dad's added help on the business side, she would be sorted. Also, after tonight, she knew she'd be able to ask advice from the other stall holders, who seemed a lovely bunch, and the thought gave her heart and courage. And it wasn't as if she needed the money – not right now, anyway; it was more the challenge and the distraction that she craved.

The party had been in full swing, the booze had flowed free, and the music was banging but without her alter ego, she had found it hard to go up to people and chat and although it was lovely to take in the view of the estuary by night, there was only so much small talk she could bear. It had made her wonder, under the grease paint and show tunes exactly who Sabrina Swift was. It also worried her that if people meeting Sabrina Swift, daughter, sister and friend, rather than Sabrina Swift, soap actress extraordinaire, would even like her.

She batted the thought off, as her therapist of old had told her to do in moments such as these. Belle liked her, Isaac liked her. It was OK. She now knew both Frank and Monique. Plus, she had been introduced properly to the legendary Charlie Dillon, who had stayed for just one drink after telling her that he couldn't be bothered with all the niceties and 'would rather be having a couple of cans of Strongbow at home with the missus'. Billy and Kara seemed lovely, too. But despite all this, she had executed a stealthy French exit as she didn't think anyone would care if she was there or not. Just as she was leaving, she had passed Star, who was just arriving arm in arm with a short, bearded man, whom Sabrina assumed must be her husband.

She began to walk along the harbour path. It was only nine-thirty, but the measures of vodka she had been poured made it feel like eleven-thirty. The last bus was long gone and after specifically being told by Belle to call a cab in plenty of time, she didn't dare call her now and disturb her evening. Maybe she should have skipped the market stall idea and set up a cab company. Surely Uber would make a killing down here? Who'd have thought that getting from A to B would be this difficult. It made her realise how easy life in London was – with regards to public transport and accessibility, at least.

A wry smile crossed her face. Of course! Lowen might come and get her. She reached for her phone and dialled. She was just about to hang up when he answered, sounding out of breath. 'Jilly, are you OK?'

'Yeah – well, no, actually. I'm stuck in Hartmouth as no taxis and was hoping maybe you could give me a lift home. I'll make it worth your while...' She giggled.

'Are you drunk again?'

'Pot kettle black, matey. Just a little tipsy, maybe.'

'I'm really sorry, Jilly, but I can't tonight. Erm...

like I said before, my sister is coming home from holiday later and my house is a tip. I don't think I mentioned but err... she lives with me and will go mental if the place isn't how she left it.'

'Ah, OK. I've never been turned down for a duster before.' She giggled again.

'Yeah, I'm literally rubber gloves-deep in polish and bleach – and before you ask, I wish that was a euphemism.'

'No worries. Another time.'

'I'll be seeing you next Monday at the market for sure, though. Better get on. See ya.'

'See ya.' Sabrina hung up and put her handset back in her bag. Next Monday? That seemed like eons away.

She noticed a bench along the quayside overlooking the estuary but far enough away from Frank's to remain inconspicuous. Sitting down under the streetlamp, she was startled by a lone gull squawking disapproval of his quiet night being disturbed by Elvis being *All Shook Up*.'

She was just about to bite the bullet and as a last resort reluctantly call Belle, when she heard footsteps approaching along the path. A familiar voice greeted her. 'Jilly? Is that you?'

'Kara? Hi. I thought you were staying up the hill?'

'I am, but whilst I'm down this end of the lane, I thought I'd check in on the flat to make sure it's ship shape for guests – which could be you, of course.' The pregnant woman yawned. 'God, I'm knackered. I hope you understand if an Airbnb booking comes in, we will grab it.'

'Oh my god, of course.' Sabrina stood up. 'I just need to make my mind up, sorry. Is Billy still partying?'

'Yeah. I told him to stay. He needs to get as many nights out as he can 'cos when these two arrive, I dread to think how little time to ourselves we'll both be having.'

'You two seem so happy.'

'We have our moments, like anybody. But yes, I found a good one there.' She yawned again loudly. 'So, Billy boy has told me he's cleaned the bathroom properly, but he's from the "that'll do" school of cleaning, and I know it'll need a full inspection.' Sabrina laughed and then realised what a blessed life she had lived with Dominic, enjoying both a cleaner and an ironing lady.

'Sorry to be nosey, Jilly, but what are you doing sitting here in the dark on your own? Haven't you got a home to go to?'

'I thought I could get a cab to Penrigan, but stupidly left it too late.'

'One of the very few downsides of Cornish living.' Kara's voice lifted a notch. 'I tell you what, how about you come and have a look at the flat now? It's just here.'

The door to Number One, Ferry View Apartments, set on the first floor of a charming Victorian apartment block on the estuary side, was painted a sage green and sported a gorgeous silver knocker in the shape of a bumble bee.

'I love bees,' Sabrina exclaimed. 'Interesting choice, though. Why not a nautical-themed one? It seems like everyone else has one of those on Ferry Lane.'

'Never did follow the trend.' Kara smiled. 'And, it reminds me of my Grandad Harry, who's sadly not with us any longer.'

'Aw, how sweet.'

'Yes, he was a force of nature, that one. Made Charlie Dillon sound like an angel, the things he used to come out with. I put it there to remind me of him every time I return home. He used to say –' Kara's voice took on a strong Cornish accent – '"Family is where life begins, and love never ends – and don't you ever forget that."'

'He sounds like an amazing man.'

'He really was. I'm gutted he never got to meet my little ones. My Granny Annie, too. But that's life, and we must do the best with who and what we have left... Right.' Kara was back in the moment, suddenly business-like. 'Come in, come in.'

Pushing the door to the flat open, she switched on the light and bent down to pick up the mail. 'If you do decide to stay, it would be great if you could just pop any mail up to my shop.'

'I'm surprised your postman comes up here and you haven't got a box outside.'

'It's always been this way; he has a door code. One less thing for me to remember, emptying a blinking mailbox, so I'm happy.'

The lounge was small, with a television set on the wall, a comfy-looking beige sofa and a round dining table with two chairs filled the room. A tiny coffee table was pushed to the corner. There was a cute bay window seat adorned with multi-coloured cushions, and glass door leading out on to a balcony.

'"Bijou with a view", is how the estate agent described it when I was looking to buy. I fell in love with it on sight.'

Sabrina looked around. 'I can see why, I think it's gorgeous, even without being able to see the view.' She went towards the balcony door. 'Can we open it?'

A tiny security light came on as Sabrina pushed the

stuck door. The balcony had room enough for a wrought-iron bench and two large terracotta pots. Both were empty apart from the earth, and Sabrina could tell they would look gorgeous when planted with a smorgasbord of colourful summer bedding plants. The light of the silvery moon was glimmering its romantic pathway across the estuary to the ferry landing opposite. Sabrina took in the comforting sound of boats floating in the darkness, awaiting their next voyage, their ropes and halyards creaking softly. A whoop from the party crowd broke the peace as Abba's 'Dancing Queen' burst out of the speakers at Frank's.

Kara sat down on the bench, making a noise of relief as she took the weight of her feet. She patted the place next to her, and Sabrina sat down. 'Cushions in the airing cupboard for these, if and when required.' The redhead smiled.

'Thank you.' Sabrina smiled back, shivering slightly as the chill of the evening began to take hold. She pulled the raincoat out of her bag, put it on and sat back down.

'I take it your *long story* probably involves a man.' Kara's eyes remained fixed on the distant horizon.

'Sure does.' The actress let out a big sigh.

'Wanna talk about it.'

'Not right now but thank you.'

They sat in silence for a few minutes. Two women on quite different paths bound together in this moment of calm and understanding, just taking in the beauty of the moon filled sky, and the stars, that Sabrina had noticed seemed so much brighter down here than in smoky London town. The salty smell on the air caused by the sea being whipped up with the breeze was oddly comforting.

Until – FIZZ, BANG, WHEE! A cacophony of delighted screeches and yelps of joy as the sky came alive with vibrant colours as if a paint palette had exploded in mid-air and golden sparkles drifted down to the water in slow motion, like rain. And then the putt putt noise of extinction as the fireworks finished their dynamic display and said their goodnights into the dark water.

As the strangely pleasing smell of sulphur reached their nostrils, Kara shot up and headed inside followed by Sabrina. 'I'd better get going. Billy's mum is so good, but she'll be up at five tomorrow for market day. Oh, shit, you need to get home.'

'It's fine.' Sabrina checked her watch. 'Are there any hotels near to here?'

'I won't hear of it. How about you stay here to-night? Call it a "try before you buy".'

Sabrina stared at her, unable to believe her luck. 'Are you sure?'

'Really sure. It'll absolve my guilt of not driving you back. I'm literally asleep on my feet. There's a spare key in the key safe just in case you may need it – 2906 is the code. Not sure about make up remover. Do you need pyjamas? Oh, what else? There's no milk for tea but—'

'Kara, please – You're doing more than enough for me already. And don't worry because, well, I can sort all that out when I move in next week.'

'Wow! Really? OK cool. That's amazing news! Phew.'

'And I'd like to stay until the end of December – if that's OK, of course.'

'I could kiss you. Thank you, thank you. That's brilliant news.'

The main bedroom of the apartment looked directly out over the estuary and, despite it being a little chilly, Sabrina opened the large sash window as far as it could go, allowing her a direct view of the busy and picturesque waterway. As she lay back on top of the comfy grey fluffy throw, her mind drifted to how trusting Kara was of her, and how so very kind she was. Usually, she would have immediately gone to her Instagram to share this joyous place, but who was she doing it for? And even if she did and captioned it. "What a view" or "Guess where I am?", what would that achieve? And who would know the reality of the pain that was going on behind her scenes. Nobody had a perfect life, and who was she now to pretend that she did?

The refreshing thing was that her disguise had so far worked. And if it kept on working and nobody down here recognised her, then Dominic Best would have no idea where she was again now that she was changing towns. Not that he would probably care now, knowing that she had slept with someone else. But the look on his face had said otherwise and at the memory of it, Sabrina felt that pain in her tummy again. The pain of guilt, the pain of longing and the pain of sadness at how things had turned out.

She was just contemplating taking off her jumper and jeans and getting into bed when a text pinged in. A room with signal, how novel! If she were honest, though, this did please her. Especially if Number One Ferry View Apartments, Ferry View, Hartmouth, was to be her home for the next three months.

Hey, it's Belle, hope you're having fun. Did you manage to book a cab?

Shit! She had forgotten about kind, thoughtful Belle, who would of course be concerned about her getting back to Kevrinek.

Was just about to message you. No to cab but Kara Dillon from Passion Flowers is kindly putting me up. I didn't want to disturb you. See you tomorrow xx

Aw, good, OK. Enjoy xx

Sabrina smiled at another one of life's good people. She would explain tomorrow to the pair of them what she was doing. She also must get in contact with Dee, who still hadn't responded to her last message, which was rare for her.

She got undressed and slid into bed. On feeling something soft by her feet under the covers, she reached down and pulled it up. It was a cuddly seagull with a fish in his mouth. She put it on the top of the covers and reached to turn her phone off. BEEP! Another message coming in made her jump.

Still needing that lift home? Because all that dusting has made me super horny.

Sabrina checked her watch. Eleven p.m. Long gone were the days of her receiving a late-night booty call – but when in Hartmouth, and all that…

'Let me close the window.' Sabrina panted as Lowen Kellow started to kiss her neck and tell her exactly what he was going to do to her. 'We don't want the whole block to hear.'

'Come, on, hurry up Miss Prudey Pants. I literally have an hour before I pick my sister up from the station.'

Their love making was fast and furious. Their climaxes hard. They lay back on the top of the bed, exhausted.

'Shit!' Sabrina propped herself up with a pillow.

'What is it?' Lowen reached for his boxers on the floor and pulled them on.

'I can't believe I've let you into somebody's flat who had the decency to let me stay over for nothing. I'm sober now, too. I have no one to blame but myself.'

'You worry too much – and I did say we could go to Brian's place.'

'Even worse! At least Kara knows *I'm* here! She's so lovely. In fact, all the market stall holders I've met are.'

'Well, don't be getting *too* close to them now, will you.'

'Why ever not?'

'Forget I even said that.' Lowen bent down to brush her lips with his.

'Lowen? What do you mean by that?'

He checked his phone. 'Fuck!' He started pulling on his clothes at speed. 'Fuck! I've got to go. My sister got an earlier train. She's waiting for me at the station.'

'But Lowen, tell me…?'

'I'll call you tomorrow.' He blew her a kiss and was gone.

Pushing Lowen's cryptic words aside and knowing full well that the after-sex munchies would stop her from sleeping, wearing just her knickers, Sabrina made her way through to the kitchen in search of sustenance. She found a nearly empty jar of instant coffee in the kitchen cupboard and put the kettle on, then went to the fridge to be faced with one over ripe tomato and an out-of-date yoghurt.

However, it was like she had seen an oasis when pouring the boiling water in to her mug, as next door to the kettle was a flower painted tin sporting the word BISCUITS. She was just about to dig her hand in to see what sweet treats she could find, when she suddenly froze in fear.

What was that noise? It very much sounded like a key being turned in the front door lock. Oh god, it *was* a key being turned in the front door lock, then an absolute commotion as with a drunken 'What the fucking, Jesus', an Irish accented man had tripped on something and fallen to the floor. The something which quite possibly was the handbag Sabrina had left in the middle of it.

With her heart beating faster than a frightened bird, she looked around the cluttered kitchen to try and find something to cover both her breasts and her dignity. Failing that, she grabbed a huge wooden spoon and tried to swallow her breathing.

'Kara. Kara, is that you?' The voice slurred.

She felt instant relief that whoever this man was, he seemed to know Kara so hopefully he wasn't a burglar. However, in blind panic that she was going to be discovered in just her pants smelling of sex and eating stale biscuits, Sabrina tried to hide herself behind the door. Thank the Lord she had changed her identity, she thought as the *Daily Swine Online* could have eaten out on this for weeks!

She tried to close the door shut as quietly as she could with just one finger, but it gave out an almighty creak, leaving her with no possibility of escaping discovery. Realising that her only option was to run at speed to the bedroom so at least she could face whatever this situation was fully dressed, she crossed her arms over her chest and with the soft flesh of each E cup bulging out of the side of each of her hands, she came out of the kitchen blocks like Usain Bolt on speed.

'Jesus, Mary and Joseph, what the deuces is going on in here?' Conor screwed up his face in confusion. 'I thought I just saw a naked woman run in front of me, so I did.'

SLAM! Sabrina made the bedroom finishing line. 'I

have my phone and I will have no hesitation in calling the police if I have to.' She shouted through the closed door.

'You'd have more chance of calling a Royal Flush down here, I tell ya. And it should be me calling the old bill. Who the hell are you? And what are you doing here? I'm not gonna fecking bite.' Silence, as Sabrina started to get her breath back. 'I'm Conor, Big Frank's nephew.' A pause. 'Now, come on, everyone knows who Big Frank is down here, so you know you're safe. And put some fecking clothes on, will ya, ya heathen.'

A fully dressed but slightly dishevelled Sabrina poked her head around the door. She noticed the Irishman rubbing his elbow.

'Hi. I'm Sa… I'm sad… 'Sabrina in nearly tripping up with her name, started speaking not only in riddles but in an abnormally slow voice. 'I'm sad… yes… sad that you fell over. That you fell over my bag…' She held out her hand to the man, who now had a very confused look on this face.

'Jilly Dickens.'

'And what the Dickens do you think you're doing here, Jilly Dickens,' The Irish man smirked at his own joke. He swayed slightly, then let out a massive hiccup. 'If you'd given me a bit of warning, we could have danced around it. I take it this is yours?'

'Guilty as charged.' Sabrina started to laugh at the farce-like situation. 'And me scare you? It wasn't me breaking in!'

'How dare you. I wasn't breaking in.'

'Well, it seemed that way to me.'

The man unsteadily rested his hand on the dining room table. 'So, Jilly Dickens, what *are* you doing here?'

'I live here. Well, I will do officially, once I've paid Kara.'

Now her heart had stopped racing, Sabrina took in the characterful individual in front of her. The apple certainly hadn't fallen far from the Brady tree as he was a ringer for Big Frank. The same accent. Handsome. Broad-shouldered, with dark curly hair that tumbled all over the place and with his full lips and just the one deep dimple on this right cheek, he could have walked straight off the set of Poldark. But there was something about him so much more than a face full of perfectly formed features. An energy, not an attraction. Not unlike how she felt around Isaac Benson, and despite the chaotic situation, Conor Brady made her feel safe.

Conor screwed his face up. 'You're going to be living here, you say?' Sabrina nodded. 'Well Houston and Jilly Dickens, I think we may have a problem, because from tonight, I'm supposed to be living here, too.'

Chapter Sixteen

The next morning Sabrina awoke to what sounded like a whole flock of seagulls squawking at the top of their voices outside on the balcony railings. The strange bed had led her to sleeping in a funny position, and her neck was stiff. She felt gross from not having had a shower after her sexual exploits with Lowen. On remembering that she might be losing this lovely flat to Big Frank's nephew, she groaned. Sometimes, when things seemed to be too good to be true, they quite often were.

It was still dark, but on checking her phone, she was surprised to see that it was actually seven a.m. Dragging the curtain across to reveal a grey and rainy day – the first of such since she'd been here – she pulled on last night's clothes and crept to the kitchen. The last thing she wanted to do was wake Conor, who after announcing he was living there too, had gone straight to the other bedroom and crashed out. She had heard him tumbling to the bathroom in the middle of the night but luckily had been able to go straight back to sleep.

She made herself a cup of black coffee and sat down on the seat in the bay window with her legs curled under her so she could take in the view. Rain was now lashing in strips against the windows and balcony door. The red and yellow tug, aptly named the *Happy Hart* and now bobbing around in the rippling estuary hadn't even started its daily ritual of going back and forth to Crowsbridge. She'd overheard Billy reciting its opening hours in Frank's, and had guessed it must be a regular question from the tourists who visited here. 'Eight until dusk, January to December. Nine until four on a Sunday. Closed Christmas Day. Weather dependent, of course.'

She checked the time again. Should she get a bus or a taxi to Penrigan? It was too early to expect Belle to come and get her and she was conscious that not only did she honk but it looked like seagulls had been nesting in her hair for a week. With no shampoo, soap or towels in the bathroom she would just have to do some kind of ride of shame home.

She heard Conor's alarm go off, then a swear word, then all six-foot-two of rugged Celtic gloriousness walked into the lounge wearing just his boxers, scratching his arse in front of her as he did so. Another giant, she thought. He gave her a lop-sided grin, a thumbs up and without a word walked through to the kitchen to flick the kettle on.

'Dickens, do you want a hot drink?' he shouted through.

Sabrina laughed to herself and shouted back. 'I've got one, thanks. There's no milk, though. Why are you up so early?'

He poked his head round the kitchen door. 'Some of us have got to work, you know.' He double took her. 'Do I know you? I recognise you from somewhere.'

Sabrina reached for her bag and put her glasses on, stating calmly, 'I'm sure I'd have remembered you if we'd met.'

'Ah, maybe you just look different with your clothes on.' The Irishman laughed.

Sabrina was thankful for the knock on the door and

the sight of a flushed Kara rushing in.

'Oh my god, I'm so sorry, both of you! Jilly, I hope our Conor didn't scare you last night. Billy literally only just told me. Men and their lack of communication.' She rolled her eyes, looking stressed.

Conor paraded back through to the lounge. Both women doing their best to keep their faces at eye level to avoid gazing at his crotch. 'Me, scare her! I tripped over her fecking handbag, so I did. Look.' He pointed to the red mark on his elbow. 'Let me get my jeans. It's too early to be given you two lovely ladies a show. Although, old Dickens here already gave me one last night.' He winked at the pair of them.

'Less of the old, you.' Sabrina shook her head, then smiled at his effortless banter.

Kara lifted a couple of towels from her bag. 'Thought you may want a shower. And here's some milk.' She popped everything on to one of the dining chairs.

'You're so thoughtful, thank you.' Sabrina stood up, put a dash of milk in her coffee and went to put the bottle in the fridge.

A fully dressed Conor appeared and kissed Kara on both cheeks.

'Look at you, all pregnant and gawgus there. Four, I hear! Four bairns! Just my Niall is enough for me, and as you know I only get to see him part-time.'

'So lovely to see you back. Billy is made up, and I am too. It's such a relief that you can help him on the ferry. Starting today, too – now that's commitment.' She turned to Sabrina and her face screwed up with guilt once more. 'Sorry again Jilly. So, what's happened is my Billy sees Conor at the party last night, who wasn't expected, but has already re-recruited him to work on the ferry and said he can stay here whilst he does.' Kara became animated with her hands. 'I, with my baby brain had forgotten to tell him that I'd mentioned this to you, hence Number One Ferry View Apartments is now double booked.'

'Honestly, it's fine, please don't worry.' Sabrina wishing she had at least put a comb through her hair, began to push her hands through it wildly. 'Conor can stay. I can commute from Penrigan and I'm sure something else will come up around here for me.'

'Ah, you work in Hartmouth too, do you?'

Sabrina could feel Conor studying her.

'Yeah. Just took a market stall. I'm there from Monday, unofficially.'

'Grand, grand.' Conor put his hand to his head. 'Ouch. That uncle of mine and his hospitality, nearly always damn hospitalises me the next day, so it does. I didn't arrive there 'til late either.' Both women laughed. 'Look, I'm a fair man. If you can bare to share your space with a big, hairy Irishman, then I'm game. I promise to pick up wet towels and I'm an amazing cook.' He burped loudly. 'Shit, pardon me.'

He smiled at Sabrina, who felt the same feeling of calm she had felt the night before. However, the thought of sharing this tiny space with this big man, who would no doubt leave hairs in the bath and clearly had few social graces, was not an option, especially when the alternative was having the complete peace and quiet of a remote cottage.

Kara's face screwed up. 'Jilly. I know I mentioned it to you first, but Conor will be such a help to the both of us being here and—'

'I said it's fine, and it's a no brainer for Conor to be here, especially as his workplace is literally a stone's throw away. Honestly.'

'Are you sure? I'm so sorry.' Kara looked pained.

'I can sleep on a rusty nail if I have to.' He pointed to a holdall on the floor. 'And that's the extent of my wardrobe, so I'll take the little room if that works for you?'

'Reduced rents of course, as I wasn't expecting two for the price of one.' Kara added, and Sabrina noticed Conor's look of relief at the comment.

'Blimey, you two should be in sales.' Sabrina smiled. 'So…OK, OK. There are going to be house rules: no wet towels on the floor and toilet seat down after you've used it. And categorically, no hairs to be left in the bath.'

'Yes, ma'am.' Conor saluted. 'Can't promise I won't snore though.'

'Don't make me want to change my mind, now.' Sabrina laughed, catching Conor's eye. What kind of look was he giving her now? One of amusement maybe?

Kara looked relieved. 'And I guess you're only here for three months, Jilly, so if you can't live together at least there's an end in sight – or you could always make him sleep on the balcony if he gets too annoying.'

The ladies laughed.

'Oi! Ganging up on me, the pair of you, but it sounds like you've got a deal, Mrs Dillon.' Conor took a sip of his black coffee and grimaced.

'Yes, I'm so happy that's sorted. Poor old Billy got a right earful this morning, and I was so worried about letting you down, Jilly.'

Conor pointed to Kara's tummy. 'You're clearly getting good at this two-for-the-price-of-one lark.'

They all laughed.

'Anyway. There's a solution to everything except death, so I don't know what everyone gets in such a flap about.' Conor said nonchalantly whilst checking his phone for the third time. 'And when those three months are up, Dickens here will be begging to stay longer, you mark my words.' He winked at Sabrina.

'You behave yourself, Conor Brady.' Kara made her way to the front door.

'You know, I'm just kidding with you both. I'm on a break from wine, women and song. OK, maybe just the women. And I'll be working six days a week, including weekends, so it's just a place to rest my head. And I've got Frank's place and the Ferryboat to go to on my day off. So, it's all good.'

Kara reached for her van keys. 'Are you wanting to head back to Penrigan this morning, Jilly?'

'Yes. I need to get out of these clothes and chat to Belle and Isaac about me moving out of the cottage.'

'Dirty stop out.' Conor smirked.

'There were no bloody taxis.' Sabrina cocked her head to the side with a face of faux annoyance.

'OK, good.' Kara put her hand to her bump. 'Skye, who works for me, is delivering flowers to Penrigan View – you know, the hotel near Kevrinek. If you'd like a lift, come with me in the van to the shop now and she'll take you from there, no problem. You'll need to forfeit your shower though.'

'That's our Star's girl, isn't it?' Conor enquired. 'She's not so little now, I guess. Driving too! And how is the lovely Star doing?'

'She's a happily married woman with two babies herself now. So don't you be getting ideas.' Kara tutted.

'I knew about the one, of course I did. She didn't mess around having another. Both with Jack, I guess?'

'Yes, of course with Jack.'

Conor seemed wistful for a second. 'It seems an age away now. I may be a mouthy so and so, but you know me, Kara. If she's happy, then I'm happy.'

'I must pee before I go.' Kara ran to the bathroom.

Sabrina pushed her bottom lip out at the sweetness of Conor's reply.

'Are *you* happy, Dickens?'

BEEP. Saved by the text this time! *That was SO HOT last night. Sorry I rushed off. Chat later, L x*

Sabrina bit her lip.

'Ah, I see, you are now.' Conor nodded his head knowingly.

'You see, too much, Conor Brady.' They held a glance for a second.

'I saw too much last night, to be sure,' he joked, and Sabrina felt herself flush from head to toe.

'Right! Are you fit, lady?' Kara headed for the front door. 'I've got a market stall to run.'

Chapter Seventeen

'I really appreciate you doing this.' Sabrina's voice lifted an octave as Skye Bligh took yet another bend at speed in the branded Passion Flowers van.

'No worries.' Skye, the nineteen-year-old daughter of Star and employee of Kara, shouted over the 1975 track she was playing at volume. As they reached a sign that said five miles to Penrigan, the van slowed, and Skye turned the music down to a comfortable level.

'Phew, I thought we were going to be late delivering, but I've caught up now. Sorry for the hair-raising ride.' The young girl laughed. 'The hotel manager here can be a real stickler for time, you see.' Sabrina found the girl's light Cornish twang endearing. 'And we have such a good gig going on here, what with a huge weekly display of fresh flowers for the grand reception desk, a smaller one for the spa, plus we are the hotel's preferred wedding supplier, so we like to keep them happy.'

'That is one good contract.'

'Yes. Kara is good at her job, that's for sure.' Skye indicated right. 'Do you mind – Jilly isn't it? – if we stop off at the hotel first? Before I take you to Kevrinek, I mean.'

'No, not at all I'm just so grateful for the lift.'

'You should come and take a look inside. It really is a stunning place. People travel from all over to escape down here. It's tourist prices but you'll see it's set at the top of a cliff, with panoramic sea views. Oh, yeah, and Kara told me it's just won a Michelin star for its VISTA restaurant. The spa is top notch too, if you fancy a bit of pampering.'

Sabrina grimaced. 'Look at me – I've got the same clothes on as last night and you could cook chips in my hair. I'll wait in the car.'

'People only worry about what they look like themselves, they don't give a damn about anyone else, so I shouldn't worry. But it's up to you.'

'So, you've got two much younger brothers, I hear. How's that for you?'

'I love it. Me and mum are like sisters anyway, and Jack – that's her husband – he's great. It's all worked out well.'

'Mum says you're moving into the market for a few months.'

'Yes, that's right. And I've just agreed to move into Kara's place down the front too, sharing with a guy called Conor.'

'Not Conor Brady?' It was Skye's voice's turn to go higher.

'Yes. Big Frank's nephew. And, oh god, don't say it like that. I was in two minds as it's such a small space.'

'I thought he had left for good so it's a bit of shock, that's all.' Sabrina was desperate to ask about his relationship with her mum, but it turned out she didn't need to.

'He's a lovely bloke. Mum dated him for a while. Asked her to marry him, he did. He thought the world of her. It was amicable when they split. He said he was leaving because he had work elsewhere but I'm not so sure. I think he was sad.' They pulled into the trades-men's entrance of an impressive, gothic-looking dark-bricked building. 'Here we are!' Skye switched off the wipers causing the torrential rain to run down the windscreen in little rivers. 'I won't be long – put the radio on if you like.'

That afternoon, a freshly massaged and showered Sabrina sat in a window seat at the Penrigan View Hotel, a cream tea on order. Skye was right: the spa *was* amazing. She peered down at her nails. Instead of Polly Malone's shade of bright red, and despite her recent aversion to the French, she had chosen a classic French manicure.

The hotel was Edwardian and charming and with its wood panelled walls, dark furniture, and deep red sofas, its bar area felt really cosy – especially with the rain still pouring down outside. Pampering over, she'd thought it would be silly not to come and make use of the free WIFI and to treat herself to some scrumptious food.

Sabrina's mouth watered as a smart waiter dressed fully in black delivered her tray of delights. Two huge home-made scones, a pot of thick clotted cream and another of very fruity looking strawberry jam. An antique teapot with a beautiful floral design with a non-matching floral-painted teacup, and a plain white jug of milk, completed the delightful repast.

As she poured her tea through a tiny, ornate metal strainer, one of two white-haired ladies, on the table adjacent to her whispered way too loudly: 'Now let's see if she's Cornwall or Devon, shall we?'

Sabrina smiled to herself. After years of holidaying down here, she knew exactly what they meant. Taking the first scone, already halved, she put a big dollop of cream on, followed by a sweet helping of the delicious strawberry jam. She did it the opposite way on the other one, then as she took a big bite, causing cream to fall down her chin, she did a little wave across to the two staring ladies.

She was just about to take a sip of her tea from her pretty bone-china mug, when Lowen's name popped up on her phone screen. *Mad busy today and sis wants us to visit her parents at the weekend in Somerset, so let's meet Monday as planned. I've got the paperwork. Signal at theirs is same as the cottage where you are, SHITE! See you soon L x.*

Before she had a chance to read it, another message came through.

Der, I meant our parents!

Cup and saucer in hand, Sabrina gently put her head back in the old-fashioned winged chair and looked out over the rainy vista. The huge sea-facing windows, adorned with luxurious, long red-velvet drapes, had steamed up and despite it being only mid-September, the day had taken on a wintry feel. She took a sip of the deliciously hot and aromatic tasting tea, and let her mind run away with her recent antics.

Was it mad, what she was doing? She had not only taken on a market stall unit but had now agreed to move into a tiny space with a big and from what she had seen friendly but slightly uncouth stranger. She had taken on a new identity and had had rampant sex with a near stranger. She had turned down a huge fee for the second most popular reality show in the UK and as far as her irate agent was concerned had committed career suicide in making the decision to stay off social media until after Christmas. All this in the space of two weeks! No wonder she felt tired and a little confused. She thought back to what her mum might say to her and then smiled as she went through the list in her head of what Gillian Swift *had* said to her in her final letter of love.

She was certainly taking chances and was definitely starting to be her beautiful unique self by stripping herself back from all pretentions, at least. She now had something to do in getting this market stall up and running, as well, and maybe it would become something she loved once she got her head around it. As for something to hope for and following her heart and not getting lost – well, they were the tricky ones. For love had hurt her in many ways, and if she was ever going to let somebody else in romantically again one day, then she surely had to let somebody go. But as easy as it was for her head and everyone on the outside to call Dominic out for showing he was a loser, if she was honest with herself, her feelings hadn't quite caught up with everyone else's opinions.

An unexpected tear started to roll down Sabrina's face, one of the two white-haired ladies stopped on her way through to the toilet. Expecting some comforting words, Sabrina gave her a weak smile. What she got instead was a strong Cornish accent, saying, 'That's what happens when you put the cream on first.'

Chapter Eighteen

On Monday morning, Sabrina drove tentatively onto the car ferry.

'Ah, Dickens, look at you now, in your fancy car?' Conor stooped down to her open window. She was never sure what she should be doing when she drove on to one of these and quite often got into a fluster. Nervously pulling on her handbrake, as the sign instructed, she waved her debit card over the wireless terminal that he held out to her.

'I've been missing you already, so I have.' Conor grinned.

'God, did you eat that Blarney Stone, rather than kiss it?' Sabrina then put on an affected and prude like posh comedy voice, 'And I'll have you know, that us living together is purely a professional arrangement.'

'I see I'm going to have to keep my banter battle pants on with you around.'

'Please do.'

They both laughed.

'Rumour has is, Dickens, that I'll have the pleasure of your company later on?'

'Ooh I do love a rumour. I find out so much more about me that even I didn't know.' Sabrina tipped her head back and laughed.

Conor smirked. 'Or maybe you're heading to a better offer over in Crowsbridge?'

'Better offer than living with an uncouth, hairy Irishman? Nah.' She grinned at him. Sabrina could now see the sign for the Crowsbridge ferry port as the car float took its short journey across the estuary. 'It'll be tonight. Not sure exactly what time yet. Got to get the market stall paid for today. Is that OK with you? About me moving in tonight, I mean.'

'Conor!' Billy shouted for the Irishman to get ready as the ferry slip was fast approaching.

'Look, it's our place, not my place. I'll make sure the bath is a hair-free zone and that toilet seat will be glued down. And of course, if I'm around, I'll give you a hand with your things. Better go, the boss is calling!'

When Sabrina found a space straight away in the Ferry Lane Market car park, she sent out a silent prayer of thanks. Turning off the engine, she double counted the money she had just got from the bank in Crowsbridge. She had already done the verbal deal to pay Lowen in cash, so she would honour that. Also, out of anyone, she really didn't want him to ever find out who she was, as it would no doubt affect things and she didn't want to spoil the fun they were having.

Putting the notes safely back in the white envelope the cashier had given her, she checked herself in the rear-view mirror and applied a light smudge of gloss. Her roots were already starting to grow out and she made a mental note to find a hairdresser to colour it professionally, plus tidy it up a bit. Although Belle had done a respectable job, it wasn't quite the usual Mayfair salon finish she had become accustomed to.

She secured her nose ring and put on her glasses. It was only Lowen who had really seen her without them. Worried that he may recognise her, she had slipped into the conversation that she was a big soap fan and did he watch any of them. She was relieved at his flat no, although he did mention that his sister never missed an episode of any of them.

Checking her watch, Sabrina rushed into Passion Flowers. 'Hey Skye, is Kara around?'

Skye was busily arranging a multicoloured array of blooms. 'Wotcha, Jilly. She's got a doctor's appointment, will be back around one thirty, she said. Can I give her a message?'

'Can you please just tell her I'll be moving into the flat tonight and not lunchtime as planned.'

'Sure. Is everything OK?'

'Yes, fine, fine. I had to go to the bank this morning over in Crowsbridge and wasn't very organised yesterday. I know where the key to the flat is, so it was just to let her know, really.'

Sabrina waved at Star, who had come outside to check her window display. Crossing the road to the market unit, she took a deep breath and centred herself. It felt like an age since she had seen Lowen and despite her gut beginning to twinge against him over the last couple of days, she was looking forward to seeing him again. Maybe, she mused, she felt an element of distrust of him because she had been cheated on by Dominic. Maybe this was how she would feel about all men moving forward. The thought made her go cold with dread. But he hadn't given her any particular reason to distrust him, and surely lightning didn't strike twice that quickly? And maybe deep down she didn't really want to know if it had...

For Lowen Kellow was sex, nothing more, nothing less. A distraction. She was doing nothing wrong. Just consenting sex between two adults – what was the harm in that? She'd once read in a magazine article that the best sex you would ever have in your life wouldn't be with the man you ended up with. For completely emotionally unattached sex without the internal dialogue of "does he like me?" "Did my arse look big when I bent over?" "Did I taste good?" or "was it good enough for him?" was *always* the best sex. Because you were doing it for you and nobody else. The take away on Sabrina's terms anyway, with the few one-night or casual relationships she had experienced was simply to have steamy, no-holds-barred but safe sex, with a hot man, ending with an orgasm for her, ideally before his. Maybe a bit of foreplay, but certainly no after play or meaningful chats required. Bish bash bosh. Job done. Satisfaction guaranteed. No contract required.

Then she became famous and had to become more guarded to a man's intentions. Annoyingly, once she was public property, everyone felt they could try and take a piece of her – men and women alike. Boy oh boy had she had a lengthy line of potential suitors, and a lot of very handsome ones at that.

Until she met Dominic, that was. And then she'd had eyes for no other. He was the first man whom she had genuinely loved and had allowed in. For her complex relationship with her mother and sporadic one with her kind but workaholic father had put paid to her ever forming any healthy romantic relationships. Not without doing a lot of work on herself first, that was. Therapy ('the work') had helped a bit, but she had only had ten sessions, had left before they got to the crunch point of the whys and wherefores of her inability to have a decent relationship. And her relationship with Dominic *had* been decent, until he'd ruined everything.

She went to open the door to *Brian's Books & Beats*, but it didn't budge. Pushing again as she thought it may just be stiff, the same again. It was locked, and no sign of Lowen. She checked her watch. Five minutes past midday. Maybe he was just caught in traffic? She rung him. Straight to message. Strange... He had clearly stated midday on the Monday for them to meet here.

A rotund woman came bustling past and on noticing Sabrina trying the door again, turned back. Sabrina recognised her as the woman who served the rocket fuel coffees in Monique's. 'You alright, love?'

'Er, yes, I'm supposed to be meeting someone here today. I've taken on the unit.'

'Ooh, I didn't know that.'

'Yes, I'd arranged to meet the market inspector here, but he's obviously late.'

'Lowen Kellow, you mean?'

Sabrina nodded.

'Rumour has it, he's moved on, got the old elbow, the heave ho, you know, the sack. I'm not surprised. He did bugger all and none of us really liked him, to be honest.'

'Has he indeed?' A deep Devon accent interjected causing both women to jump out of their skin as a suited Lowen Kellow seemed to appear out of nowhere. He cleared his throat noisily. 'Mrs Harris. In the words of the indomitable Terry Pratchett, "A lie can run round the world before the truth has got its boots on." So, you best get your facts right, eh, before you start spouting such vitriol.'

Linda Harris, her mouth practically dropping to the pavement, let out a loud harrumph and scuttled back up the hill.

Before putting the key in the door, Lowen looked surreptitiously around him, and then with the flat of his hand pushing into Sabrina's back, he whispered into her ear, 'Come on in, Missy. Let's get this Christmas show on the road.'

He shut the door behind them and put the folder he was carrying on the empty shop counter and opened it. Sabrina put her hands loosely around his neck and in pure drama school voice purred, 'Alone at last.'

He gently pushed her away. 'Not today. I can't.'

'Oh, baby. Doesn't Santa want to come down my chimney? He can be as quick as he likes.'

'Jilly.' Lowen's voice tightened. 'I'm so busy and I need to get out of here and back to work, pronto.'

Sabrina's strong feeling of hurt at this brush off caught her off guard. She coughed to steady herself. 'OK, OK. Why on earth would that woman say you'd got the sack? I don't get it.'

'I'm surprised at you, Jilly Dickens. Gossip usually dies at a wise person's ears. Now, have you got the cash?'

'Blimey, I'm just asking you a straight question. No need to bite my head off.'

He kissed her on the forehead. 'Sorry, darling. That stupid old bitch rattled me, but we will arrange to see each other properly again soon, I promise. I've just got lots to do today.'

'I think I need to get back in the real world. I've clearly been off work for too long.'

'From that international woman of mystery job you have, you mean?'

Sabrina smiled. 'Exactly.' She rustled about in her bag for the envelope of cash and handed it over. 'It's all there.'

Lowen took it with a smile. 'I trust that I don't need to count it. Bugger!'

'What is it?'

Lowen flicked through the paperwork in his folder. 'I've put everything in here, except the contract.'

'No worries. Just pop it in. I'll be in here getting set up from tomorrow.'

'I'll do that. Right. Here's the key. And I've gotta run.'

'Before you go, what *did* you mean by me not getting close to the locals?'

His eyes shifted away from hers. 'Well, you've just had proof of it, haven't you? Keep your head down and your business to yourself, Jilly – and like I said, that includes you and me.' He kissed her on the forehead and gently squeezed her bum. 'It's been a pleasure doing business with you.'

Chapter Nineteen

'Dee! Thank God, I've been so worried about you. Is everything OK?' Sabrina was sitting at the bottom of the cottage garden, a big mug of tea in hand, her phone on speaker.

'I'm so sorry, Rini. Honestly so much has been going on. Phoebe broke her arm. Stu is travelling all the time. It's just been mental, to be honest.'

'Oh, bless darling Phoebe. How on earth did she do that?'

'Netball – you know how competitive she is. But she's doing fine.'

Sabrina took a slurp of tea. 'I'll send her some Cornish goodies. But you said you wanted to talk to me, it sounded urgent, and Dom arrived and then all that kicked off and I feel like I've been a terrible friend.'

'You really haven't – it's the other way around. I take it you are not getting back with Dom after seeing him. Please say you're not.'

'No. But I can't lie, he is still in my head. Let's FaceTime. I have something to show you.'

Sabrina pressed the video button on her phone and on seeing her friend on the screen waved furiously. 'Aw. I've missed seeing your ugly mug so much!'

'Me too and oh, my fucking god! Your beautiful hair.'

'Don't say that – you sound like Dom.'

'No. I mean I like it. It really suits you.' Sabrina put her glasses on to give the full effect. 'Mad! You look SO different.'

'I thought it would hopefully give me some freedom after Dom put that wanted poster out. He told me he did that just so that he could confirm where I was.'

'Tosser!'

'Yes, tosser! And, Dee, I've made some huge decisions and I don't know if they are for the best, but I felt my gut was leading me and I feel like I'm not ready to step back into the media circus.'

'Just go with it, darling. Life goes on. I got your email. You don't mess about, do you? What with shagging Lowen, taking the market stall and pissing Caroline off all in one fell swoop!'

Sabrina grinned. 'Crazy, right?'

'Well, I think it's brilliant, mate, I'm so proud of you. You'll be pleased to know that the press has slowed down talking about you. Even the comments on your Instagram posts are lessening.'

'Good.'

'Are you not worried about that? Losing your popularity, I mean.'

'No. I'm a good actress, Rini, I know that. Everyone needs a break and Polly Malone is such a big character, I'm sure she will be returning.'

'*So*, you're not running away forever then?'

'Never say never or forever Delilah Dickinson. I'm just grateful that I filmed all her prison scenes before this all kicked off so I can have this break.'

'Yes, I watched one the other night, where you were fighting with one of the inmates. Couldn't believe it when she nearly ripped your top right off. Bit risqué for before the watershed, I thought.'

'Oh god, yes. She wasn't meant to be quite so rough, but they decided to keep it in. I don't miss it one bit. In fact, I seem to be filling my days really well down here.'

'Your boots, too, by the sound of it, with Mr Market Inspector.'

'Ha. He's a weird one. When he gave me the key for the unit today, he flatly refused having a quickie in the flat upstairs like we did before, said he had to rush off.'

'Just busy maybe, not weird. You have to keep that imagination of yours in check, you know that. And people do have work to do.'

'I know. The village gossip, Linda Harris, told me he'd got the sack, which was odd as he vehemently denied it.'

'Again, you have to trust. Didn't you say there was a lot of jealously around the locals and incomers taking on stuff? Maybe she was angry with him for letting you take it. And as for a quickie – what's that? Maybe it was a good job you didn't get married because as soon as the milk is on tap, honey, you both become lactose intolerant.'

Sabrina laughed. 'How very Gen Z.'

'Yes, I saw that online somewhere, been wanting to use it for ages.'

'Are you and Stu really OK, Dee?'

'We're ships that pass in the night, but yes, I think so. We have such a deep connection and I do love him dearly. It's just life gets in the way of the good bits sometimes. We're planning a family holiday for next Easter, though, so that'll be lovely to look forward to. Show me your view?' Sabrina stood up on the bench and gave Dee a three sixty of the rolling fields and the cliffs in the distance. 'I can see you why you are staying. It's so beautiful.'

'Just come down, Dee.' Sabrina paused. 'Ah, I'm going to be staying in a flat in Hartmouth near the market from today, so not as easy, but that's alright. I'll book a hotel.'

'Actually, my mum and dad are taking the kids away to Centre Parcs. I think it's the second weekend in October and Stu is at a golf tournament, so yes! Let's do it then. And I'm happy to crash with you, that's fine.'

'Well, that's the thing. I'm sharing this new place with someone else?'

'You, sharing!?'

'It's for convenience really, an Irish guy called Conor.'

'Ooh! Tell me more.'

'Oh god, nothing like that. He's very funny, got a great energy but not my type at all. The kind of "wherever he lays his hat is his home" type of vibe. But the apartment is lovely. Well, the view is for sure, has a balcony that looks out over the estuary and Conor will be working most of the time anyway. I kind of thought I wanted to get amongst the community a bit. It's amazing in the cottage but it is so remote up here and when winter comes the roads will be icy.'

'You've really thought this through haven't you.'

'Yes, look at me being a grown up. I might as well have the full 'working girl' experience. So, what was it you wanted to talk to me about?'

'Honestly, it can wait until I see you.' Dee suddenly looked a little pained.

'Dee?'

'It's fine.' She blew a kiss. 'I better go, school run time. Oh, the monotonous joy of motherhood. I'll let you have the exact dates for October.'

'Fab! You'll have to help me work on the Saturday as I plan to be open by then.'

'That'll be fun.'

'You say that now.' Sabrina laughed. 'Love you, mate. Big kiss to the girls and say hi to Stu.'

Sabrina had just walked back into the cottage to start packing up her stuff when there was a tap on the door. She opened the door with a smile.

'Only me.' It was Belle with a white envelope in her hand. 'So, you're leaving us today, then?' She put the card down on the table.

'Yes, but I'm only down the road.'

'I know, and you're so welcome to come and visit me and Isaac anytime you know that. In fact, I expect it. We must arrange a walk or dinner or whatever fits with you soon, and I will of course be coming to inspect your Christmas wares. I can't wait, in fact. It's exciting.'

'Exciting, yes, but do you think I'm mad, Belle?'

'Clearly. But we knew that the minute you allowed me to cut off all your hair and stick a fake nose ring in your nostril.' They both laughed.

'Actually, that reminds me. Can you recommend a hairdresser please?'

'What, you don't want me to cut it for you again?'

Sabrina smirked. 'Just needs a little shaping on the ends, as opposed to it looking like it's been chewed by Beethoven.'

'Mortally wounded.' Belle smiled. 'But yes. There's a salon called Giselle's in Penrigan High Street, that's where I go. And, despite being in the depths of Cornwall, the woman who runs it does seem to be able to do more than just a purple rinse or a wash and blow dry.'

'That's a shame – I was thinking of going a light mauve next.' They both laughed. 'I'll get in there before I start work. Do I owe you two any money, by the way? I'm not sure what day would have been the last day of our…stay.'

'Not at all. It's been a pleasure having you here. I'll miss popping by and although you haven't been here long, I feel we've developed a nice little friendship.'

Sabrina grasped her hand. 'Nice and little are not big enough words for what I feel our friendship has grown into. Thank you, Belle. Thank you so much, for being an absolute angel. For supporting me and for keeping *me* secret and making me feel so at home. And... for helping me to trust again.'

They embraced.

'Do you need any help packing the car?'

'No, I've only got the two cases. I'll put the key back in the key safe when I'm done. See you soon.'

Sabrina waved Belle off from the back door. Going back into the kitchen, she noticed the card with her name on it on the table and ripped it open. On the front a black and white photo of an empty windswept beach and the words:

> *The quieter you become, the more you are able to hear.*
> *RUMI*

And inside, *Keep Listening, Sabrina. There are rare people who will show up at the right time, help you through the rough times and stay in your best times. Those are the keepers.*

With much love,
Belle, Isaac and Beethoven XX

And as Sabrina began to empty her clothes from the old pine wardrobe into her Louis Vuitton case, she realised that it had taken her a heartbreak and a six-hour drive to Cornwall to be lucky enough to have come across two of those very rare finds already.

Chapter Twenty

'I don't mean to be rude, but can I ask who cut your hair previously?' The willowy ebony-skinned hairdresser exclaimed as she lifted a section of Sabrina's hair and started to paint bleach on to the roots.

'Err. I usually have it cut in London, but I've been down here on holiday.

The fringe was getting on my nerves, so I had a go at it myself. Is it really that bad?' Knowing full well it was, Sabrina smiled sweetly at the woman in the mirror.

'Just the fringe, you say?' the hairdresser laughed. 'I'll get the bleach on, you need to sit for half an hour, then I'll get these ends tidied up, don't worry.'

'I love your colour.' Sabrina wished she could be so brave at having such a close crop, but for now her pixie disguise would do.

'Thanks. I'm going through the rainbow, a different shade each month.'

'That's fun.' Sabrina took in the woman's perfectly made-up face. Her full lips were shiny with a burgundy gloss. She lent in and took a sniff of Sabrina's neck. 'What's that perfume you've got on? I love that.'

'Jean-Paul Gaultier. *Scandal*, I think this one is. I loved the bottle.'

'The one with the legs sticking out, isn't it. I've put it on my Christmas list.'

'That's it.'

'So, you're on holiday down here, you say?'

'Yes, just visiting Hartmouth and surrounding areas.'

Sabrina took a deep breath. She wasn't quite ready to go into detail that she had just set off from the cottage and had called them to get a last-minute appointment before she headed out of Penrigan to her new estuary fronted home. She had learnt in the past that loose lips about anything, especially in a hairdresser's that wasn't familiar to her, could get her into trouble of some sort on social media.

'Yes. It's been lovely. Gorgeous area, you live in. Beaches are amazing.'

'Yes, we are incredibly lucky. Ooh, your nails are beautiful. I take it you didn't do those yourself, too?' The woman laughed.

Sabrina grinned at her. 'I treated myself at the Penrigan View Spa.'

'Very fancy. Right, that's your bleach on. Would you like a coffee? And do help yourself to a magazine. Helen will wash it off when it's time.'

'I'm fine with my water, and thanks again, Giselle, for fitting me in at such short notice.'

'Like I said, we had a late cancellation. We close at six on a Monday, so you were lucky.'

The salon was small, just two workstations. Helen, a petite redhead, was washing up the bleach bowl in a small, private but open area to the back of the salon. Giselle joined her. Sabrina stuck her head in a magazine, then quickly shut it again as for there on the *Who's On, Who's Off* page was a photo of her at last year's soap awards, arm in arm with Dom, with the caption *Sabrina Swift flies away from her love rat fiancé*. At least this editor was on her side and the photo of her was a good one.

Feeling slightly sick, she reached for her earbuds and pushed them in. She was just fiddling with *Spotify* to put some tunes on when her ears pricked up as she began to overhear the conversation behind her.

'Lowen's changing jobs.'

Sabrina felt her back go rigid. Sitting back in her swivel chair, she pretending to jig along to music. She could see in the mirror Giselle reaching for a couple of mugs and switching the kettle on.

'Oh, I thought he'd just started one at the council over in Hartmouth, this time.'

'Yeah. He was mainly looking after Ferry Lane Market. But...umm. He didn't really like it.'

Sabrina's knuckles were white as she gripped the arms of her chair.

'Has he got something else lined up?' Helen reached for the milk from the tiny on counter fridge.

'You know my man, he's like a cat. Never fails to fall on his feet.'

Sabrina put her hand to her mouth. Her man? The man she had been shagging with no idea he had a girlfriend? Did she have the word "mug" printed on her forehead? How could she have been so stupid? Again!

'Well, I guess that's a good thing, at least.' Helen added.

'Yes, and he did an amazing deal before he left. Gave me three hundred quid towards my Ibiza trip, so it was a win-win for me.'

Sabrina held back the tears as she thought back to the tales of Lowen Kellow's imaginary sister! Oh God, she had slept with him at the apartment the night that he had rushed off to pick his GIRLFRIEND up from the station. What a bastard! Yes, what they'd had had been mainly sexual, but they'd also had fun and a real connection – or so she'd thought. She had also felt that he was the safe reintroduction to sex, after Dominic cheating on her. More importantly, she had trusted him.

'Nice one.' Helen took a slurp of her tea.

Sabrina's lip started to wobble.

'He needs a little break before he starts his new job. So we're going to his parent's place in Marbella for a few days. Sammi from *Cutting Edge* is taking holiday from there and covering here as she's saving for a hot tub. Hope that's alright.'

Helen shrugged. 'I guess it'll have to be.'

Sabrina took her earbuds out and gestured to the women. Helen came over immediately. 'It's got ten minutes to go on here.'

'I'm so sorry, but I'm feeling quite unwell. Think it must be something I ate. I'll pay the full amount for the colour and cut.'

Gisele came over. 'Let us just wash the bleach off, at least.'

Sabrina's, 'NO!' came out far louder than she had wanted it to.

Dragging her hairdresser robe off in her hurry to escape, she caught her t-shirt with it to reveal her left shoulder and the distinct tattoo of a Swift in flight with her mum's birth date in roman numerals under it.

'Let me help you.' Gisele went to assist with the robe.

Sabrina pulled away. 'No! Get off. I have to go.' Hurriedly pulling her t-shirt back up, she reached in her bag for her purse. And without another word, she threw eighty pounds on the side and ran to her car as fast as her legs and newly bruised heart would carry her.

Chapter Twenty-One

S abrina was thankful of the parking space outside Number One Ferry View Apartments. She was also happy to see the *Happy Hart* in the harbour but with people still on it. The last thing she needed was to have to explain to Conor why her hair was soaking wet and covered in bleach. And worst still, why her face was streaked with tears. She searched on her phone for the code to the key safe, then, leaving her cases in the boot, she grabbed her handbag and took the stairs two by two to reach the first floor, and the door to her new home for the next three months.

Her face fell as she pushed it open to a Niall Horan track blasting out of the small Bose speaker on the dining room table and the smell of garlic wafting from the kitchen.

Conor, wearing just a pair of joggers and oblivious to what she looked like, gave her a massive grin and started to dance towards her singing along to the lyrics – something about not getting complicated and enjoying the view.

Head down to avoid his eyes, she rushed towards the bedroom, but it was too late. Before she had a chance to shut the door on him, he had already turned the music off. 'Dickens, what the Dickens? Your hair fecking stinks.' She looked at him with her big blue eyes tinged with red and burst into tears. 'Jesus, here I was minding my own business, cooking my signature dish, listening to my boy Niall, and all of a sudden we have a hysterical woman on our hands.' He drew the sobbing Sabrina to his hairy chest.

'You'll get bleach all over you,' Sabrina gasped.

'I don't fecking, care. What's happened, Dickens?'

She immediately pulled away from him. 'I really do need to wash my hair before it falls out!'

'OK, OK, you go and do that. How about I pour you a nice glass of cold white wine and we sit out on the balcony and put the world to rights.' Sabrina nodded and made her way to the bathroom.

Half an hour later, Conor smiled at her as she walked out on to the balcony, her hair wrapped in one of the fluffy white towels that Kara had left for her. He had put on a grey hoody and even through her sadness, Sabrina noticed how effortlessly cool he looked.

'Tell me his name, I'll get him for ya.' The Irishman put up his fists in jest.

'If it was just the one, I could maybe deal with that.'

'Jesus, lady. I've only got the two hands.'

Sabrina plonked herself down next to him and took in the beautiful vista in front of her. The sun was a bright orange fireball disappearing behind the cliffs over Penrigan Head. The yachts full of late holiday-makers were making their leisurely way home to harbour. Seabirds soared and dived for their suppers. The water was still and calm, unlike Sabrina's mind.

She had assumed Lowen Kellow was no angel where women were concerned, but she hadn't suspected for one minute that he had a girlfriend. And it sounded like he'd handed her three-hundred-pound deposit over to Giselle, too, which meant he could quite possibly have conned her – and, well, that was a whole new level of deceit.

It was awkward to chat on the small bench. Conor

clearly felt the same way, because he stood up and leant on the railings, facing her. 'So, what *is* your story, Jilly Dickens?'

'A sorry tale of love, loss and fucking up.' She replied dramatically. 'But, in short, I was engaged and got jilted at the alter under three weeks ago. I decided to come to the honeymoon cottage we had booked. And I don't want to talk about the rest.'

'I think I'd be crying too at just the first bit.' He smiled warmly at her. 'When you're ready, you can tell me more, eh? These big Irish ears were made for listening.' He pushed his hair back to reveal one of them. 'And what's going on with the hair?'

'Oh, I felt a bit sick so had to rush off from the hairdressers.' She really couldn't go into detail about Lowen, not now, it was still too raw. 'I just hope it doesn't fall out – it feels like wire wool at the roots now.'

'Aw, bless you. Are you feeling better now?'

'Physically yes. But slightly poco loco in here.' She pointed to her head.

'Poco loco eh? That's a new one on me.'

She ran her hands through her hair. 'Oh God. At my age you'd think I'd know better.'

'About your hair or your situation.'

Sabrina laughed slightly manically. 'Both, I guess.'

'And just look at you – you're no age?'

'Thirty-eight and holding – that's what I say now.' Sabrina smiled weakly.

'Depends what you're holding on to, I guess? But you're looking good for it, girl. Us late thirties dudes are still in our prime, I say.'

'I just need to wise up a bit.' Sabrina pushed the towel back to balance it. 'And I'm sorry. I doubt you realised there would be such drama on day one.'

'Living with a woman in such close proximity? I'm surprised it's taken so long, to be honest.'

They both laughed.

'Did you finish early today, then?'

'I know I just started, but I negotiated with Billy to have Mondays off. I like to graft but seven days a week is just a bit too much for anyone. Got to have one day to recharge the batteries and drink some Guinness.'

'All work and no play makes Conor a dull boy.'

'Exactly. Now, I've made a spaghetti bolognaise if you'd like some? Garlic bread? Bit of salad?'

Sitting at the small dining table, Sabrina pushed her plate away and put her hand to her stomach. 'That, Conor Brady was the best meal I've had since I've been down here.'

'Well, you can get used to that, then, because I love to cook. And it looks like you could do with some looking after.'

Tears pricked Sabrina's eyes.

'Jesus, girl. I'm being nice. Don't you be gurnin' on me again.'

'Thank you so much.' Her voice was wobbly. She went to the kitchen to get herself a glass of water and sat back at the table, more composed now. 'So, I've told you a bit of my story, Conor Brady – how about yours?'

He flopped down on the sofa, his long legs hanging over the side. 'We'd need all night for that, and I've got to be up at seven.'

Sabrina was wise enough to ask no further – not tonight, anyway. Instead, said quietly, 'Everyone has a story, Conor. Good, bad, ugly. Some people just have a plot line that stays level, and others are set off on a roller coaster of twists and turns.'

'So, Dickens, are you on the carousel or the Incredi-coaster?'

Sabrina stood up. 'The rides have been fun, but I'm kind of feeling I'd like to get off now, please.'

Conor sighed. 'Me too. There's something about this place that levels me out, you know? In a good way.'

Sabrina nodded. 'I get that, I really do. Well, it's been great to meet you properly, Conor Brady, and thanks again for dinner and for lifting me up.'

'Strong arms, me.' He tensed his right bicep through his hoody. 'And are you sure we've not met before? I do really recognise you from somewhere.'

Sabrina screwed up her face in denial. 'Like I said, I would have remembered you.'

Despite the stiff breeze that was whistling around the estuary, Sabrina lay back on her bed with the window wide open, taking in the fresh, salty air. She checked her phone for messages. Nothing. Since seeing her at the cottage, Dominic had gone silent and she didn't like it. Yes, he had been angry when he had realised she'd slept with someone else, but she was sure his face had also shown that he cared. She picked up her phone to message him. Then, she realised she was too tired and emotional to deal with anything now – and that included the possibility of him NOT answering her message. Sighing, she threw the handset back on to the duvet.

And why would Lowen message? He was busy at home with his darling Giselle, getting ready for their holiday. It all made sense now – no wonder he had insisted they had sex on such neutral, safe ground, had never invited her back to his place. She looked back through their message chain. '*Her* parents!' How could she have let that go without picking up on it? And as for taking her money, she had the key to the market unit now, so surely everything would be alright. It was common knowledge that Brian was away until the end of December. And maybe Lowen had just given Giselle the three hundred pounds as that was his commission from the market deal. She had no proof that he'd duped her or the council. As Dee would say, she was making things up in her head again.

She did, however, hope that nothing was going to jeopardise her new venture as she was really looking forward to the freedom of it all.

She checked for messages one last time, then lay her head back on her pillow to hatch a plan for the next day. She decided she would head to the market unit and act as if everything was alright. Some of the orders she had put in were arriving, so she could busy herself by unpacking those. And if somebody from the council came to call her out then she would call out Lowen for the rat – love or otherwise – that he was.

She started to draft a message to him but then realised that every time she went to put something, she had no idea what to say. Yes, they'd had a connection, and she did care about him, but not enough for her to demand that they be together. She had no urge to blow his relationship apart – what would be the point of that? She was more hurt than angry. Plus, annoyed that she had yet again fallen foul of another cheater. And as much as it hurt, she had to deal with this practically. Another lesson. But what more could she have done to protect herself? She had asked about this life, and he had lied to her. He had told her that he was single, and she had believed him. Plus, thinking about it, she had also lied to him, hadn't she? And an even bigger one at that. At least he hadn't lied about who he was. She had to look at it as a godsend that she had found out so quickly and just make sure she was on her guard for any other potential suitors who decided to come her way. She would wait and tackle him face-to-face. The satisfaction of seeing him squirm when he knew she'd found out would be the closure she needed.

It made her cringe inside that she wasn't telling the truth to all the lovely people in the market, too. Kara and Star and Frank and now the lovely Conor, who in just the fleeting time she had known him, came across as the kind of person who'd not only have your back, but he'd make you a new one out of clay as a reserve if you needed it.

Her thoughts then turned back to Dominic, and the burst of longing she felt was followed swiftly by frustration at herself for wanting him. Why was it that when you'd been hurt, you quite often craved for the touch of the person who hurt you? It didn't make sense. But her whole life at the moment didn't make sense. As far as she was aware, Dominic Best had treated her with respect and love, right up until he hadn't. Well, that was what she assumed, and maybe it was much better not knowing anything else. She sighed and looked out to the twinkling lights on the harbourside. Dominic would love it here. The peace of it all. She reached again for her phone to message him but still something within stopped her. Instead, she stretched down to the floor to reach for her handbag and found the crumpled letter from her mother tucked inside. "'If a man shows you he's a loser, believe it,'" she recited aloud. A seagull flew down outside the window, let out a massive squawk then set off again. Sabrina laughed. 'You've got it, mate!'

And with the mantra of "no more losers" flying around her head, Sabrina Swift fell into a fretful slumber.

Chapter Twenty-Two

Despite such a disturbed sleep, Sabrina woke at six-thirty a.m. Not wanting to wake Conor, she tiptoed to the kitchen and made tea and toast. It wasn't quite being warm enough to sit outside, so she sat down on the window seat to take in the view whilst having a leisurely breakfast.

A lone beam of golden sunlight made its jittery mark across the wooden floor as it seeped through the open crack of the balcony door. The comforting sounds of mewing seagulls and creaking yacht masts in the estuary harbour rose from below yet, did nothing to ease the gnawing feeling in her stomach.

The whole Lowen debacle didn't sit right with her. The thought of Dominic and the French stick, probably now sleeping back in the Bloomsbury flat bed together after her own misadventure, didn't sit right with her. And now her plan to help her forget and try to enjoy a few months for herself out of the spotlight, may now also be in jeopardy. She had one day before he ran away on holiday to confront the wayward market inspector and find out exactly what was going on.

'Shit!' Conor clattered through from the bathroom. 'I'm going to be late.' He grabbed a piece of toast off Sabrina's plate. 'You don't mind, do ya? I'm fecking starving.' Before Sabrina had time to answer, he was careering down the flat stairs two at a time, shouting,

'See you later, Dickens. Have a good day.'

She laughed to herself. It was going to be anything but dull living here. Finishing off her tea, she messaged Lowen with a simple, but provocative, *Buy one, get ME free at the unit today x*. His love language towards her was plainly sex and money, but two could play at that game! And at least seeing him face to face, she could find out what was going on directly rather than let him get away with fobbing her off with some easily misconstrued message. The positive card she held was that he was oblivious to her knowing anything, so hopefully it wouldn't take long for him to take the bait.

She stood up and checked the time. Eight-fifteen, a quick shower and off to the market at nine. She had made sure to check that the WIFI was strong at Brian's place, so she could start setting everything up from there. A feeling of excitement ran through her as she got up to leave. Picking her keys up from the shelf above the fireplace, she took in the canvas above it, full of words. She went up close and then her jaw dropped at the sight of the author's name at the bottom: RUMI. It was as if he was following her around. She read.

The Guest House

This being human is a guest house.
Every morning a new arrival.
A joy, a depression, a meanness,
some momentary awareness comes
as an unexpected visitor.
Welcome and entertain them all!
Even if they are a crowd of sorrows,
who violently sweep your house
empty of its furniture,
still, treat each guest honourably.

He may be clearing you out
for some new delight.
The dark thought, the shame, the malice.
meet them at the door laughing and invite them in.
Be grateful for whatever comes.
because each has been sent
as a guide from beyond

RUMI

She touched the yellow topaz of her ring and heard
Star's words going through her head: "It helps you
bond with the people who are good for you and keeps
you away from those who are a harm to you."

Without doubt, this whole place had a certain magical air about it. Rumi had been right in the fact that
the quieter you became, the more you were able to
hear. By making her life smaller, her inner thinking had
become bigger. And like her thoughts, Sabrina Swift
would be grateful for whatever and whoever came to
her and had to trust that she would act accordingly
when it or they did.

Chapter Twenty-Three

'Who doesn't love a big, juicy, succulent pear. Come on, ladies, you don't get many of these for the kilo.' Charlie Dillon blew Sabrina a kiss as she walked passed him on her way to Monique's, causing her to humour him with a reluctant smile.

Star, who was busily cleaning the front window to her shop, waved her over. 'Hey, Jilly. How you doing?'

'Good, thanks. Going to the unit today. Getting some stock ordered. I need to get a move on.'

'You've gone blonder, haven't you?'

Sabrina put her hand to her head and cringed. 'By accident.'

'Looks great!'

Kara was watering some of the flowers in pots out the front. 'Everything OK at the apartment? I trust that Conor's behaving himself?'

'He stole my breakfast this morning, but I have a feeling that's par for the course with him.' They both laughed. 'But he's being a good boy. Cooked me dinner last night.'

Star overheard. 'Did he now? He only does that for people he really likes.'

Sabrina shifted, feeling embarrassed. 'There's nothing and will be nothing going on like that, I can assure you.'

'You don't have to worry on account of me,' Star

responded sincerely. 'I'm a happily married woman. Me and Conor, well, we had our moment.' She looked slightly wistful. 'He's a great guy. But when you know, you know, Jilly. And I knew the minute I saw Jack that he was my man.'

'That's cute.'

'Cute, yes, but it was a long road to happy families. He lived in New York with someone else when I met him.'

'Bloody hell. You must have known you loved him, then, to follow that through.'

'Took him a while to realise but... here we are. Married with two kids in the space of two years. That heart of ours isn't really that complex. If you follow it, it does usually know where it's going. Sometimes men just need a better compass, that's all.'

Sabrina smiled. 'Do they ever! Coincidentally, my mum said similar about the power of the heart.'

Star walked over to Sabrina and squeezed her hand. 'Nothing in this world is a coincidence, Jilly.' Shutting her eyes for a minute, the petite blonde then said abruptly. 'Swifty, you've got this girl!'

'Woah.' A startled Sabrina pulled her hand away, heart pounding. 'How did you...?'

'It's all good.' Star was undeterred. 'She loved you so much and she'd be so proud of what you're doing down here.' With that, Star Murray and all her ethereal beauty walked back into her shop and shut the door.

Sabrina wasn't sure whether to laugh or cry. How could it be possible that another human being could channel the *exact* words of her dead mother? But maybe the spirited Gillian Swift *had* come back to Hartmouth, a place that she herself had loved dearly, and was flying around causing mischief here now. Sabrina looked to the sky as if it would give her some kind of answer. She then looked down the lane and saw the calming sight of the estuary. Surprisingly, knowing her mother may be circling around her didn't scare her. It was more of a sense of peace that she was feeling.

This aura of calm was abruptly disturbed by Linda Harris greeting Sabrina with an, 'Oh, it's you. I know it's not my business, but he *has* been sacked you know. And are you taking Brian's place? He'll be back at the end of the year – I hope the lizard told you that.'

'And that's not *your* business either. It's Linda, isn't it? I'd like a large cappuccino to take away please.'

They completed the transaction in silence.

'Ah yes,' Sabrina said aloud as she walked back down Ferry Lane and spotted the a-frame outside The H*art*mouth Gallery, where the artist Glanna Pascoe resided. The bell on the door to the white walled gallery rang as she opened it and was greeted by a trendily dressed guy with a smart buzz cut. He reminded her very much of Idris Elba.

'Morning.' Sabrina smiled at the friendly face looking back at her.

'Hey. How you doing? Feel free to browse, or was it one of our courses you were interested in?'

'I actually just wanted to say hello to Glanna and tell her how much I admired her work. I've been staying over at Kevrinek Cottage and one of her paintings is displayed over the fireplace there.'

'Aw, amazing. Yes, Isaac Benson is one of her biggest fans.'

'Is that so? He's a master in many ways, that man.'

'He really is. She's not around this morning. I'm Oliver, by the way, Glanna's partner. And I will of course be happy to pass the message on for you.'

'Good to meet you.' Sabrina nodded. 'I'm Jilly, and no worries. Actually, I've just thought of something. I'm taking over Brian Todd's place until December and I want to cover his sign with a vinyl. Is that something you might create for me here?'

'Not specifically, but I tell you what, I could get one of our students to rustle something up for you. If you get me the sizes, no problem.'

'That would be amazing, thank you.'

'What are you going to be selling?'

'Christmas stuff. It kind of made sense as I've taken the place just for the three-month run up to it.'

'I like that.' Oliver nodded. 'And what would you like on the sign?'

'Oh, now, that's put me on the spot.' Sabrina looked to the sky, her brain whirring for Christmas puns. She took a sip of her coffee. 'Hmm. I hadn't even thought about a name. Jilly Dickens's Christmas Emporium?'

Oliver shook his head. 'That's too much. Umm. How about, Jilly's Christmas Crackers?'

'Just Jilly's Crackers would fit with me at the moment.' They both laughed. Sabrina then gasped. 'I've got it! How about Tinsel Town?' As soon as she said it, Sabrina knew it was The One. It felt good to have a nod to her old self – even if it had to be a secret.

'We couldn't be any further removed from Hollywood in Hartmouth, but I love it.' Oliver nodded. 'And you definitely have the sparkle to carry it off.'

'Thanks Oliver.' Sabrina became animated, excited anew at her project now that it had a name. 'OK. That's brilliant. When do you think you might be able to do it? And just black print on white vinyl and maybe add a few images, like some holly and a cracker, maybe? And some tinsel, if that's easy to do? Oh, god, is Tinsel Town in the Hollywood sense one word or two? One, I think, but I want it as two anyway – it will look better.'

'You've clearly thought this through very carefully,' Oliver said sarcastically. 'But I promise, we'll do a good job and we can get it to you in a couple of days, I'm sure. Is eighty pounds alright for materials and everything? Here's my card, just text me through the dimensions.'

'Perfect. I'm glad I came in now!'

'Me too,' Oliver added. 'Always good to see a new face down here. You must meet Glanna. You two have a very similar look, actually.'

'I look forward to it.'

'Will you be selling Christmas trees?'

'Ooh are you my first customer? Do you want me to reserve one for you?'

'Actually, it was to say that most people down here get theirs from the forestry place at Penrigan Head so it might not be worth your while.'

Sabrina initially felt deflated, but then perked back up. 'Actually, thinking on it, they are big things to manoeuvre on my own and I don't want to be left with any, so that's a great pointer. Thanks, Oliver. I may just get some smaller ones in pots. So much to think about! Right, I'd better go – I've got a market stall to stock.'

Sabrina smiled as she pushed open the door to her temporary unit and locked it behind her. Her plan was to just get cracking today with no interruption. Other than Lowen, of course. She checked her Whatsapp, but the bastard hadn't even read her message yet.

She finished up her coffee and looked for a bin. There was one in the kitchen, so that was good. She figured the fewer things like that she had to buy, the better. There was also a fridge and a microwave, so she could sort her own coffee and bring lunch if she needed to. Although, working in the market, there would never be a shortage of goodies on offer.

She plugged in her laptop and set it up on the counter. It was a joy to have such fast WIFI for a change. She was just going into her email when a new gossip piece flashed up with the headline, *"The Best is Yet to Come"*. There was a picture of Dominic and the French stick coming out of the lobby of their Bloomsbury apartment. Despite the initial burst of dismay that coursed through her, she was pleased to see that neither of them looked that happy – but the article claimed otherwise. *Dominic Best has chucked fiancée Sabrina Swift, most well known for her gritty soap role as Polly Malone, out of his two million pound Bloomsbury penthouse to make way for his new French girlfriend, Françoise Bardot, 21, and their baby to be. A source told us that Swift, 38, has not been seen since their break up, which happened just after her and Best's aborted wedding at Soho Farmhouse. Swift also turned down an extremely high offer to perform on Prancing on Ice. Which brings further speculation as to where her acting future lies and begs the question: where, exactly, is she? Her agent Caroline Smart, declined to comment.*

'Pregnant!' Sabrina rasped aloud, not quite believing what she had just read. She stared at the picture. Of course there was no bump yet, the French Stick was far too skinny to be showing. Somehow, though, she knew the vultures weren't lying this time.

Making sure the front door was locked, she went through to the back kitchen. She couldn't believe that Dominic hadn't had the balls or heart to tell her. He had said he needed to tell her something when he had come to the cottage but in all the kerfuffle of condom-gate, maybe he felt she didn't deserve to know. Just the thought of the pair of them in what used to be her home with a kid on the way made her feel sick. But Dominic with a baby? The woman at twenty-one was barely out of nappies herself. The whole lot of it would drive him crazy. The deluded man was reaping what he had literally sown. But whatever was going on, it certainly seemed like Mademoiselle Bardot was a lot smarter than he had bargained for.

Sabrina dialled Dee's number. 'Have you seen the news?'

'Yes. I wasn't sure whether to message you straight away. I hoped you'd see it before I was the bearer of it. How are you feeling?'

'Like shit.' Sabrina sighed deeply.

'Oh, Rini. I'm so sorry.'

'Do you think she was up the duff when she came to the wedding?' Sabrina flicked on the kettle.

'We won't know that until you speak to Dom, but does that really matter, mate?'

'I guess not, but it does make more sense as to why someone would travel all the way from Paris to interrupt a wedding.'

'Are you going to call him?'

'No, what's the point.' Sabrina sniffed. 'If he couldn't have the decency to tell me before it hit the press, then he can fuck off. At least it confirms one thing?'

'What's that?' Dee said quietly.

'There ain't no going back from this.'

'I'm here twenty-four-seven if you need me, you know that, darling.'

'Thank you. Catch up soon.'

'And Rini. Everything will work out OK. I promise.'

Sabrina blew out a huge breath and logged into her

email. Thankfully, this would be old news soon but bless Caroline, for all her faults, she was a loyal lion. Pretending that none of this was happening, and with tears slowing flowing down her cheeks, Sabrina turned off her phone and began to undo the boxes that had arrived at the back entrance. Instead of Christmas trees, she would see if she could get hold of some real mistletoe nearer the date, and of course she had to have some holly – again, ideally real. She had found some really classy-looking faux holly garlands with lights to either hang down doors or put over a fireplace. And also some cashmere socks in all sorts of Christmas designs. She would have to get some tinsel in, of course, in honour of the name she had chosen for her shop. Plus some paper chain kits for the kids and some delicate, more expensive baubles than the traditional metal effect ones – all with Monique in mind, of course. Remembering what Lowen had told that her about the stallholders liking to decorate their stalls, she put outdoor lights on the list as well. She found some crackers, too – high end with recycled gifts, plus some cheaper ones with the ridiculous cracker prizes that actually she preferred. Give her a Fortune Teller Miracle Fish a.k.a, a *Fickle Fish*, that moved around with the heat of your hand and told you what love mood you were in, and she would be happy for hours.

She thought back to Christmases in the Swift household, where such crackers had been a family tradition. They had been such happy affairs before the accident. Then, after her mum's death, more often than not, it was just her and her dad and whichever girlfriend at the time he was seeing, sitting in a restaurant as her brother generally wanted to stay at his care home with the friends who didn't have families to go to. Sabrina felt a terrible guilt that this was a lot easier for everyone as her brother's swearing was usually off the scale and if they made it to the Christmas pudding without a distressing and sometimes violent tantrum, they were lucky. Poor Simon. He had been such a vibrant and ambitious lad. The whole scenario was just so sad. But he seemed mostly content in his new world and they couldn't go back, not ever. So, it just had to be how it was.

After a couple of hours of Sabrina ordering more stock from the wholesaler that her dad had recommended, she was happy with her choices. Knowing that being left with too much stock would be a waste, but to order too little would also be to her detriment, she had created a spreadsheet of the items, with expected delivery times and costs against each. One of her concerns was how did she know what would be popular or not? Just because she liked certain things, it didn't mean other people would. Maybe this shop lark wasn't as easy as she thought it might be...

'Right,' she said aloud, refusing to allow her mood to dip and her to wallow in misery at the pregnancy news. 'Come on, Swifty.' She started to look online for the wireless payment device that Lowen had suggested she buy.

With a new payment account set up and a wireless card reader machine on order, she made a contented noise of achievement and shut her laptop. She was just locking up the unit when Lowen messaged. She felt a surge of weird excitement go through her. Yes, he had used her as a mistress – but just knowing that she'd busted him, she felt that it allowed her to hold the power over him and boy would he feel that power when their paths crossed next. Her face fell slightly as she read, *Try before I buy will have to wait, foxy lady. Sorry I didn't tell you but I didn't get fired, I was made redundant with immediate effect. I've got a new job lined up, though, and I'm going to be away on a training course for the rest of this week. My phone and laptop go back tonight, so I will let you know my new number when I get it.*

Sabrina shook her head in disbelief. If you could get a PhD for deception, this man would surely get the top grade. She felt like replying. "Have a great time in Marbella with your girlfriend". Instead, she replied with the universal, most powerful retort: SILENCE.

Chapter Twenty-Four

D ays began to fly past, mainly spent by Sabrina in a whirlwind of cleaning, taking stock in and generally getting the unit and window as shipshape as possible ready for her planned grand opening day of October the first.

She had managed to fit in a couple of beautiful walks with Belle, Isaac and Beethoven over at Penrigan Head and most evenings, completely knackered, her nights had consisted of staying in with beers, wine, tasty food and general chit-chat with Conor before going to their separate rooms and snoring until the seagulls broke their deep slumber. She had surprisingly had no word from Dominic. She was so hurt by him not telling her the pregnancy news that her pride and respect for herself would no way let her contact him. And of course, there was no word from Lowen either. But no contact from either of the shallow bastards meant no drama for her, and with no social media of her own to scroll or update, her quiet life on the estuary front with a man who asked nothing from her except company, who made her laugh and cooked her dinner, was such a calming and pleasant change from everyone wanting a piece of her.

The first day of October fortuitously fell on a Friday, and with it being outdoor market day, she figured she would open Tinsel Town with a bang. She had decided that as it was just a short-term pop up, she wouldn't have a grand opening as such, but had put a small advert in the *Hartmouth Echo* main paper and on their online page with a ten percent off voucher for any purchase made on opening day. At Conor's request, Billy had also agreed to give out vouchers offering the same discount to every customer who drove on to the car ferry.

On the morning of that day, a bleary-eyed Conor walked into the kitchen in just his underpants to find her making scrambled eggs. 'What's happened to you? You're putting food in a pot yourself and it's not even my birthday?'

She laughed. 'Cheeky bastard. Need to get my strength up – big day, today. How many slices of toast do you want?'

'Two is grand. And of course.' He opened his long arms wide and stretching noisily, declared, 'Tinsel Town is open for business! Hartmouth's very own answer to Hollywood.'

'I really do think you're going mad.' Sabrina laughed.

'Just going?'

They both laughed out loud.

They sat in comfortable silence with their breakfasts on their laps on the small sofa.

'Shit, it's freezing in here.' Conor shivered and in doing so his bare arm touched Sabrina's. She didn't flinch.

'Well, if you put some clothes on...'

'Not a statement many young ladies in my company make.' He stood up and without thought kissed her on the top of her head. 'Good Luck today, Dickens. I'll try and run up between crossings, but it may be too busy. I tell ya, though, I'll be pushing those vouchers hard, girl. Saying that, I don't think we discussed my commission.'

He winked as he went through to his bedroom to get dressed.

'I'll walk downstairs with you.' Sabrina held the front door open. She was wearing what she called one of her 'classy' Christmas jumpers – plain black with a tiny brown reindeer with a sparkly red nose on it – under her black silky bomber jacket. It was one of the five designs that she was going to be selling at the market.

Reaching the bottom of the stairs, Conor stopped in the lobby. He looked right at her.

'Thanks a million, Jilly Dickens.' He ruffled her hair causing her spectacles to slip.

'For what?'

Serious for once, he sighed. 'Bringing back my faith in women.'

Before she had a chance to answer, he was running towards the ferry port and shouting back in an atrocious American accent. 'Geez, that Jilly Manilli has only gotten herself a shop called Tinsel Town in Hartmouth town.'

A grinning Sabrina shook her head. Conor Brady was one of life's decent men and she was beginning to realise that maybe a decent man was exactly what she needed…

Chapter Twenty-Five

As Sabrina walked up the hill to get herself one of Monique's bionic coffees, she began to feel totally overwhelmed with gratitude as the few market stall holders she'd got to know began to greet her.

Charlie Dillon came round the front of his stall that he was lining up with huge pumpkins and deep orange sweet potatoes. 'You make sure you tell those customers of yours that Dillons do the best figs in the area for their figgy puddings, won't you, girl.' He handed her a brown paper bag containing two huge figs.

Pat shouted from behind it. 'I think what he's trying to say – actually, what we are both wanting to say, love – is good luck today, love.'

Star was delicately placing necklaces on her moon-shaped display stand, whilst baby Storm snoozed in his papoose. She spotted Sabrina, walked over to her and touched her shoulder lightly. 'I don't believe in luck. We all forge our own paths, in our own time.' She jiggled on the spot as Storm began to murmur. 'And you will know when the time is right.' She kissed the little one's head. 'For everything. Now enjoy your day.'

'Thanks a million, Star.'

'Thanks a million? You've been spending too long with that Conor Brady.'

Sabrina laughed. 'I'll be doing an Irish jig down the lane next.'

It was Kara's turn to apprehend her. 'I've made up a little flower display for you and popped some sparkly bits in. It's nothing much but thought it would brighten up your counter.'

'I feel so blessed.' Sabrina bit her wobbling lip. 'Thank you.'

'My grandad Harry – you know, who had the bees – he used to say to me that every soul was a flower blossoming in nature.'

'That is the sweetest thing.' Sabrina immediately thought to her troubled mum and wondered if there was a flower that represented strength and sadness all in one go.

Kara was smiling at the thought of her dear grand-father. 'Every flower has a spiritual meaning, too.'

'Wow. I didn't know that. What with you and Star here, I'll be fully covered for my spiritual journey to wherever I'm supposed to be going.' Sabrina laughed.

Kara put both hands to her lower back. 'I popped in a few asters. They're associated with the planet Venus, which represents beauty, love and art. They also symbolise the unfolding of inner thoughts and the importance of being patient and waiting for life's natural progression.'

'Is that so?' Sabrina didn't want to be rude, but she was dubious at best. Could a flower really hold such power? 'This is all so amazing. Umm...I'll just grab a coffee and get it on the way back down if that's OK. Can I get you anything from Monique's?'

Kara put her hand to her stomach. 'I shouldn't, but I will. Can you get me an almond croissant and a chocolate one for Skye, please?' She went to her money belt and shouted across her stall, 'Star, anything from Monique's?'

'I'm good, thanks.'

Sabrina put her hand up. 'On me – it's the least I

can do.'

Linda Harris greeted her at the café counter. 'Large cappuccino? No chocolate sprinkles?'

'You've got it Linda – and err, I'm sorry if I was a bit short with you the other day.'

Linda was a bit twitchy. 'Oh. Well, we all have a difficult day sometimes, don't we dear, but...' she dropped her voice to a surreptitious whisper. '*He* does seem to have disappeared, so I do think my sources were correct.'

'And what are we without a good source, eh, Linda.' Sabrina smiled falsely and, as she walked back down to Passion Flowers, thought to herself that living in a small town like this was like living in a permanent soap opera. And as her alter ego Polly Malone would say, it was advisable to keep your friends close, and in this case, the gossips closer.

'Surprise!' Isaac and Belle cried in unison on seeing Sabrina approaching Tinsel Town.

Isaac was hurriedly hanging a red ribbon across the front door as Belle scrabbled in her handbag.

'Aw, you two, this is so sweet. Thank you.' Sabrina felt a fizz of happy energy go right through her.

'You couldn't just go in without some kind of fanfare.' Belle announced, as Beethoven barked his approval. 'Go on then.' The pretty blonde urged, taking Sabrina's coffee cup and handing her the scissors she had just retrieved from her bag.

Sabrina cut the ribbon and grinned broadly. She assumed the accent of the Queen when naming a boat.

'I hereby declare Tinsel Town officially well and truly open.'

The three of them laughed.

'And we wish you every ounce of success with it,' Isaac declared, awkwardly kissing her on the cheek.

'You should be so proud of yourself,' Belle added. 'And we can't wait to have a look around.'

Sabrina's first day as a market trader flew by in a blur of stallholders being nosy and new customers getting excited about Christmas already. She was happy that her bestsellers had been baubles as there was a good mark-up on those, plus they didn't take up too much space. The jumpers had also been a big hit. And because she had only ordered in one size and one colour of each of the five assorted designs, she had taken various orders with individuals who were excited about how cool they would be for either their work Christmas parties and for Christmas day at home with their loved ones. Conor had literally run in and out to tell her that he'd given out nearly all the vouchers and that he was having dinner at Frank and Monique's place that evening and would be back in the morning. He had also promised they would have a celebratory drink for sure on the Saturday night.

She sat back in the uncomfortable high stool and checked her takings. She was amazed to see three hundred and fifty pounds on the screen of the handheld payment machine. And that was without counting the cash. Of course, she'd have to take off the money she'd spent on stock, but she knew it would still be a tidy profit. Now, if she could do that six days a week then that was incredible; the rent would be covered in no time. Yes, she felt tired, but nowhere near as tired as she used to feel after a day of filming and hanging around on a TV set. And what she was doing here was all about her. Just for her and nobody else. She was the boss. No pesky directors shouting at her. No makeup being caked on. But what she didn't have was a Dominic to go home to. To share some food with, to talk about her day. To make love to her and cuddle her in bed. She sighed loudly then smiled. For she had all of that with Conor, aside the intimacy. And it was the intimacy side of a relationship that caused all the complications. Dom had had a friend who, to the abhorrence of his wife, would announce when drunk that it would make more sense and save a lot of heartache to have a good network of friends and a brothel around the corner.

With thoughts of her old life and in particular Dom now running through her mind, she put her hand to the little embroidered reindeer covering her heart and suddenly felt very alone.

Not keen to sit with this feeling, she jumped up and went outside to start bringing her stock off the stall. The market rules were that Ferry Lane had to be clear by six p.m. latest so that the traffic could flow through again and she didn't want to get into trouble on her first day.

She was just wheeling in the rail of jumpers when her phone rang.

'Sabrina, it's Caroline, and I'm sorry. It's not shocking news but it's not great news, either.'

'Go on.'

'They do want Polly Malone back on the street, but not until next summer.'

'So filming will start February time, I guess?' Sabrina replied casually, pulling the rail fully inside. 'When do I need to confirm?'

Caroline was silent a moment. 'I thought you'd be pissed off about that?'

'No.' Sabrina replied casually. 'I've started working down here, now.' Sabrina surprised herself at how relaxed she felt about the whole situation. If someone had told her two months ago that she would have to wait so long to start filming for her major soap role again, she would have thrown a complete hissy fit. She wasn't even bothered about the money. It was great to feel like this, but why *did* she? Maybe it was just being out of the limelight? No one to judge her on the way she looked or which restaurant she was eating in. Had she at last found her peace and didn't even realise it? Down here, she could just be unapologetically her. And she was beginning to realise, thanks to all the new good people around her, that being unapologetically her was alright. In fact, more than alright.

'Working? What on? Why on earth didn't you consult me?'

'I'm running a market stall.'

Caroline laughed out loud, then after nearly sucking the back out of her vape laughed again. 'Well, I've heard it all now. What are people saying?'

'I've cut off my hair and dyed it, I'm wearing glasses and a nose ring, so nobody is saying anything because they don't recognise me.'

'I told you that coming off social media was career suicide.'

'Well, clearly it doesn't matter what I do or don't do, as I still have a job next year if I want it.'

'Your beautiful hair, too.'

'It will grow. The same as I am now that I'm not having to deal with so many negative idiots. Dom included in that.'

'It needs to be long again for filming, though.' Another long drag on the vape. 'I'm so happy they want you back.'

'Caroline, there are wigs and we could even make it so that somebody cut it off in prison. Anyway, good to hear that you're happy. But does it matter if little old Sabrina Swift is happy or not?'

Caroline's voice softened. 'Oh, here she is! The little fighter. Of course, it matters. Contrary to your beliefs, I've been worried about you.'

Sabrina sighed. 'Thanks for not commenting to the press.'

'That doesn't even warrant an answer.' A brief silence. 'I'm sorry about the kid news, by the way.'

'I'm not. It means I won't go back to him even if I want to.'

'You're a strong woman, Sabrina, and I admire you for that.'

Sabrina's face lit up. A compliment from Caroline Smart was equivalent to receiving an OBE. A slight pause.

'How *are* you doing about it all?

'I'm fine and he's a cunt.'

'Sabrina Swift!'

'Cried the woman who practically invented the use of the C-word.'

They both sniggered. It was good to have a laugh together for once.

'Mrs Batty is being hysterical.' Caroline let out a little snort.

'Why?'

'She cleans my place straight after Dom's now. Thanks again for the recommendation, by the way. She's like a Henry the Hoover on acid. Anyway, she evidently splits up his socks into odd pairs and told me that the other day, she'd rubbed her false teeth around his toothbrush.'

They both laughed again.

'I'm guessing you're getting some action, too as you're certainly not sounding as morose as usual.' Sabrina began to rearrange the jumpers on the rail.

'I've been fornicating with a personal shopper from Selfridges, as it happens. You know me, darling, I'm all about the extra. She's only an eight out of ten, but who's counting when the discount is twenty percent? Anyway, I'll email the new TV offer over. I guess you are still checking your e-mail?'

'Send it over, but I'm not making any promises.'

Sabrina could hear the vape getting blasted again. 'I know you don't mean that. You'd better not mean that. I've told them that you're working with monks at a donkey sanctuary in Outer Mongolia during your time out. And, well, if the press get hold of that, we can revel in their stupidity. Plus, we'd be relieved of course that they are not going to find you, working a market stall in the depths of Cornwall with a ridiculous new short haircut. Anyway, ciao darling. Enjoy being a cashier and let's talk soon.'

The call ended abruptly, and a message came in. *Rini. Hope today was fun! Can't wait to see you next week and dive into that spa hotel. It looks sublime. Complete bliss, in fact. Love you. DD XX*

Chapter Twenty-Six

It felt weird going into the apartment and knowing that Conor was not going to be home for the night. Most evenings after they'd eaten, usually together, they'd sometimes put a coat on, sit out on the balcony, and have a drink and a chat. There was always a lot of laughter. Sometimes they went off and did their own thing or just retired to their bedrooms where they each had a television. Wherever he was in the flat, it was just nice to have a heartbeat in the same space. To know he was there. She had felt safe around him from the minute that she had met him. Probably because there wasn't an instant attraction, and she had no qualms in being one hundred percent herself around him. After all, because they were sharing a bathroom and such a small living space, she could be nothing but authentic.

She ran a bath and turned on the television for company. She had bought herself a bottle of wine and was going to have an early night, for it had been a long day on her feet and tomorrow she had to do it all over again. It was a bit nippy to sit out, so comfy in a tracksuit, she poured herself a large glass of Merlot and lay on the sofa with her feet to the balcony door so she could have a good look at what was going on in the darkness of the harbour. The nights had suddenly drawn in and she really wasn't looking forward to the clocks changing. Kara had told her that Hartmouth, in fact all of Cornwall, was a quite different place out of season. With no sunshine and not as many tourists, it wasn't quite the picture postcard destination that visitors or second homers imagined. The benefit of that, though, Kara had explained, was that the roads were clearer, and you could at least get a seat in your favourite restaurant.

Going to the kitchen to refill her wine glass, she found some left-over pasta in the fridge, she put it in the microwave then set about her feast whilst scrolling through the TV channels to find something light to watch. She rarely watched herself acting, but on seeing that her programme was on and now feeling a bit tipsy, she decided to give it a go – but got herself a pillow to put over her face if it was too cringey. She turned straight on to a prison scene where her screen son, whom she had taken the rap for, was visiting her. Thinking of it, where was he now? And where were the other few friends she had on set now she was in this predicament? She took a large glug of wine. It felt odd now to see herself with long dark hair and she cringed at how rough she looked. The dark bags under her eyes weren't make up, they were real. She had been so busy and tired whilst filming those scenes, which was great for the character, but she realised now looking back that despite her pending wedding, if she had been honest with herself, she had not been truly happy with her life. She switched the TV off.

Yes, a couple of texts had come through the week after the wedding – the wedding she hadn't invited them to, granted – but they'd soon stopped when she said she was keeping a low profile. She wasn't really surprised. They were colleagues, not friends. They knew little about the real her, even after working together for five years. She checked her watch: nine p.m. She messaged her dad to tell him how well she had done on the stall and asked after her brother, then with food eaten and wine drunk and completely knackered from her day on the market, she nodded off in a dreamy slumber on the sofa.

She was awoken by the flat intercom incessantly ringing. Half asleep and thinking it was Conor coming home after all and not bothering with his key, she pressed to open the exterior door. Knock, knock, then a familiar voice, 'It's me. Let me in.'

'Lowen? What are you doing here?'

'Are you alone?'

'Yes. What the—? You sound angry, is everything OK?' Sabrina yawned and shook her head to try and wake herself. Lowen's eyes were wide, she could smell drink on his breath. Her memory kicked in.

'Angry? Of course, I'm fucking angry. Of all the hairdressers in the area, what on earth led you to go into Giselle's and have your hair done? What kind of trouble were you thinking of causing me, eh?'

'Woah, there. If you mean why did I decide to have my hair done by *your* girlfriend, I had no idea who she was until I overhead a conversation she was having with her assistant.'

'Why didn't you tell me this before?'

'I haven't seen you since. Besides, I don't think that's the issue, do you, Lowen? You're the one who told me you were single. I'm the innocent party here! I was as shocked to realise who she was, as you obviously were when you found out I'd been there.'

'Really? You're such a good little actress, though, aren't you, Sabrina Swift, so what do I believe, eh?'

Sabrina felt a surge of fear go through her from head to toe. 'You're drunk, Lowen, what are you going on about?'

'So, I'm lying on a sun lounger in Marbella.'

'With your girlfriend...' Sabrina now felt anger

rising within her.

Lowen snarled. 'Yes, with my girlfriend. And she tells me that some blonde tart comes in for a root touch up, nothing out of the ordinary there but as you rushed out to leave, she sees a tattoo on your shoulder.'

'And?' Sabrina closed her eyes in anticipation of knowing exactly what was coming.

'The very same tattoo of a swift that that Polly Malone, big-shot soap star, has.'

'Lots of people must have tattoos of birds.' Not liking the tone of his voice, Sabrina moved away from him towards the balcony door.

'Not with the same birthdate under it they don't. When we got back, Giselle froze it on the screen to show me as she was so excited it could be you.'

Lowen lunged towards her and roughly pulled at her top.

She pushed him away. 'I think you should leave.' Sabrina's fear escalated.

'Why have you lied to me, Jilly, or whoever you are? And why go in and try and cause trouble for me with my girlfriend?'

'I really don't care enough about you or her to spill even a drop of tea. And I didn't know! I honestly didn't know who Giselle was!' Lowen stood shaking his head. 'We had sex, Lowen. Yes, it was fun but I'm not a cheater and don't intend to ever knowingly be one.'

'You're a two-bit soap actress, not Elizabeth bloody Taylor. I wouldn't even have known who you were if Giselle hadn't told me. Saying that, I've never fucked anyone remotely famous before, so I guess I can add that notch to my bedpost, at least.'

'You're vile.' Sabrina felt tears pricking her eyes. 'And I don't have to tell you anything.'

'And as for working the market, surely you're loaded?'

NICOLA MAY

'Do you have to be so cruel? Just fuck off, Lowen. My life is none of your business.'

Lowen raised his voice. 'Tell me! You lied to me. I have a right to know.'

Sabrina centred herself. 'OK, although clearly you are far more concerned that I will out your infidelity than caring who the hell I am!' She then began an uncontrollable rant. 'My fiancé *cheated* on me. My honeymoon was supposed to be at Kevrinek. I came away to escape from the drama and vitriolic comments that were all over social media. Because you may not know who I am, Lowen, but many people do. And I'd had enough.' Her bottom lip began to wobble. 'And I wanted to escape, and I want people to like me for who I am and not the character I represent or the fame I have. Because the man I thought loved me, couldn't even do that.' She began to cry.

His drunken mind tried to compute. He went to embrace her.

'No.' She pushed him away. 'Go home to your girlfriend, Lowen. But before you do, please tell me that my giving you the money for the market stall was legitimate. I heard you *have* been sacked.'

'You hear too much.' Lowen growled. 'You got the unit you wanted at the price you wanted. I don't know what all the fuss is about.'

'That's not an answer. And what did you mean about not getting too close to anyone in the market? How dare you even think of being jealous over me, when you are the one with a girlfriend.'

'I didn't realise quite how stupid you were to even think that.' Lowen shook his head in mock disbelief.

'Just go. Please leave. I don't want or need to know anything else,' Sabrina shouted.

The man's mood changed again. 'Look at the little actress pushing me, away. I said don't get too close to anyone because by next year, the outdoor market is going to be no more, and it will mean a lot of the businesses may not survive.'

'You're talking rubbish, Lowen. You're drunk. It's been an outdoor market for over a hundred years. Ferry Lane Market is part of the history of Hartmouth.'

'And times need to change, don't they? I'm now working for the planners of a big new housing development and we're looking to build a brand-new housing estate at the top of Hartmouth Hill. We need access to Ferry Lane, seven days a week to act as a bypass to cope with the new volume of traffic heading out on the coastal road to Penrigan. And with the council workers I've kept in my back pocket, they will be getting their pockets filled with backhanders from me when they push it through.' Sabrina's mouth dropped open. 'You can't do that. *They* can't do that – and I wonder where you got that backhander cash from?'

'Watch us.' An evil grin spread across his face. He took hold of her hand. 'You can't deny we had great sex. Come on, how about one for the road – or shall we say, lane?' He laughed manically.

Sabrina ran to the front door and opened it. 'Get *on* the fucking road and *out* of my life.'

'I'm going. I've said too much.'

'You really have.' Sabrina was shaking.

Lowen turned as he was at the top of the stairs. 'I think we need to make one more deal, don't you?' Sabrina remained silent. 'You stay away from my girlfriend and keep your mouth shut about the market and I don't blow your cover, because the last thing you want is the press running all over town and that includes your ex-boyfriend.' Lowen smirked. 'Quite a babe he's got on his arm, now, hasn't he? *Au revoir, salope.*'

Sabrina slammed the door shut and put her back against it. Sobbing, her first thought was to call Dom, but then the kind face of someone she really did trust crossed her mind. Shakily, she scrolled for his number.

Sabrina was still sobbing when Conor arrived back at the flat. He was sweating profusely and out of breath. Realising the state she was in, he pulled her on to his knee as if she was a baby and held her tightly. 'Jesus, Dickens. I haven't cycled like that for years. Had too much Guinness to drive back from Uncle Frank's and I tell ya, the hills on that Penrigan road are fecking deadly. I feel like I've just done a leg of the Tour de France.'

'I didn't...' A hitch. 'Expect...' Another hitch. 'You to come back now...' Three hitches in a row.

'Now, you tell me.' Conor stroked her hair, then gently moved her off his lap back on to the sofa. 'Coffee, tea, me?' He winked at her.

'Tea please.'

He came back in with a pint of water and placed a steaming mug of tea on the edge of the window seat. He unwrapped a large bar of chocolate and handed it to Sabrina, then opened the balcony door. 'Sorry, I need some air.' He wafted his t-shirt up, broke off a strip of chocolate and handed it to her. 'And get some of that sugar down you, girl, it looks like you've had a shock.'

Just the presence of this solid Irish man calmed her, as he had done from the minute she set eyes on him. She took a sip of the hot, sweet tea. 'I didn't mean you to cut short your evening. I'm so sorry.' She stuffed in a square of chocolate.

He joined her on the sofa and put his hand on her knee. 'Now, do you wanna tell me what all this is about or not? I can be a shoulder or a shotgun, whichever is required.' His curly hair was tumbling all over the place, his brown eyes soft and sincere looked caringly at her. Sabrina put her hand to her forehead and looked at the floor.

'I'm really worried that what I'm going to say to you now will ruin our friendship.'

He gently put his hand under her chin and lifted her head. 'It would have to be something pretty bad to do that.'

'Well, I have lied to you about something pretty big.'

'That your name is not really Jilly Dickens and you're actually a big shot actress, you mean.'

Sabrina's mouth fell open. 'Woah! How on earth…?

'I went in your bedroom to nick some of your deodorant, your driving licence was out on the side and yes, I admit, I checked out your photo.'

'When?'

'Oh, a couple of days ago.'

'Why didn't you say something?'

'Because I'm a Brady and coming from a family such as mine, your secret is yours until you want to tell it.'

'You're not angry, then?'

'Angry.' Conor pretended to straighten an imaginary tie. 'I've seen Jillian Swift's tits. Not many men can say that.'

It felt weird hearing him say her christened name out loud. She laughed and hit him on the chest. 'What? When?'

'The night I met you, silly. You ran through and—'

'Shit, yes, that seems so long ago.'

Sabrina suddenly felt more held and respected than she had done in a long, long time. What a man Conor Brady was. He had found out who she was, and there was no drama. He had realised that her secret had a reason and that reason was no business of his and more importantly, even though he had found out she had lied to him, he had understood and treated her no different-ly. He cared about *her* feelings and what was going on for her. Yes, Dominic may have driven all night to see her in his fancy car, but this wonderful man, on realising how distressed she was, had got on a bike and ridden miles in the dark on steep and treacherous roads to be with her. His actions had spoken more than a million words, and maybe it was time she started listening to them.

'I'm going to admit it now: I have a huge fucking crush on Polly Malone. I mean, those leather skirts she wears. Fire! And a Best Villain award! Literally, that does it for a Brady.'

Sabrina's jaw dropped and she felt her cheeks flush. 'You can't be saying that.'

He laughed loudly. 'Not going to lie, I Googled your passport name, and despite your acting name being Sabrina Swift and not Jillian Swift, with you being so famous and all, pretty Polly obviously came up. Well, a whole bunch of photos did anyways. I didn't know of you. I don't care you're an actress. To me you're Dickens, kind, slightly scatty, vulnerable, friendly, intelligent and a good laugh.'

Sabrina put her hand to her chest. 'I'm sorry I lied to you. Or rather, didn't tell you the whole truth. Really, though, you've known the real me – Jilly – all along, and not the fake Sabrina persona I use with the rest of the world. It's felt amazing to be known for just me – even if I couldn't tell you what it meant to me before.'

'You're an amazing girl and I'm sorry you've been through such shit – that ex of yours is a fool. Is that why you're upset?'

'No, the plot has thickened. Oh, Conor, I want to tell someone, but it must have the Brady seal of silence on it.'

'See, you don't know me that well, do you, yet? Because that's an unspoken rule. Unless it involves my family, of course.'

Suddenly feeling an undeniable level of trust for this man, Sabrina took a deep intake of breath. 'I slept with the market inspector.'

'Ah, I see. That's how you got that unit, then?' Conor's face remained dead pan.

She hit him on the arm. 'No, I was the first person in to see it and paid for it fair and square. Anyway, he's got a girlfriend and he just came round here drunk being abusive and said that if I said anything to her, he would out my true identity to the market.'

'Blackmail.' Conor downed his pint of water, an ugly look twisting his face.

'I guess it is. And please don't think badly of my actions – he told me he was single.'

'Dickens, judgement defines who the other person is, not you.'

'I wouldn't have ever told her anyway. I didn't like him that much to cause a scene. The awful bit is I met her, completely coincidentally or I may have never found out he was a cheater too.' Star's 'nothing is a coincidence' comment suddenly resonated with her.

'You met her?'

'It was mad. Belle, you know Isaac Benson's Belle who I told you about. She put me on to her because she's her hairdresser.'

'Ah, the day you came running in stinking of bleach. I get it now.'

'Yes. I freaked when I realised what was going on. This place is so interlinked in such a weird way.'

'Tell me about it. I've lived in London before, too, where you can hide amongst the masses. Anyway, why would it be so bad if everyone knew who you were? I think you're grand, Jilly, I really do.'

'You're not so bad yourself, Conor Brady,' Sabrina said through watery eyes, then shrugged.

'I guess I'm happy just being known down here as Jilly Dickens, market stall holder. I don't want people treating me differently. And yes, I'm not a huge movie star, but I am well known in this country and people do treat you differently when you're a bit famous. The main reason, though, is that I don't want the press sniffing around. It's been joyous being so free.'

Sabrina started to well up again.

'Houl your wheesht, lady. It's all good.'

'Houl your what?'

'Come here.' He pulled her to his broad chest and held her tightly.

'Oh my God, hugs are the best.' Sabrina melted into him and assumed a girlie voice. 'Your hugs are the best.'

With a contented smile, Conor Brady tightened his hold and nuzzled his chin into the troubled woman's blonde mop. As he did so, Sabrina made a little groan of pleasure. It was so lovely to feel held by a man whose only agenda was to do right by her. Telling him about the market could wait, for she was enjoying the moment. A moment of peace. For the market news was big, and maybe it was something she could handle herself, because as soon as she involved the Brady bunch, goodness knows what would happen then!

Chapter Twenty-Seven

On seeing Dee coming out of the train station, Sabrina leapt out of her Audi convertible to greet her friend.

'AAAAAhhhhhhhh.' Dee screamed as she ran over to the car dragging her weekend case as fast as it wheels would allow. 'Oh my God, it's so bloody good to see you. And your hair! It looks better in real life. Really does suit you. I had to double take, especially with those glasses on. Sexy lady!'

Sabrina gave her friend a huge hug. 'I've missed you so much. And look at you, nice jacket!'

'Thanks, these curves ain't going nowhere with my current chocolate intake, so I'm just cinching in the waist and owning them, girlfriend.'

'Hurrah to that.' Sabrina placed her friend's suitcase in the boot.

'This area is just so gorgeous. I'm so glad I got the train – it went right along the coast for the last few miles and it's so green and lush down here, too.'

'You sound like you've never left Essex before.' Sabrina laughed.

'I've got a kid and husband free pass. I'm on my holidays. I wouldn't care if I just sat in a field with a box of wine and a picnic basket for the whole time. Just to get the peace.'

'Well, I'm sure I can arrange that, but I think you'd

much prefer the Penrigan View Hotel. It's proper five-star luxury.'

'But I also have to meet this Irish stallion you are living with and see the market and—'

'We will do it all. But I've been working all week and it was market day today, so I'm knackered, so tonight I thought we could have a few drinks in the hotel and a nice dinner and tomorrow, it's up to you. You can come and work the Saturday outdoor market with me, and I'll give you the key to my place so you can chill there when you want to. Or you can explore over in Crowsbridge – a ferry goes across every thirty minutes – and of course the market is amazing for shopping. Or you can just stay here and enjoy the spa, beach and pier if you so desire.'

'Options, options. I love it. But yes, let's go check in and get a drink down us. It sounds like we have a lot to catch up on.'

'Happy Noneymoon.' Dee clinked their champagne flutes gently together as they sat perusing their menus in the packed posh restaurant of the hotel.

'Thanks for that. But I guess, if it's right that everything happens for a reason I must have been led here.'

A young, chiselled waiter in his all-black uniform smiled between them as he refilled their glasses.

'Bloody hell, Rini, you didn't warn me that this place was teeming with such totty. We will be ordering room service every hour on the hour at this rate.'

'They're half your age!' The reminder of the age gap between Dominic and his new lover caused Sabrina to blow out a big sigh.

'Shit. Sorry.' Dee's face looked pained. 'Looking at the photos, I don't think he's that happy.'

'Well, he may be happy with her but a kid on his coat tails is everything he didn't want at his age.'

'He made his bed, Sabrina.'

'I know.' Sabrina took a big sip of bubbly. 'And now I have to make my own bed and move on.'

'So, being led here for a reason? Does that mean you're feeling alright about everything? About Dom, I mean?'

'Yes, considering the enormity of it, I actually do.'

'Good girl.' Dee gently placed her hand on her friend's.

Sabrina sighed. 'Don't get me wrong, it's been difficult dealing with the fact I feel rejected by him. And then finding out she was pregnant – well, that was a huge kick in the teeth. But it's only been six weeks and I don't think I'm missing a man I was supposed to be marrying like I should be. I cried more when I broke up with Sammi Jenkins in sixth form.'

'Oh my God, Sammi Jenkins. Wasn't he the blondie with the cock ring?'

'Trust you to remember that.' Sabrina laughed out loud. 'Yes, him – amazing in the sack, but thick as pig shit. I still stayed with him for two years, though.' Sabrina laughed. 'God, you'd have thought I would have learnt my lesson by now, wouldn't you?'

Dee took a drink. 'Life is one ongoing lesson, mate. But it's brilliant, isn't it, that you're not missing Dom? And I'm so relieved you're not, Rini.'

'It was you who said to think about what it really was I missed about him, and do you know what, I must still be fickle now as I liked the crazy lifestyle that being with him brought. I liked the fancy London restaurants and having him on my arm at the soap awards red carpet. But through all of that, I never really felt held. I don't think he ever got to know who I really was. Do you understand what I mean by that?'

'Oh, Rini.'

'And I'm not sure he *ever* had my back really. He loved himself more than me and that's not a quality I find attractive in a man. I look at Isaac and Belle, and their love is so pure and real. And I know you and Stu have your ups and downs, but the foundation is still true love. You two just work.'

'That's because we still laugh together. We have this standing joke of leaving a dog-eared Koala with one eye somewhere funny that the other will find – it was one of Phoebe's old toys. This morning it was tucked in the top of my case with a note just saying, *Love you, Chops.* It is the little things.'

Sabrina nodded, so happy for her friend in her choice of husband. 'Yes, it is. Not going to lie, I was feeling a bit morose the other night and I looked up the piece I read on your wedding day. I remember it was harder than learning any lines as I kept crying when I read it out in front of the mirror.'

'Aw. You donut. You never told me that.' Dee reached for her friend's arm. 'The only piece out of the Bible I would allow; we are such heathens.'

Sabrina was a little tipsy, she began reciting a little too loudly. She saw the woman on the table next door raise her eyebrows to her partner, but didn't care.

'"*Love is patient and kind. Love is not jealous or boastful or proud or rude. It does not demand its own way. It is not irritable, and it keeps no record of being wronged. It does not rejoice about injustice but rejoices whenever the truth wins out. Love never gives up, never loses faith, is always hopeful, and endures through every circumstance.*"'

Dee put her hand to her heart, tears in her eyes. 'It

is the most beautiful prose.'

Sabrina took a large slug of champagne, 'I've been worried that something is wrong with you and Stu.' Dee looked awkward for a second. 'Oh no, there is, isn't there?' Sabrina grimaced.

'I don't know how to tell you this, but just after you left to come down here, Stu and I had the hugest row, because he doesn't think you should know about something.'

Sabrina felt a wave of dread course through her. 'What are you on about?'

A waiter came over to take their order. 'Five more minutes.' They said in unison.

'Oh my god, Dee, what's happened?'

Dee took a deep breath and ran her hand through her messy brown bob. 'Rini, you know you have been my friend for years and years and I love you very much.'

'You're scaring me now.' Sabrina felt her stomach lurch. 'You're not splitting up, are you?'

'Worse than that.'

'What? Just tell me.'

Dee rushed her words out at one hundred miles an hour. 'Dom did something inappropriate at my birthday drinks this year.'

Sabrina swallowed loudly. 'Go on.'

'He was drunk, Rini.'

'I see the pattern, here.' Sabrina tried to mask her disappointment with sarcasm but knew her friend saw through it.

'It was discreet. He brushed passed me gently, touched my arse, then gave me a wink and that was it. But it was enough, Rini.'

Sabrina's face contorted. 'He was joking though, right.'

'No. He wasn't.' Dee was quietly adamant. 'It was

creepy, not friendly. I felt physically sick for you, not me. It reminded me of when someone at the Houses of Parliament did similar to me once. Stu had a drinks thing going on with work with proper posed photos, and I was his plus one. One of the ministers of sleaze there jostled next to me for the photo and put his hand on my muffin top and squeezed it, saying, "I guess you're OK with that?" If it hadn't been a work do, I'd have twisted his gnarly old todger right off.' Proper #MeToo stuff. Discreet, but seedy as hell.'

'You could have told me, Dee.'

'No, I couldn't. You were so excited with the wedding coming up and seemed so happy. If he'd offered sex, then yes, of course I'd have told you, but he just brushed passed me. But the fact that he did that is enough to prove he's not for you, Rini, and then when he shagged the French stick, I was kind of relieved as being honest, you deserve better than him. And a man in a relationship just shouldn't behave like that. Imagine Stu doing that to you.'

Sabrina shook her head. 'He just wouldn't.'

'Exactly. He loves you and we both know that, but he will kiss you on the cheek openly goodbye or hello. And basically, he said if I did tell you about what Dom had done, it would open an unnecessary can of worms and pain for you that you didn't need. Would you have stopped the wedding if I had told you?'

'He's such a sleazeball!' Sabrina said far too loudly, the champagne now taking effect. 'And it looks like Little Miss Frenchie did me a favour as it left no doubt that I should leave him. No wonder you were relieved.'

'I love you so much, Rini, and I'm so sorry if I handled this wrongly, but you know me and you, we have never had a secret between us.'

'I can see both your and Stu's sides. And I'm so sorry this has caused you such anguish and that you fell out with him over it. And now, I am genuinely so happy you told me.' Sabrina squeezed her friend's hand.

'Really?'

'Really. How mad is Stu with Dom on a scale of one to ten.'

'Let's just say it's a good job he hasn't seen him since the wedding that never was. I'm surprised he didn't lump him one then, to be honest.'

Sabrina's brow furrowed. 'Now I think back, there were so many times that Dom was over-flirty and just a little too edgy with women. You've cemented my decision. My head was clear, but my heart wasn't and yes, as I say, it's only been six weeks, but I don't want to be with him. I really don't.'

'Hurrah to that! And as for me and Stu, we're fine, now. I mean, Colin the Koala is back leaving me messages, so the Dickinson household is clearly business as usual.'

They both laughed.

'And Dominic Best is clearly a cock.' Sabrina announced.

'Let's drink to that.' Dee lifted her glass. 'Then let's order some bloody food. We've got a market stall to run tomorrow and I'm starving.'

Chapter Twenty-Eight

'Remind me never to invite you down on a market weekend again.' Sabrina croaked as both she and Dee stood outside Tinsel Town nursing huge hangovers and wearing saucer size sunglasses.

'It could be worse – it could be freezing cold. At least this Autumn sunshine is putting some brightness on the matter,' Sabrina said. 'And I did tell you to stay back in that huge comfy hotel bed.'

'No. I helped get us in this mess, so I'm here.' Dee was resolute. 'Can't say I'll be here all day, but I'm here now.'

'We planned it so wrong.' Sabrina yawned. 'We are missing out on a legendary Penrigan View Hotel breakfast, too.'

'It's fine.' Dee caught Sabrina's yawn.

'We have two more nights there to relax.' Sabrina brushed a stray leaf off the market stall. 'And, to be honest, it might have to be an early finish. I am the boss, after all.'

The sound of an Irish accent caused Sabrina to instantaneously smile. 'Ah, here's my girl. Jesus, Dickens you look like shite, and that's only seeing half your face.'

'Thanks, mate! Conor, this is Dee, long-term friend and mischief maker. Dee this is Conor. My roommate and...' Sabrina felt herself waiver and flush.

'Shoulder to cry on.' Conor gave one of his lop-sided grins.

Dee held out her hand. 'Lovely to meet you. I've heard all about you.'

'All bad, I hope.' He grinned again. 'Looks like you had the craic at that fancy hotel last night, for sure. Good on you, ladies.'

'What are you doing up here, anyway?' Sabrina acknowledged a customer who had started browsing the new Gisela Graham baubles she'd just ordered in.

'Just waiting on a bacon bap from Uncle Frank, so I am, and wanted to check you two had a good night.' As he looked to Sabrina, his voice softened. 'You needed that.'

'I did. But not this bloody hangover.'

'I tell you what, have you had breakfast?'

'No, we literally skidded in without so much as a cup of tea earlier.' Dee groaned.

'And we've been too busy to make one, since.' Sabrina added mournfully.

'I've got to get back on the ferry now, but how I about I order you in some bacon baps and a couple of cappuccino from Frank's and I'll get young Kirsty who helps him on a Saturday to drop them up to you?'

'Amazing! Here.' Sabrina went to give him some money.

He waved her hand away. 'Don't work too hard.' He then bolted off back down Ferry Lane.

'He fancies you,' Dee said matter-of-factly as she started going through the rail of Christmas jumpers.

Sabrina gave a feeble laugh. 'Don't be silly.'

'What man goes out of his way to run up a hill to say hello and then go and get you breakfast?'

'A decent one?'

'Exactly – someone who gives a shit. About you! And you told me last night that when you were distressed about Lowen, Conor not only gave you the best hugs but also cycled all the way from his uncle's place to you in the middle of his night out. I mean, if that doesn't smack of someone who cares about you a lot, I don't know what does.'

Sabrina kept her eyes averted from her friend's. 'Maybe.'

'Actions, Rini. Actions. They *do* speak louder than words. And he's hardly been hit with the ugly stick either, has he? In fact,' Dee put on an Irish accent, 'he really is quite the ride!'

Sabrina laughed, then groaned. 'Stop it, my head hurts. And I don't want just a *ride* – I had that with Mr Market Inspector. When I'm ready, I want *a romance*.'

The morning flew by in flash of selling baubles, candles and lights. The candles and lights were good for any time of the year, Sabrina figured, but it was great to see that the dedicated Christmassy stock was also moving and that the decision to sell festive stuff had been a good one.

Both she and Dee went inside the unit whilst there was a bit of a lull to make a much-needed cup of tea. Sabrina leaned on the window ledge to keep an eye out for any customers, and Dee swung her legs on the high counter stool.

Sabrina sighed. 'I've got a moral dilemma.'

'Well, with my recent track record with you on morality, maybe I'm not quite the right person to ask about this.' Dee smiled. 'But go on, let's talk around it like we always do.'

Sabrina cleared her throat. 'The delightful Lowen in his drunken rage told me that he is now working for a developer who wants to shut the outdoor market down. Basically, this company is planning on building a housing estate at the top of Hartmouth Hill. And they are wanting access to Ferry Lane seven days a week to act as a bypass to cope with the new volume of traffic heading out on the coastal road to Penrigan. This market has been here for over a hundred years, Dee. If it goes through, the livelihood of the stallholders will be deeply affected. It's disastrous!'

Dee gasped. 'Oh, no, that's tragic. I've only been here a few hours and I can tell what a lovely community it is. It lives and breathes for both the sellers and the customers.'

'I know. Ferry Lane Market *is* Hartmouth.'

'Everyone will still be able to sell from inside their shop units, though, right?'

'Yes, but it won't be the same and the footfall is huge on the Friday and Saturday market days. It would really affect everyone's businesses, plus extra traffic down these cobbles would take the magic of the place away.'

'So, what's the dilemma?'

'Lowen said if I say anything, he will out me for who I really am.'

'Oh.' Dee's face fell. 'That's not good.'

'Yes. I'm so enjoying the anonymity. I love acting with a passion, as you know, but I want to see if I can do something other than that. It's all I know, Dee, and yes, the money's good, but being honest, I've got savings and I've realised money doesn't make me happy. I mean, look at me swapping a Dolce & Gabbana cashmere for a twenty-quid jumper with a reindeer on it. Which I have to say, I do rather like.'

Dee laughed. 'I like it so much that I'm getting one each for the whole family for Christmas Day – including the dog.' Dee took a sip of tea. 'But what are you going to do about it? The market, I mean.'

'I don't know. I'm only here for three months, so selfishly I'd quite like to do nothing. I'm trying to get my head around it. Conor knows who I am, and it didn't faze him one bit, but Conor is Conor and I know what my soap fan base is like. I can't walk down the street at home or go to the supermarket without some kind of catcalling. And it's not always pleasant. The madness of people mixing fantasy with reality, it's not normal and just from my social media I know there are some weird people out there. Plus, the press would be all over me within seconds.'

Dee yawned loudly. 'Have a really good think about this Rini. It sounds like you've got a lovely thing going on down here. And talking of cats – in a different sense, maybe – I've just proved that sometimes, letting the cat out of the bag *is* the right thing to do. And not just for you, but for the greater good.'

Chapter Twenty-Nine

On Monday morning, Dee ran in to the apartment and waved frantically at Conor, who was spreadeagled on the sofa in just his underpants, eating dry cereal from a bowl.

'Just wanted to say a quick goodbye before I go back home.'

'Aw, that's nice. How was the meal at the hotel last night?'

'Amazing, thank you. VISTA is definitely worth its Michelin star.'

'Grand. Where is that housemate of mine?' Conor turned the television down.

'I'm here.' Sabrina came through the front door with a carton of milk in her hand. 'I knew you'd be doing that – take this.' She handed him the milk, which he poured straight into the bowl, then placed the carton on the floor.

'Thanks a million, gorgeous, and so glad you had a nice time.' Conor turned the TV back up and started tucking into his Frosties.'

'Shit, is that the time? Rini, I need to be at the station in twenty minutes. I promised my parents I'd be back for the afternoon school run.'

'You're up early on your day off, Conor Brady?' Sabrina grabbed an apple from the fruit bowl, which was perched precariously above the fireplace.

'Yeah. I thought I'd go for a walk up on the head. I'll wait for you, if you fancy joining me?'

'Definitely, I could do with stomping off some of this weekend's excesses. I won't be long.'

Dee went over to Conor and, trying not to stare too hard at all his taut flesh on show, leant down and kissed him on the cheek. 'It's been lovely to meet you, and thanks for making this one smile.'

'Likewise. Safe journey, and I hope to see you again soon.'

Sabrina headed to the front door.

Dee followed. Thinking they were out of earshot, she gushed, 'He's so lovely, Rini. Are you going to tell him? I think you should for his uncle and Monique's sake, at least.'

Sabrina glared at Dee and put a finger to her lips to shush her.

She looked through to Conor, who was still face-forward, intently watching the news, then shut the door quietly behind her.

Conor took Sabrina's hand to steady her as they walked up the steep path towards Penrigan Head. 'It'll be worth the climb in a minute, I promise.'

After fifteen minutes of solid walking, they reached the end of the cliff path, which flattened out to reveal a jaw-dropping vista. The cloudy autumn sky mirrored the flat of the calm sea below, where coastal birds bobbed up and down on the white-tipped waves. On spotting a shoal of fish darting under a rocky shelf at the bottom of the cliffside, some dived at them, shrieking their approval.

There were two large rocks right at the top of the cliff. Both had flat tops and were facing the awe-inspiring view. Sabrina pulled her scarf tighter around her to protect herself from the sea breeze that was whipping around them. 'It's like these have been put here by Mother Nature on purpose so that we can sit quietly and appreciate what she has created around us.'

'You're so sweet.' Conor smiled at her. 'Here. Let's sit on the grass between them if you don't mind. It'll be more sheltered down here.'

'Ta da!' Sabrina pulled a flowery flask of coffee out of her bag, along with two take-away cups. 'I found it in the cupboard when you were in the shower.'

'I wouldn't have put you down as a girl guide.' Conor laughed. 'But good work, Dickens.'

They sat in silence for a second drinking their coffee and taking in the view.

'Conor, do you mind me asking why you came back here?'

The Irishman blew out a big breath. 'It's painful.'

'Breakups always are.' Sabrina put her hand on his.

'Oh God,' he cleared his throat, 'it's not a woman. It's my Niall.'

With the passing thought of Conor now being in a gay relationship, Sabrina squeaked. 'Do you want to talk about it?'

'Niall is my son, so he is.'

Shocked at the strength of her relief, Sabrina's voice became softer. 'Ah, I see.'

'Yes, he's thirteen now and such a good kid. I've tried so hard to do right by him but his mother Maeve, my ex-wife, has met someone new. He's a Kiwi and, surprise surprise, he wants to go back to New Zealand to settle and she is of course happy to follow. The only good thing about it is she's not living with my mate any longer. She left me for him years ago, you see.'

'Wow, that's all so harsh.'

'Yes, it's been an ongoing source of grief for me. My boy and making sure he's provided for and happy. It irks me so much, him living with these different men, but that's life and it goes on.'

'Is Niall happy, do you think?'

'He's really excited about the move and assures me we can chat every week, and I guess it gives me an excuse to visit a country I've never been to before.'

'And I'm assuming he has grandparents and other family here that he may come back to visit.' Sabrina soothed.

'I hadn't thought of that. I think this new bloke's not short of a few quid, so hopefully that's an option.'

'So why has this led you back to Hartmouth? I don't understand.'

'I left here the Christmas before last. Niall was still in Ireland and Maeve said I could see a lot more of him, but only if I was in London as Cornwall was too far to realistically manage visits. And I got that, so I went back and worked with a cousin of mine who has a landscaping business. The intention was to set up on my own, but it never happened. And, if I'm honest, the reason why is because I missed it down here too much.'

'It is so magical, isn't it?' Sabrina cupped her hands around her coffee.

'Yes. I grew up in a beautiful area in Ireland, but I had to leave for fear of what I might do to the mate who nicked my wife. I never went back and until I came here I'd never found somewhere else to call home. Does that make sense?'

'Yes. It really does.'

'Where is *your* home, Dickens?'

Sabrina sniffed back tears. She spoke quietly. 'I don't know, yet.'

Conor put his hand on her knee. 'You had the rug pulled right out from under you, didn't you?'

'That's the problem. A lot of my stuff is still in the London flat we shared. Not that I care about that per se. And if I'm honest with you, I never saw that as our forever home. Dom has big retirement plans, but he also had a terrible fault of never living in the moment. It was all about the big future, the big dream. My plan was to get married and ditch the acting so I could start an acting school. That *was* my big dream.'

'And why can't you still follow that?'

'I have to admit that Dom was my security, as I had looked into it and needed a big chunk of money upfront if I wanted to set something up in the city. That's not to say that the money was why I wanted to marry him, of course. It was just a bonus. I also need to get my head around being single again. It was a bit of a shock, him shagging a waitress, you know. More fool me for relying on a man.'

'Look at me putting my size nines in it. I read all that, too, and I'm so sorry.'

Sabrina sighed. 'I guess my real home was with my family in North London. I wanted for nothing there, apart from my mum to be mentally well and my dad not to be at work quite so much. But there *was* love. We used to come down here on holiday, to that beach.' She pointed down to a tiny strip of sand in the distance. 'Hence my pull to here and the honeymoon cottage, I guess. I had my first kiss here too – my very first holiday romance, in fact. Cried for days when I got home. He lived in Manchester, so it was never going to go anywhere.'

'Aw, that's cute and sounds idyllic.'

'Ironically, it was the one year that we didn't come here, that my brother decided to cliff dive and damage his brain and my mum, reasoning that if we'd been here, it never would have happened, blamed herself. A logic I could never quite understand, but she was mentally ill and the stress and guilt of it, led her to commit suicide.'

'Jesus.' Conor put his arm around her. 'You poor, darling, angel.' He pulled her in close. 'How the feck do you ever get over that?'

'You don't. I must try and fill the emptiness with love evidently. And I'm realising that shallow, adoring love from fans or from an ex-fiancé who never really knew me isn't cutting the mustard on that front anymore.'

Conor gave her one huge squeeze, then helped her up. He grasped both of her hands and held them to his chest. His eyes met hers. 'What would you say if I said I really wanted to kiss you, right now?'

Sabrina felt the butterflies in her tummy start to come alive again. 'I'd say it might make things a little complicated.'

'And does that matter? I really like you, Dickens. From the minute I set eyes on you, I felt an attraction. There's something about you. You're an incredible person.'

Sabrina made a little groaning noise and pulled away from him. 'Oh God, we can't. I can't.'

Conor smiled sadly. 'Why not?'

'I'm scared.' Sabrina's voice was childlike. She felt like she wanted to run and never stop running.

'Of what, darling girl.'

'Of getting hurt, of fucking up, as losing you as a friend as to be honest you are the best wing man any girl could want. It's not you, I just... I just don't think it's the right time. I just...'

Conor pointed to a lone yacht on the horizon. 'See that boat over there.'

Sabrina nodded. 'It's free in the wind, but it will

come back to its harbour and be safe. I will wait for you in our harbour, Dickens. Because even though you don't feel it at the moment, I've never been so certain of a connection like this in all my life.' He pulled her to him, hugged her tightly, then kissed the top of her head. 'And the reason I will wait for you, is because you are so worth waiting for.'

She pulled away and looked into his eyes. 'And you Conor Brady are a beautiful man.'

They began to walk back down to the car park. 'I know what else I meant to ask you.'

'Go on.' Sabrina grabbed Conor's arm as she lost her footing on some loose stones.

'See, you are falling for me already, so you are.' They both laughed. 'Yeah, Dee asked you earlier if you were going to tell me something?'

'Oh. Umm. You heard…'

'You know you can tell me anything.' Conor softly squeezed her hand.

Sabrina grimaced. 'You have to promise you won't do anything to get me into any trouble if I tell you.'

Conor sighed. 'Please trust me. I'm not Dominic, or Lowen, or any of the other men who have treated you badly. My word stands.'

They reached Sabrina's Audi and relished the instant warmth of the heater as she turned the engine on. She looked across to Conor. 'This is really huge and really horrible, and I didn't want to say anything as it does indirectly affect your family.'

She could see the light drain from Conor's eyes. 'Go on.'

'Lowen is now working for a developer who wants to shut down the outdoor market. They're going to build a huge housing development at the top of the hill, which means that the excess traffic will have to go through Ferry Lane seven days a week.'

'What an absolute eejit.' Conor bashed his hand down on the dashboard. 'But he's seriously deluded. The planning will never go through.'

'Well, this is why Lowen had a short-term job at the council. He's got some of them on his side ready for some backhanders if it does.'

'The cunning piece of...'

'Yes. He really is a nasty man.'

'I guess the positive of you having your dalliance with him is that you found this out.'

'Everything for a reason, and all that.' Sabrina's face dropped. 'But I don't want you or Frank or anyone else getting involved because he will know I've said something, and I really do want to keep my anonymity around here. He said that if I say anything, he'll tell everyone who I am around here and inform the press. It will be a circus, and I'm not ready for that.

'What a wanker.' Conor looked pained.

'So, I'm going to handle it by myself.'

'How?' Conor stared at her.

'You don't need to know that. Give me a week, please, and if I haven't put some kind of halt on it, then you can take over. OK?'

'But—'

'Conor, I've trusted you with a lot. In return, trust me on this one. Please. You must promise me.'

Conor sighed deeply. 'Next Monday, we walk and talk again. Deal?'

'Deal.' Sabrina put her hand out to shake his and he immediately put it to his mouth and kissed it.

'But, after that, I can't promise you what might happen.'

'Conor!'

'This is serious shit, Dickens, and affects a lot of people.'

'I get it – of course, I get it.' Sabrina sighed.

Conor gave her one of his lop-sided smiles. 'You're an amazing woman, and don't ever forget that.'

And despite her preoccupation with the question of what on earth she was going to do to save the market without exposing her own secret, she blushed. 'I try.'

With Conor dropped off at Bee Cottage doing some gardening for Billy and Kara, Sabrina let herself into the flat and made herself a cup of tea. So happy that she had taken the decision to take Mondays off, too, she positioned herself on the sofa so that she could look out over the busy estuary. As she focused on the *Happy Hart* making its way over to Crowsbridge, she thought back to Conor wanting to kiss her. Every ounce of her gut had told her to. In fact, she had never felt so certain of wanting something or someone in her whole life. His touch felt so right, he smelt so good. But more importantly she could tell that his intentions were true. And as certain as what she had experienced with Lowen Kellow was pure lust, she knew that if she were to kiss Conor Brady right back, it would undoubtedly lead to something far deeper. If she would let it, that was. Because, despite convincing herself and everyone around her that everything about Dominic Best was wrong, there was a tiny part of her bruised, fragile and clearly deluded heart that was still telling her that she still loved him. And until that feeling passed, she wasn't ready to move on.

Chapter Thirty

The Ferry Lane Market Stallholders Monthly Meeting was a far more relaxed affair than Sabrina had imagined it would be. She had arrived at Monique's, promptly at midday to find four tables pushed together, each with a delicious looking platter of sandwiches, jugs of water and a coffee jug.

Linda Harris was in her element chatting to everyone, pouring the coffee and basically busying herself to make sure each stallholder had what they needed. Once everyone was sat and settled, she looked over to Big Frank. 'Ready?'

He nodded and with an air of importance, the plump woman scurried to lock the door and hang the *Private Meeting until 1* sign on it.

Kara and Star had beckoned Sabrina to join them at their end of the table, which she was pleased about as she had felt a bit of imposter even being invited to the meeting, especially as she was so part time and not a local. She obviously knew Frank and Charlie, too, and for her sake, Frank had kindly asked everyone around the table to give her a little introduction as to who they were, and which stall they were connected to. Gideon Jones who ran the antique stall had given her a leery smile; Nigel from the fish stall, still wearing his blue-and-white-striped apron and smelling slightly of haddock, gave her a half smile. Ben Clark, the butcher sat quietly doing a word game on his phone, looked up and cooly just nodded his head at her; and Alicia, who seemed as sweet as the fudge and honey she sold at The Sweet Spot, gushed a huge welcome.

Frank cleared his throat. 'We wish you all the best, Jilly, and welcome to the Ferry Lane Fold. It's great that Brian can keep his slot on the market, thanks to you. So, if anyone has any problems with Jilly taking the unit, then I suggest they talk to me about it.' Sabrina suddenly felt warm inside. Accreditation from Big Frank and a justification that she was in fact helping one of their own was, she realised, a big step towards her acceptance into the market community.

'Anyway, it's good to see a few of you here today. I have had apologies from the other stallholders, and I will send a brief email out after the meeting to all.'

'Great end-of-season party, by the way – thanks, Frank.' Gideon Jones grinned. 'Took me a week to recover.'

'Hear, hear.' A resounding thumbs up from the whole group.

'My pleasure, but you bastards best keep coming in through the winter, now.'

They all laughed.

'Has anyone heard from Brian?' Nigel piped up as everyone started tucking into the sandwiches.

'Yes.' Frank nodded. 'He's loving Australia and his mum is so pleased that he has made the trip to see her. He emailed me this morning and wanted to wish you well, Jilly.'

'Aw.' Sabrina blushed, realising more than ever that she had to come up with a plan to put a stop to the huge and damaging changes to the outdoor market that were afoot.

Frank looked directly at her. 'He also said that he'd got the signed contract from yourself, but the rent hadn't gone through yet.'

Sabrina suddenly felt cold. 'OK. I will check with Lowen Kellow as I paid him in cash directly, but can you share Brian's email please so I can find out…umm…when he receives it.'

Frank scribbled on the scrappy piece of A4 paper in front of him.

'I thought that useless so and so had been sacked?' Charlie chipped in. Linda, who was polishing the glass counter, stopped what she was doing, ears pricked to high alert.

'Bloody hope so. I never liked him – something I couldn't quite put my finger on.' Gideon Jones sniffed loudly.

Frank refilled his coffee cup. 'Until we get confirmation of that, we carry on as usual. He's been as much use as a chocolate teapot to be honest, anyway, so I shouldn't worry too much.' Frank stood up and checked his watch. 'Let's get going properly. I wanted to say that this is our tenth meeting and I think you'll agree, that we have already achieved quite a lot between us. News, aside Jilly joining us, is that the Christmas lights are going to be going up at the start of November and my *decent* contact at the council, Roger Terry, has promised that they will be slightly more decadent than last year's paltry offering. Also, Ben, thanks to your suggestion, a bi-weekly rather than monthly street clean has been confirmed as I agree market days do take their toll on the pavements.'

Star raised her hand. 'Are we going to be doing the Victorian Christmas Fair again this year? It was on the first Saturday in December, from memory, and it did attract a huge crowed.'

There was a mumbling in the group.

Frank tapped on his cup with his pen. 'I guess it just involves us dressing up and Charlie roasting his chestnuts on an open fire. Plus, we got the Salvation Army band playing before and the snow machines I managed to acquire were also a nice touch. Hands up if you'd like to go ahead with it this year.'

'You know me, I'll get my old chestnuts out any time of year.' Charlie laughed, and the group joined in.

'That's unanimous, then.' Frank made another note on his piece of paper.

Star interjected. 'Sorry, but I won't be able to be as hands on this year with the marketing of it. One toddler, a newborn and keeping my bespoke service running is proving quite a challenge.'

Kara tutted. 'Just the two babies… come see me in January, you'll feel like you're on a permanent holiday.' Star smiled and dug her sister in the ribs.

'I'll take it on.' Alicia piped up. 'I'm sure Glanna will produce some flyers for us, if we ask her nicely, and I'm happy to contact the local papers and all that.'

'Good idea – and thanks, Alicia,' Frank said. 'She'll be back in the gallery later; she's doing a talk at the university this morning.' He sat back down. 'OK, that's all sounding grand. Let's set the Victorian Fair running and if anyone has anything else during the month they want to discuss, just pop down to me or send an email. Before we go, any other business?'

Everyone shook their heads.

As chairs scraped back for everyone to leave, Frank looked directly at Sabrina. 'So, definitely no other business from your side, then…Jilly?'

Being faced with all these lovely people whose livelihood depended on market days and who generally did care about each other's wellbeing caused a gnawing of guilt within her. Maybe Dee had been right, as she usually was, that her being selfish here was not for the greater good. But her fear of having to face everything, including herself, was just too much to bear at the moment.

But Frank was asking her very pointedly... did he know about Lowen's plans? Her gut told her that he did. And yes, Conor had promised her, but blood was thicker than water and she had come to realise that Brady blood was undoubtedly thicker than most.

She smiled weakly back at him. 'Not yet, Frank, no.'

He put his big hand on her shoulder. 'We've got your back.'

Without her needing to reply, Frank began to put the tables back into their original café positions.

Sabrina hurried her way to the front door that everyone else had already streamed out of and then, BANG!

'We really must stop bumping into each other like this.' Lowen Kellow gave her a wry smile.

Sabrina's nostrils flared as she glared at him. 'And you need to start looking where you are going?'

'Mark, meet Jilly Dickens. She runs our pop-up Christmas gift shop, Tinsel Town. She should have been a Hollywood actress with a shop name like that.' He laughed. The suited man looked slightly awkward. Sabrina felt sick. 'Mark is from County Homes.'

'Hi.' Sabrina rushed past him. 'Must get on, Tinsel Town,' she exaggerated the two words, 'sadly isn't able to run itself.'

Lowen turned his attention to Linda. 'Ah. Just the lady. I'll have one of my special coffees, please. And Mark, what's your poison?'

Frank looked over at Linda and winked. 'All OK, Mrs Harris?'

She gave the big man a thumbs up and turned to the coffee machine.

Sabrina was just unpacking a box of silver and gold tinsel when her shop bell went. She was faced with an attractive woman, the same height as her, with a white-blonde crop and black statement spectacles.

'Hi.' Sabrina smiled and stopped what she was doing.

'Hey. I'm Glanna Pascoe. From the *Hart*mouth Gallery.'

Her partner, Oliver had been right. Aside from the woman's plumper, currently bright red lips and doe-shaped brown eyes, she could see there was a similarity between them.

'I'm S… Jilly. So lovely to meet you, at last.'

'Yes, sorry, I was going to fit your sign for you, then I had an exhibition going on in St Ives, so it's been all go the last few weeks. Good old Oliver. It looks great!'

'Yes, I'm so pleased with it, and the fact we can detach it so easily when Brian comes back is the cherry on top, so thank you.'

'We aim to please.' Glanna's eyes went to the expensive baubles in a box on the countertop.

'Also, I've been wanting to see you and say that the painting of yours in Isaac Benson's holiday cottage is so gorgeous.' Sabrina grinned.

'Remind me, is it the ferry coming in with the rainbow in the distance'?'

'That's the one. You are so talented.'

'Thank you. I feel so blessed to have been gifted with a creative talent.'

'You really should.' Sabrina found her thoughts

leading to her first drama class at school realising that all she had ever wanted to do with her life was act. Oh, to be young again with not a care in the world and the dream of Hollywood still a possibility. Where had that passion gone? Did adulthood just kick your dreams out of you? Or maybe with everything that had happened recently, her priorities had just been reset.

'How's your day going, anyway, Glanna? I guess like all of us, your weekdays are far quieter than the weekends?'

'I was giving a lecture to the art students at the University this morning, so I enjoyed that.'

'Ah, yes, Frank mentioned that at the meeting this morning. I'd love to be able to teach.' She stopped herself from saying 'my craft'. 'I expect your ears were burning. Alicia is going to be in touch about some flyers for the Victorian Fair.'

'That's fine. I try and make as many of the meetings as I can but if I can't the big man is particularly good with the minutes after. I just had a bit of a weird moment in the gallery, though. A reporter from a publication I didn't even recognise came in, looking for someone whose description fitted mine. A well-known actress has evidently gone missing or something and there is a reward out to find her.'

'Oh. How odd.' Sabrina put her head down and started to fiddle about with some tinsel, heart pounding. 'Right. Well, I hope the woman's OK.'

'I take it no one came in here?' Glanna started looking through the jumpers.

'No, but I've not been back from the meeting long. What did the reporter look like?'

'It was a woman – short, ginger hair. I saw you arrive earlier and assumed as you and I have kind of the same hair and big glasses, they might have put two and two together and made eight, like local reporters usually do.'

'Did they have a photo of the actress?'

'No, they just described her as blonde haired, with statement glasses.'

Sabrina felt an overriding anxiety that somebody was on to her. They hadn't mentioned her nose ring, so at least that was a bonus.

'Anyway, Jilly. I will come and have a proper look at your stuff nearer Christmas as it looks like you have some lovely bits that I could dress my window with. Better get on. Great to meet you.'

'You, too.'

Sabrina went to the door, locked it and turned the *open* sign to *closed*. Lowen surely wouldn't have contacted a reporter – he had two much skulduggery going on himself. And who would actually know to describe her with her current look? With a loud, 'Shit!' She put her hand to her head. How could she have been so naive to think that Giselle wouldn't make herself busy trying to find her. It probably still showed online there was a reward if anyone spotted her, and Lowen had said what a soap fan she was. And now that the woman knew she was in the area and had changed her hair, maybe she was pulling out all the stops to locate her even without knowing her boyfriend had been unfaithful with her. She knew she hadn't given much away, but it was a small town and if you were looking for someone with the same description as her, in a place where even the walls talked, it would be quite easy to find her if someone was on a mission and had a photo or her pre-haircut, and a description of what changes she had made to her appearance.

She quickly called Belle. 'Hey, it's me.'

'Hey, Sabrina, how's it going?'

'It was going amazingly, thanks, but I need to change my hair.'

'What colour?'

Sabrina smiled; a no-questions-asked friend really was the perfect one to have.

'I don't care, as long as it covers this blonde. Will you be home in an hour?'

'Sure. Come over then. We can hatch a plan.'

Sabrina chose a Beanie hat from another box of stock that had come in that morning. She pulled it completely over her hair and, happy that the sun had come out, donned her sunglasses. She was just on her way to get some honey to take to Belle from Alicia's place when she saw Lowen and the man from County Homes leaving Monique's.

She watched with surprise as an over-friendly Charlie Dillon called them over. 'Alright gentlemen. Cox!' He paused and smiled sweetly. 'Got a basket full of 'em here. Fancy trying one?' The greengrocer was polishing one in his hand. 'All free of charge. My lad's missus has got a glut of 'em in her garden. And isn't it right, we must give to receive and all that, and I've got twenty quid on *Hey Jude* in the four twenty at Haydock.'

The men laughed as Charlie handed over the apple he'd been polishing to Lowen, and the other man took one from the basket. As they made their way down Ferry Lane, Sabrina took off her sunglasses and rubbed her eye.

'Now, I know you've declined my ripe and juicy Cox before, Jilly, but—'

'You're alright, Charlie.' Sabrina grinned.

With a pot of honey in hand, Sabrina headed back down to her apartment to get her car. She smiled as she saw Conor and Billy getting the ferry ready for a crossing, and Frank chatting amiably to a passer-by as he swept the benched area outside. Despite there being a nip in the air, the sky housed not a single cloud and the still expanse of the sea below offered twinkling reflections from the warm Autumn sun. The mesmeric sounds of sea birds swooping, feeding and going about their daily feathery business were carried on the soft breeze. She still had to pinch herself that this was currently her home. And a home that she wanted to remain as peaceful as this for ever. Lowen had no reason to tell the press she was here, for she had kept her side of the bargain and there was no win for him in her being outed – quite the opposite, in fact, as if he did tell the world, it would only give more reason for her to reveal his plans. And an angry market-stall-holder mob was in fact far scarier than a few members of the gutter press.

She was just about to get in her car and head off to Kevrinek when she noticed Lowen, now alone, heading towards Frank's. He caught her eye. She couldn't help herself. 'Don't see you for days then you're everywhere. Busy day?'

'Busy? More like hungry.' He sneered. 'All-day breakfast here and then plans a-plenty to get my teeth into back at the ranch.'

Sabrina shook her head in disgust. 'Oh, yes. Whilst you're here, Brian says he hasn't received his money. Are you intending to send it?'

'Yes, of course I am.' He started to walk away.

'When?' Sabrina shouted after him.

He turned back. 'When I'm ready.'

Sabrina messaged Belle to say she was on her way, and with her roof down and feeling melancholic, she put on her Songs to Make you Cry, playlist on Spotify.

Speeding out of Hartmouth and on to the coastal road, she began to sing along at the top of her voice to George Michael's 'Careless Whisper'.

It really was a spectacularly scenic route to Penrigan Head, with rolling fields to her right and, when the tall hedgerows and hand-built granite stone walls allowed, glimpses of the sea to her left.

She was just about to turn into the quiet lane leading up to Isaac and Belle's farmhouse when Belle's name flashed up on her phone. Sabrina put her on speakerphone and spoke first.

'Hey, sorry, have I been ages? I'm literally just turning into your lane.'

'It's not that.' Sabrina could hear an edge in her friend's voice. 'Dominic's here.'

Chapter Thirty-One

Sabrina looked pensive as Dominic Best tentatively opened the door to Kevrinek Cottage and greeted her with a weak smile.

'Well, this is a bit of a turn up, you staying in *my* cottage.'

'Yes, Isaac didn't have much choice – I just showed up and asked him if it was free and thankfully he said yes. I figured it's a peaceful and private place to meet. I also gave him another five hundred pounds for Headway.'

'At least money talks, eh, Dominic?' Sabrina said tightly.

'I know I've been a complete dick but I'm here now. I had to see you. To talk face to face.'

'How long are you staying?'

'Just tonight. It nearly killed me driving down and back in one day when I saw you before. And I'm off to a...err... a work event in Cannes on Friday.'

'Won't it be a bit cold in Cannes this time of year? And...I'm certainly not apologising for you doing all that driving before.'

'I'm a big boy, Sabrina. I make my own decisions.'

'Yes, and lately, most of them have been wrong.'

'I asked for that.' Dominic lowered his eyes.

'Yes, you did.'

'Are you going to stand out there all afternoon? At

least come in for a cup of tea.' He ushered her inside.

With mugs of hot tea in front of them, they sat at the pine kitchen table.

Dominic put his hand over to touch Sabrina's, she pulled it away.

'What do you want, Dom?'

'To talk like adults instead of screaming at each other.' Nodding, Sabrina instantly felt tears pricking her eyes. She sniffed them back and took a large gulp of tea.

'It fucking hurt to find out she was pregnant from a newspaper article.' Dominic squirmed in his chair. 'All you had to do was ring me. What did you think I was going to do?'

'She hadn't even had her first scan and if I'm honest I hoped she'd change her mind. We did talk through that option.'

'But she didn't, and you are going to be a father again. I bet Mercedes is delighted about that.' Sabrina said cattily, letting out a little laugh at the thought of his spoilt daughter hearing the news of Dominic not only being involved with a woman younger than her, who was also with child.

Dominic looked to her left hand. 'Who did you sell your ring to, then?'

She managed a smile. 'You can take the girl out of North London and all that.' A pause. 'Of course, I haven't sold it. You can have it back if you'd like it.'

Dominic's face dropped. 'Sure, I'm that kind of man, aren't I? Auction it for the charity if you like. How is your brother, anyway? It's a long old trek for you to visit him from here, isn't it?'

The man in front of her sure knew how to play her emotions.

'I've called him every fortnight, as usual. He seems happy and the staff constantly tell me he's living his best life so he's as good as he can be. And I guess that is all we can hope for.'

'Well, if I'm honest, I'm not living my best life without you, Swifty. I miss you. I miss you a lot.'

Sabrina took a deep breath. 'You made your bed.' She looked up to the ceiling to push back more tears. 'Alright. I miss you, too.' She paused. 'Actually, I only miss parts of you and parts of our life together. If I'm honest, being apart from you has made me realise how shallow our existence together was most of the time.'

'I've had time to think, too. If you come back, we can change all of that. I promise.'

'Do you plan to leave your job, then?'

'No. You know the life plan: I want to retire at fifty-five.' Her frown didn't go unnoticed. 'But, not so many dinners out, more planned holidays with you and without the phone on. I will delegate more. I need to cut down on the booze because if I hadn't been pissed, what happened wouldn't have happened and we'd still be together.'

'Yes let's blame good old Jack Daniels, shall we? He's such a cad, leads everyone astray.' She screwed her face up. 'Except those men who have the upmost respect for their partners, that is. Is *she* still in the flat?'

'Yes, *she* is.' Dominic sighed deeply. 'Look, I haven't driven for six hours for the fun of it. I love *you*, Sabrina. I don't love her. I hardly know the girl. And that's all she is: a girl. She is a pretty face who is carrying my child. If there was no baby, there would be no 'us'.

'So, there is an 'us' with you and her then?' Despite everything, the pain of reality felt like a thousand knives turning in her heart.

'I can't abandon her, not yet. Her English is good, but she's young and never been to London before, and I don't want her working. Not at the moment.'

'She's pregnant, not sick, Dom.'

'Sabrina! Listen to me.'

'No, you listen to me. I assumed the plan was you find a place for her and support her. Isn't that the French way, anyway – the majority of men over there take a mistress, don't they? She'll be expecting it.'

'I'm not here to argue with you. And it's not as if you didn't shag someone else here in this very cottage. Eurghh, I just realised that I'm sleeping in the same bed, too – if you did it in the bed, that is.' Dom grimaced.

'Do you have to be so vile? It was just sex, Dom. Payback sex because I hated you and I hated myself. And the reason I hated myself was for not being good enough for you.' Sabrina started to cry. Dom rushed around to her side of the table, scooped her up and held her in his arms.

'And it was just sex for me, too. You know that. A stupid, stupid mistake.' Dom ran his hands through his floppy silver fringe. 'I will do anything to get you back. Life is not the same without you. It's shallow and boring and dull. Give me a second chance, please. Let me show you I can change. And as for being good enough for me, you make me a better version of myself, every day.'

Sabrina pulled away, grabbed a tissue from her bag and blew her nose. 'I don't want you to change. You are you and you've spent a lot of years being you.'

'So, how long do you plan to stay down here on holiday, then, Sabrina? Surely you're missing London. You can't have bought any news clothes for at least a month either.'

Sabrina rolled her eyes. 'It's Cornwall, not the bloody moon. They do have shops and online shopping here, too, you know.' Sabrina extricated herself from his arms, went to the sink and got herself a glass of water.

'Why did you come here, Dom?'

'You know why. I just told you. To ask you to come home. Well, I need to get Françoise out first, which as soon as you say you are coming back to me, I will, I promise.'

'Keep all your options open, Dom. You wouldn't want to be alone now, would you.'

'Stop, Sabrina, just stop.' He walked towards her and grabbed her to him again. The touch and smell of familiarity caused her to gasp, and the tears to continue. Dominic turned his face to kiss her, but she moved away, forcing him to nuzzle into her neck, which caused her to make a little groaning noise.

'See, you love that, don't you?' Dom said breathily.

'I do,' she said, her own breath now coming in pants.

'I want you so much, Sabrina.' She could feel him hardening against her. The pull of lust became unbearable. Until –

'No!' She pushed him away. 'No, Dom. No.' She ran to the bathroom, locked the door and sat on the toilet.

After ten minutes she came out to Dom looking through emails on his phone. He put the handset down on the table. 'You felt it, too. I know you did.'

'I've never stopped loving you, Dominic Best, and with that comes all the trimmings that love brings. But what I have stopped doing is respecting you, and now it's time to start respecting myself.'

'Oh, darling, listen to me.' Dom stood up. 'Give me one more chance. I will show you how I can change. I will make sure that Françoise is out of the flat. Maybe you just need some time to think. I will give you as long as you need, but I can't lose you. You are too special a person.'

'I don't know. I feel so confused.' Sabrina put her

hand to her forehead and in sudden recollection, shouted out. 'Fuck! Yes! You touched my friend up for god's sake, too.'

'What are you on about?'

'Dee told me.'

'Oh, that. Dee was drunk. I know she doesn't like me, so anything to cause trouble. It was a mere friendly tap on her bottom.'

'Alcohol can't be used as an excuse for everything you do wrong,' Sabrina shouted then began pacing around the kitchen. 'What am I thinking? Would I ever be able to trust you again? I don't know…'

'It's down to me, I know. And if I fuck up one more time, then you can go – but I promise you, the thought of life without you has shaken me up enough to turn me into the man you do respect again, and who you truly deserve.'

'Are you still sleeping with her?'

'No, I'm not. She's in the spare room – has been since she came over. How many times do I have to say it, but I love you. I want you.' He tapped his head. 'I know! November the fifth, Fireworks night and your birthday! *And* the date we met!'

'You remembered an anniversary, well done you.' But Sabrina took the crumbs gratefully.

'How could I not. Bloody hell, we banged all night in the Hyde Park Hotel.'

'So, what about it?' Sabrina felt so confused. How could a heart still possibly be drawn to a man who had wronged her so badly? What exactly was this thing called love? For it certainly didn't make any kind of sense. Even her usually strong mind was doing its darned best to shake the remnants of any feelings out of her and was failing miserably.

'Yes! Your birthday. Let's set that as a date. Françoise will be out by then, I mean it. We can go on holiday. Somewhere like St Lucia, you love it there. We can start again. And when you're ready, we can get married, and I'll help you set up the acting school that you so wanted. So, yes, let's do it, let's give it a go from then!'

'And they all lived happily ever after.' Sabrina shook her head.

'Don't shake your head at me.' He gave her a sexy smile, and her breath hitched. 'That gives us both time. Me to sort out this bloody stupid situationship that I've got myself into, and you to hopefully start realising exactly what you are missing.'

'I can't just drop everything at a whim. I'm working down here now.'

'Doing what?'

'Running a market stall.'

Dom looked horrified. 'Why?'

'Because I want to.' Sabrina shut her eyes for a second. Could she really imagine life without this man in it? Hadn't she been doing just that for weeks now? But now he was offering himself and their life back to her, did she really want to say no?

'You don't have to do anything, just think about us and the amazing future I can give you.'

Suddenly the good times she had had with this man were running through her mind. 'OK.'

Dom gasped. 'OK, you'll think about it?' His face lit up like a full moon.

Sabrina nodded. 'Let's see how I feel leading up to November the fifth. But I'm not making any promises, and don't book any holidays because I need this time. You've hurt me so much.'

'I know, but never again.'

'And Dom?'

'Yes, my love.'

'You know you said you'd do anything for me.'

'Anything.' He nodded his head wildly.

'Well, I really do need help with something – and with your connections, I think you could be just the man...'

Sabrina was hoping that Conor would either be out or in his bedroom when she got back. In fact, he was lying with his legs draped over the sofa, beer in hand with the credits of the film, Notting Hill running. 'She was just a girl standing in front of a boy asking him to love her.' He grinned. 'How is my favourite actress?'

'She is just a girl, standing in front of a boy, asking him to shove up and share his beer with her.'

He moved his legs and patted her on the thigh as she sat down.

'Good day?'

'Shit day.'

'Do you want to talk about it?'

'Not really. Dom is staying at Kevrinek Cottage.'

'Oh.' Conor's face fell to the ground floor. 'What does he want?'

'It's complicated.' Sabrina took a big swig from the can of beer.

'When is it not, when the heart's involved?' Conor kissed her on the cheek and handed her the remote. 'I'm going to bed.'

'Oh.' She felt a thud of disappointment. 'I've just got back.'

'We'll chat tomorrow, eh?' He stood up.

'Don't be like that, Conor, please.'

'Like what?' His voice was flat. 'I'm just tired and,

being honest, I don't like the thought of you wasting your time with that eejit.'

His bedroom door slammed shut.

Sabrina turned the television off and listened to the silence. Isaac's quotation of Rumi had been right, for the quieter her life had become, the more she was beginning to hear. The thought of hurting honest and reliable Conor was too much to bear, but was the thought of not following her heart an even greater burden? This was what she had meant about ruining friendships. As soon as intimacy got involved, it was a whole different ball game – literally! She got up to go and knock on his bedroom door to try and ease the tension, but swiftly sat down again. For there was nothing she could say to make the situation any better. Because at this precise moment in time, she was completely unsure if she wanted to be back listening to the chimes of Big Ben in fancy London, or be in Number One Ferry View Apartments, Hartmouth taking in the simple, methodical ticking of the kitchen clock above the fridge.

Chapter Thirty-Two

Friday's market day arrived with a huge rainstorm. Sabrina pulled back the curtain then let it go and snuggled back under her duvet.

Conor lightly tapped on the door. 'Tea for madame.'

'Aw, you angel.' A smiling Sabrina sat up, relieved that their familiar dynamic seemed to have returned to normal. Nothing had been said after their words about Dominic and unless he brought anything up about him, Sabrina had decided that she would just remain silent about the whole situation.

'It's raining cats and dogs out there today.' Conor put the steaming mug of tea on her bedside table.

'I've seen. You'll be being sick over the side of the *Happy Hart.*'

'Thanks for that! Actually, since Star gave me a tiny sapphire to rub and I started chewing the joy that is raw ginger, I've actually been pretty good.'

Sabrina propped up pillows on both sides of the bed. 'Come and chat with me.'

Conor lay on top of the bed and checked his watch. 'I've got ten minutes.'

'Is that what you say to all the girls?'

'If they're lucky.'

They both laughed.

'If you don't mind me asking, what happened with

Star? She seems so lovely; I can't imagine her hurting you.'

'She didn't. Well, OK maybe a bit.' He sighed. 'In short, she had a brief fling with Jack, her now husband. He stayed here in this very room. Anyway, he went off and did his thing with his girlfriend in New York and then me and Star met, and she found out she was pregnant.'

'Woah! That's big.'

'I know, tell me about it. I didn't love the girl – we'd only known each minutes – but I proposed as I wanted to do right by her.' Sabrina put her hand to her heart, for here lay another significant difference between Conor Brady and Dominic Best. Conor smiled. 'But it turned out the bairn was Jack's after all, so he came to find her, and the rest is history. It was all very romantic on her side.'

'That must have been so hard for you.'

'I wasn't ready for another child, so it was a bit of a relief, to be honest. Niall is enough for me.'

'But your relationship ended.'

'Yes, but she loved someone else, and love always wins.'

Sabrina took a gulp of tea and sighed.

'You're so matter of fact.'

'I like to call that being romantic, myself.' Conor yawned. 'Do you want children?'

Sabrina checked her watch and laughed. 'Ah, you've got ten minutes before work then.'

Conor grinned. 'You can mock but it would be the best ten minutes you've ever had, I'm telling ya now.'

They both laughed until Conor's voice was serious.

'Joking aside, *do* you want kids?'

'No. I think seeing the mental suffering of my mother and the complex relationship I had with her has put me right off.'

'That's sad.' Conor's bottom lip poked out.

'It's reality, plus I'm a bit selfish. I like my own space. I'd resigned myself to having no kids with Dom and I was happy with my decision. Anyway, back to you, please. Did you leave Hartmouth because of what happened with Star?'

'No, I think I told you that the main reason was because Maeve wanted Niall closer when he visited me. But it did help me getting over Star by being completely away from her.'

'And how about you. Are you done with having any more kids?'

'I never say never about anything.' Conor took a deep breath. 'I take it your ex is wanting you back?'

Oh, God, Sabrina thought, feeling that she wasn't ready for this conversation right now, this early. She nodded.

'Are you thinking about it?' Conor's voice wobbled very slightly. Sabrina remained silent. 'I mean, don't worry.' Conor did a fake punch to his forehead. 'I'm used to playing second fiddle down here, clearly.' He managed a smile.

Sabrina pulled herself together. 'I'm surprised anyone wants me. I mean, look at me this morning. Hair like a cock's comb.' She put her tongue to the side of her lip. 'And yum, appears to be a bit of dried dribble this side.'

'Just how I like my women. Hair all over the place and a mouth full of dribble. Delicious.'

Sabrina shook her head in mock horror. ''Ew! I can't believe you said that!'

Conor grabbed her knee over the covers causing her to squeal and nearly throw her tea over them both.

'It looks like we both turn into jokers when we don't know how to deal with something, doesn't it?' Conor got up, went to the door and turned back. 'Just give me some warning if you are going to leave, eh, Dickens.' He paused. 'I'll need to get someone else in to pay the rent.'

With Conor's comments reverberating around her ears. Sabrina put her mug on the bedside table, sat up and pulled her duvet back up to her chin. The wind was howling around the apartment block now, causing torrents of rain to smash against the windows and balcony door.

She let out a massive sigh and tried to place herself back in London, mentally. In Dom's luxury flat with all the mod cons. With it's Raindance shower, where the water was supposed to mimic an outdoor spring and the huge bathtub with lights inside that doubled as a jacuzzi. The all singing all dancing coffee machine. The cinema room that Dom had created in one of the bedrooms. She looked around her basic room and despite the turmoil within her, felt suddenly peaceful. For it didn't matter how comfy the bed was or how plush the curtains. How big the diamond or how credible the designer, what mattered were the people in her life and since being down here, she had met people who shone brighter than anyone she had ever met before and had clothed her in both love and honesty.

So, why couldn't she just tell Dom it was over? What was she hanging on to? Love had so much to answer for. Because she was trying so hard to fathom that if you did really love someone, could you not like them at the same time?

She took a deep breath and went to her Instagram account for the first time since coming down here. Underneath her last post, where she had stated that she was taking time away for personal reasons were a variety of comments, seventy per cent were lovely supportive messages but around thirty per cent were vile. She began to read though them. *Who the fuck does she think she is? So rich, so beautiful and she has to run away/You poor deluded woman/Grow some balls, you thick bitch. You can't even act anyway/ If I looked like a stick insect, I'd fuck off too/Call yourself an actress, it's no shock you never made it to Hollywood/ No wonder he left you, you ugly whore.*

Without a second thought, Sabrina deleted her profile. Had these keyboard warriors won by her doing this? No, she decided – and even if they felt they had, give them that little victory, for she didn't care. They were the sad ones. In fact, she wondered what on earth had happened in their lives to have made them become so bitter and twisted. They clearly needed mental help. And for her to keep hold of her own sanity, she didn't need affirmations. She needed to hold tight to herself and make space and time for some of the biggest decisions of her life.

Pulling on a t-shirt, she went through to the lounge and flung the outside doors open wide. Then, standing if she was the glorious Kate Winslet at the end of the Titanic, with arms outstretched and the wind and rain whipping around her whole body, she shouted at the top of her voice, 'I'm flying.'

She checked her phone when she got back inside. *What the feck are you doing up there?* Conor messaged with a googly eyed emoji.

I was flying, she replied with a grinning face.

Flying? Well, you better get yourself dressed, as Lowen Kellow could be dying!

Sabrina immediately called Conor. 'What the fuck?'

Conor was shouting against the weather. 'When you said you were going to sort it out, I didn't expect you to fecking try and kill him!'

'What are you on about?' Sabrina shouted back.

'He's in Penrigan General – been poisoned, according to Mrs Harris, anyways.'

Chapter Thirty-Three

Sabrina quickly got dressed and walked up to the market.

Knowing exactly where she would find out all she needed to know, she pushed the door open to Monique's to see an effusive Linda Harris holding court to Ben the butcher, Nigel the fishmonger and Kara, who was getting her daily pastries.

'I take it you've heard the news, too Jilly?'

'What news?'

'Well, Gideon's new girlfriend, she's a nurse and, well, yes, Gideon popped in earlier to tell me. I'm not supposed to say anything, of course, so please don't gossip, but yes, Lowen Kellow has been poisoned, evidently. Weedkiller, of all things! He was rushed to Penrigan General yesterday with terrible stomach pains and nausea. His breathing was affected too. His girlfriend, who runs a hairdressers in Penrigan, was distraught. Screaming the place down, she was. Josie, that's Gideon's new squeeze, said anyone would think he was going to die the way she was carrying on.'

'Shit. That sounds serious.' Sabrina felt slightly faint. Yes, he was a cheating bastard, but she wouldn't wish something as terrible as this on anyone.

'Is he going to be alright?' Kara's brow was wrinkled with concern.

'Yes, it was only a small amount, I think. and I'm

sure we'd have heard if he'd croaked it.'

'He's a tricky fish, that one.' Nigel chipped in. 'But who on earth would want to do that to him?'

'Jilly, you've gone a bit pale. Wasn't you, was it?' Linda Harris laughed and then started shuffling around behind the counter. 'You never know what goes on behind the scenes, do you? Now, what can I get you all?'

With coffee in hand, Sabrina had just started walking down to Tinsel Town when she noticed Conor calling.

'Monique has just called to say it looks like the old bill have just pulled up outside your shop. If they're coming to you, say nothing. No comment all the way.'

Sabrina felt her heart skip. 'Conor, you're scaring me now.'

'Say nothing, you hear me.'

She pulled her shoulders back and approached the waiting policemen with a smile.

'Jillian Swift?'

Shit, they had already done their homework, Sabrina though. 'Yes, that's me.'

'It's PC Dobbins and PC Greenway from Penrigan Police Station. We'd like a quick chat with you, if that's OK.'

'So, what would you say is your relationship with Lowen Kellow?' Both police officers stood in front of shop the counter whilst Sabrina sat awkwardly on the high stool opposite them.

'Umm. Relationship? Umm. Well, he's the market

inspector. So, what kind of relationship and I supposed to have with him? I don't know.'

'You seem edgy.' The younger of the two police officers with a neat beard announced.

'I *am* edgy, because I have two policemen in my shop.' Sabrina shifted her bum on the uncomfortable seat. It made her feel like she was back on set as Polly Malone. Who would have most definitely not seemed edgy at all. Conor's words of no comment flashed through her mind but knowing the system so well after playing Polly for so long, that 'no comment' would make her sound guilty – which she clearly wasn't. However, what she was guilty of was shagging another woman's man and pretending to be someone else and disturbingly they already had proof of the latter.

A thought occurred to her, and Sabrina's mouth fell open. Dom knew people who knew people, but she hadn't expected him to go this extreme. Maybe the darkness within the man she had been going to marry really did hold no bounds.

'Has something happened to Lowen? Is that why you are here?' Sabrina managed to keep her voice level.

'Would you care if it had?'

'What kind of question is that?' Sabrina stood up.

'Lowen Kellow has been poisoned and we need to find out who has done it.' The older police officer directly stared at her as he delivered this line.

Sabrina pulled what she hoped was a convincing face of surprise. 'Oh my God! That's terrible. Poisoned? Is he OK?'

'As OK as a man who has been given traces of poison can be, I guess.'

'You look shocked.' The bearded police officer stood up. She sat down. Her hand was trembling.

'I am shocked. How awful, poor Lowen.' She suddenly was grateful for every single acting lesson she had

had. Because if Dominic was to blame for this, then she surely would take the rap too. Terrified of what she was going to ask, yet feeling that she had to, she said slowly and deliberately, 'So why have you come to me?'

'Because Lowen's partner said that as he was slipping in and out of consciousness he was saying your name. In fact, he was repeating over and over that this was down to you.'

'As in the name, Jilly?'

'Yes – unless you have any other names he liked to call you by?'

'I'm not sure I like what you are insinuating here?'

And then as if real life had morphed right into her old working life, Sabrina Swift heard the words that she was so used to hearing as her alter ego, good old Polly Malone.

'Jillian Swift, I am arresting you relating to Section 23 Offences Against the Person Act 1861 on suspicion of maliciously administering poison to endanger life or inflict grievous bodily harm. You do not have to say anything. But it may harm your defence if you do not mention when questioned something which you later rely on in court. Anything you do say may be given in evidence.'

Sabrina sat next to Big Frank's Penrigan lawyer in the austere interview room of Hartmouth police station opposite the two policemen who had arrested her. Her palms were sweating. She shifted nervously in her seat.

The bearded cop raised his eyebrow to his counterpart. 'So, would I be right in thinking that you've spent a fair bit of time with Mr Kellow recently?'

She glanced at the lawyer and despite Conor's insistence that she say nothing, he nodded for her to reply.

'I… err… Recently took on a unit at the market, yes.'

'And did you realise he had a girlfriend?'

'It never came up. It didn't need to.'

'Right,' the bearded man held in his innuendo and smiled.

'So, am I also right in thinking you could have shared a drink with Mr Kellow at some stage?'

'Yes, I'm sure we probably did, at some stage – but I didn't put bloody weedkiller in, if that is what you are suggesting.'

'Probably? You either did or you didn't,' the bearded one stated.

Sabrina's back had now started sweating, too.

'And how did you know it was weedkiller?' The older police officer stood up and started pacing the room.

Shit! she thought. The lawyer coughed nervously. 'Because, well, I suppose I did get wind of this earlier, and umm, and you'd started talking already and…'

The bearded policemen, suddenly grinned. 'Do you think maybe Polly Malone has taught you all you needed to know on the subject of killing a man?'

The lawyer bashed his hand down on the table far too aggressively. 'Polly Malone is a fictional character and has nothing to do with these ridiculous accusations against my client.'

With the stark realisation that her cover was well and truly blown, Sabrina's voice was hoarse. 'Killing, you say? Is Lowen going to d…die?'

'I bloody love you in that show.' The bearded one suddenly blurted, much to the anger of his colleague, who scowled at him.

'Dobbins! Get out. NOW!'

As the red-faced rookie officer headed out, another officer appeared. She whispered in the remaining policemen's ear. He grunted and nodded, until his face looked as if it might burst with anger. Sabrina glanced at the lawyer again, who shot her a worried look.

The officer then turned to them and huffed loudly. 'You're free to go. No further questions required.'

'I'm sorry?' The lawyer looked as confused as Sabrina.

'Exactly what I said. Jillian is free to go. I am very sorry to have wasted both of your time.'

Chapter Thirty-Four

Sabrina breathed a huge sigh of relief as she turned the key in the door to the apartment. Conor leapt up from the sofa ready to hand her a cold beer. A big pan of bolognaise was simmering on the hob. Pre-cooked spaghetti sat in a bowl ready to be reheated.

'Hungry?'

'Starving.'

She flopped on the sofa and drank nearly a third of the bottle of lager down in one.

'Well, that's a first, being arrested for real.'

'I've been so worried about you.'

'It's fine. It was my own stupid fault.' Sabrina laughed. 'I didn't let on initially that anyone had told me already about Lowen and then I said something like, why do you think I'd try and harm him with weedkiller anyway and they hadn't even mentioned what he's been poisoned with.'

Conor laughed too. 'Oh my god, OK, that is quite funny. But don't even think of being in my gang.'

'I am never so much as stealing a carrier bag from Tesco ever again – I was terrified.' Sabrina took a glug of beer.

'I guess with them being coppers who don't get much action, you were assumed guilty before even looking at the facts. It's probably the most exciting thing that's happened down here in a while.'

'Exactly. To be fair, Lowen was evidently accusing me directly, too. That's what his girlfriend said anyway.'

'What the?'

'He's angry with me, or maybe he did think it was me, or maybe if he frames me then the heat is off him re the market for a bit, who knows.'

'Thank you so much for sorting that lawyer, though. He was shit hot.'

'Frank knows some good ones, I tell you.'

'Luckily for me he does, because Dom, who has lawyers who look after lawyers, was on a plane to the South of France when I initially called for his help.' Sabrina took another drink. 'I do have something to tell you, though.'

'Go on.' Conor was now tucking into his tasty feast.

'I did tell Dom about the development plans to see if he could do anything. He's far more of a negotiator than a murderer so I can't believe he agreed to something like this, to be honest. It's crazy.'

'It is, but a trace of poison doesn't shock a Brady. We tend to shut people up before the arrow is drawn. But you're right. It was a bold move if your ex were involved.'

Suddenly realising that she was mad to think that Dom would ever consider anything that risky, Sabrina experienced a surge of adrenaline.

'Conor, do you know who did it?' The Irishman looked away. 'Conor?' He took a slug of lager. Sabrina started twirling spaghetti around her fork.

Conor looked away. 'You asked me not to get involved with anything until you had had a chance to sort things your way.'

'OK.' Sabrina blew out a big breath. 'Well, whatever happened after my lawyer arrived, I was suddenly off the hook. I was in the interview room, someone knocked on the door whispered in one of the copper's ears. Next thing, I'm free to go, with them being nothing but apologetic for wasting my time and clearly stating that there would be no further questioning.'

'Really?'

'Yes. Please tell me if you know something.'

Conor put his hands in the hair. 'I don't... This had nothing to do with the Brady's, I mean it.'

'OK, OK. The worst thing is, I expect everyone at Hartmouth police station now know that I am Polly Malone. One of the cops was so starstruck, I thought he was going to kiss me when I left. It was so embarrassing. I can't imagine that they will all keep it quiet either. So, not only will I be the talk of the town re being accused of trying to kill Lowen Kellow, but my cover is getting nearer to being blown every day.'

Sabrina finished her plate, drained her beer bottle, then let out a massive burp. 'Oops, pardon! Compliments to the chef with that one.'

'If your trolls could see you now.'

'My trolls can fuck off and go choke on their mindless drivel.'

'Dickens! Go wash your potty mouth out!'

They both laughed.

'Please ask Frank how much I owe him for the lawyer.'

'It's alright, don't worry about that now. Another beer?'

Sabrina nodded. They sat on the sofa, both with their feet on the wooden coffee table. Charlie's prediction of the weather improving had been totally wrong for the rain was still lashing against the balcony doors.

'What was that all about this morning, you half-dressed jumping up and down on the balcony.'

'I was pretending to be Kate Winslet in Titanic.'

'Just a normal Friday morning, then.'

Sabrina grimaced. 'Shit, I forgot it's Friday, I missed a whole market day. Those pesky police officers should reimburse me.'

Conor put his arm on her leg. 'You'll be so much busier nearer Christmas, I expect, so I shouldn't worry. That's if you're still here, that is.'

Sabrina turned to face him. She bit her lip as she took in his handsome rugged features. 'You are certainly making it harder for me to leave.' Her throat tightened. Here again, this man had proved with his actions that he cared. He'd helped her through this terrible day, warning her the police were waiting, sorting lawyers via his uncle, cooked her dinner for her return. He was one big action of love. A strong man with values and morals. And the fact he was a bit edgy with his Brady moniker made him all the more sexy. So why couldn't she just succumb and be with him?

'Anyway, thank you so much for dinner – and for giving a shit.' Sabrina smiled.

'The girl doth get serious on me.'

Sabrina smirked. 'Not for long.' Conor shook his head as she went into dramatic mode. 'I want to forget all about today. We now need to talk more about me, in fact *all* about me, and why I so wanted to be cast as Rose in Titanic, even though I would have been far too young, of course.'

'Of course.' Conor grinned.

'So, this morning, I deleted my Instagram, which may not seem anything to a man who doesn't have any form of social media, but for me it was massive. And I was celebrating.'

They clinked bottles. 'Well done, Jillian Swift on the freeing of shackles both in the real and virtual sense.'

There was a sudden flash of lightning followed by a

huge clap of thunder that felt like it was shaking the whole of the apartment block. A couple of beers ahead of Sabrina, Conor got up and swung the balcony doors open. 'Come on Rose, I'll be your Jack as long as you promise to budge up on the makeshift raft, if ever our ship sinks, that is.'

Sabrina gave a disbelieving laugh. 'No, it's too nasty out there.'

'Come on. You know you want to.' He grabbed her by the hand.

'Conor! It's freezing!'

Conor Brady held a laughing Sabrina Swift tightly around the waist in the pouring rain, her arms out-stretched facing the ocean.

'You make me feel like I'm home,' The Irishman shouted to the sky.

'I can't hear you,' Sabrina shouted back.

Conor Brady threw his head back to the elements and squeezed her even tighter.

Chapter Thirty-Five

A bleary-eyed Sabrina pushed opened the door to Monique's to be greeted by a frenzied Linda Harris.

'So, tell me all about it – were they mean to you? I take it you didn't do it, or they would have surely locked you up overnight.' Sabrina imagined the woman stalking her outside the flat to see exactly when she returned.

'Linda, if you think I'm capable of poisoning someone, then you're not as good a detective as you think you are.'

'Well, who did it, then?'

'I don't know.' Sabrina sighed heavily. 'Look, I'm tired, can you just sort me a cappuccino, please? I'm sure you will be the first to find out who did it, then you can tell *me* all about it.'

'Rumour has it, you had a bit of thing with him. Lowen Kellow, I mean.'

Sabrina felt her face drop. She really wasn't in the mood for fuelling the woman's fire, and actually was past caring what anyone thought now.

'Yes, Linda. I did and he has huge feet, but a tiny little dick.'

Linda squirted the milk steamer in her face by mistake and screamed.

Kara was setting up her flower stall outside when

Sabrina marched down the hill. 'You OK, Jilly?'

Sabrina's face softened. She stopped in her tracks and went over to Passion Flowers. 'If there was an international award for gossiping, Linda Harris would win every year, hands down.'

'You're right there.' Kara's laughing caused her huge bump to jump up and down. 'Ouch.'

'You OK?' Sabrina put her hand on Kara's arm.

'Yes, just a slight twinge. I literally feel like I've got a sack of potatoes up my dress today and the terrible twosome were awake again from five this morning.'

'Oh, bless you. When are you on maternity leave from?'

'Until they pop out amidst a bed of magnolias and roses in the arrangement room out back. I expect. We are so busy.'

'Take care of yourself, won't you.'

'It's fine, honestly. I know my limits and I'm pregnant, not ill.'

Sabrina immediately thought about Dom and what he had said about not wanting the French stick to have to work. He still hadn't phoned her, despite her message about being in a police cell. And she'd heard nothing about any arrangements for the fifth of November. Granted, she had said that she would think about it, but she had expected some kind of communication, at least.

'So, have you heard anything about Lowen Kellow, Kara? I mean who would do such a thing? It's quite worrying, isn't it?'

The mum-to-be put her hand to her stomach. 'Ooh, that was a big kick. Sorry Jilly, I need a wee and the pelvic floor ain't quite what it used to be.' With that, she went charging back into the shop.

'Alright, Charlie?' Sabrina gave the tough looking bald man a wave. He didn't seem in as good spirits as usual. He gave her a tentative thumbs up. Undeterred, she went over to him. 'No free apples today then?'

'Nah, not today. Don't want people accusing my old hag of giving out poisoned ones, now, do we.' He winked.

'You're so rude about your dear wife. Where is Pat, anyway?'

'She's a bit under the weather, says it's the menopause.'

'Oh, dear.'

'Yes, she's not sleeping well. She'll be along later. I think they called it 'menopause' because it really does put a pause on us men. I've never known a woman have so many headaches.'

'In a world where you can be anything, be kind, Mr Dillon.' Sabrina assumed a self-righteous air and grinned at him.

'My Pat. I love her to the moon and back, she knows that. Anyway, hope it weren't too stressful for you yesterday.'

'I was innocent, so it was an experience. But I was a bit scared, to be honest.'

'He had it coming, that bastard. Ah, here's trouble.' He kissed his wife lovingly on the cheek. 'Right, have a good day, Jilly. My Billy informs me the first ferry is packed, so looks like it's going to be a busy one.'

Sabrina had decided that as Tinsel Town was to be in effect a general gift shop, she would sell items that would be a fit for holidays other than Christmas. Seeing as Halloween was the one that was approaching, she had great delight in decorating her outside stall with witches' hats, dreamcatchers and beanies for kids and adults alike with various spooky motifs on them. Charlie had been right: it was an extremely busy market day, probably because of half term, with lots of people taking a break in one of the various holiday lets and others making use of their second homes.

She was just making herself a cup of coffee out the back when Dom called. Before the wedding when his name had flashed up on the screen, she would feel her heart leap a little; today, she felt her shoulders drop slightly. Composing herself for a second, she pressed to answer. She could hear all sorts of noise going on in the background. 'Darling, it's me. I'm sorry I wasn't around yesterday; you know what these work things are like.'

Sabrina sighed. 'I really needed you, Dom.'

'I know, I know. But as your message said, it all turned out OK. But, Sabrina, all this really isn't good for you or your reputation. And I take it you told the police who you really are?'

'They had found out already.'

'And you really trust they are not going to blow your cover?'

'No, I don't – but until they do, I'm carrying on being me down here.'

'The press will explode on that when they find out, you know that. Polly Malone being accused of poisoning someone when she's inside for being accused of murder in your acting life.'

Sabrina could hear Dom whispering to someone. 'Who's that?'

'Oh, it's just Jessica, telling me I need to go back inside. Look, you need to keep your head down if you don't want to be found out. It's an amazing story and if I didn't care about you like I do, I'd run with that for at

least a week. If a rival redtop gets hold of it, I'll be
furious. Come back to London, Sabrina. I can protect
you here.'

'Is the flat free, then?'

'You know it's not yet, but as I said, it will be soon.
But if you do want to come back next week, I can put
you up in a hotel.'

'Did you really just say that?' Sabrina's voice raised
a level. 'Dominic, you said that if I agreed to come back
then she'd be out! I am not going to stay in a hotel.
That was my home too, you know.'

'OK, OK, sorry darling, my mind's not with it out
here, so much to do.'

'Sabrina sighed. 'Well, get with it, Dom, because
you promised me. Anyway, when are you back from
Cannes?'

'A week Friday.'

'So, it's a week-long work do?'

'Well, it is a bit of social as well.'

'Of course, it is.'

'Anyway, gotta go. Counting down the days, my
sweet. Can't wait. Me, you, alone at last. I'm planning
something super special. Make sure your passport is up
to date. Oh, and that wedding underwear I missed –
make sure you pack that, too. Ciao darling.'

Sabrina's – 'but I haven't said I'm definitely coming
back', was lost as he hung up.

She went out to the front to be greeted by a couple
of excited kids trying on the witches' hats and Conor
holding out a bacon bap from Frank's. 'Thought you
might need this.'

She grinned. 'What would I do without you.'

'I've got to get back, but whilst I remember, Frank
is doing a Halloween gig – he does it every year. Has a
candy floss maker, so the kids dress up and line up and
the grown-ups get his secret elixir from under the

counter at a discounted rate.'

'He's a good egg, your uncle. One each?' She smiled at the kids as they handed over their pocket money for the hats, then mouthed thank you to their mother.

'Just wondered if you fancied helping out, with me?'

'Sure, sounds fun.'

'Are you OK, Sabrina? After yesterday, I mean.' Conor put his hand on her arm. 'It sure was a tough day, for ya.'

'Yeah, totally fine, but thanks for asking.' She held his gaze for a split second.

'Grand. I'll see you tonight, shall I?'

'Unless Tom Hardy confirms our date, I guess so.'

'Pah. Tom who? This handsome Irishman will read ya a bedtime story, so he will.'

Sabrina laughed. Conor must have overhead Dee and her laughing about all the mums swooning over the handsome actor reading stories to the kids on a TV show.

Six o'clock came, and Sabrina sighed with relief as she locked the door to the unit behind her. She and Conor had sat up chatting until gone one a.m. the night before, and although she had only drunk four beers, a long day on her feet had rendered her completely knackered. As she walked down the hill to home, her thoughts turned to Lowen. She had been so wrapped up in saving herself, she hadn't really thought about how he was doing. And as much as she didn't want him in her life, she was human and wouldn't wish harm on him – to that extent, anyway.

She was just about to put her key in the bottom door of Ferry View Apartments when Conor's name flashed up on her phone, and she opened the message. 'You didn't mention you had someone coming over to do your nails? I've popped to Frank's for a drink with him. I've left her having a cup of tea on the balcony. See you in a bit.'

Sabrina froze. Who the fuck had he let in? It was so unlike Conor not to be more streetwise. Carefully, she walked around to the front of the block of flats to see if she could see who exactly was on the balcony. The door was shut. She then ran to Frank's and could see the uncle and his nephew having a beer together and laughing. She knocked on the door, but the music was up loud, and they were facing away from her. She texted Conor, but again, he was oblivious. There was only one thing for it: she would have to go in and see who on earth was sitting in their flat. Maybe it was an undercover cop – or worse still, a journalist.

The imposing figure of a woman scorned stood tall as Sabrina tentatively pushed open the door. Her heart began to beat at one hundred miles an hour.

'What are *you* doing in my flat?'

'More like what were you doing shagging my boy-friend, you dirty whore?'

'Can you please get out now?' Sabrina's voice remained level. She went to message Conor, but Giselle smashed her phone to the floor.

As Sabrina reached down to retrieve it, Giselle put her foot on her hand. Sabrina wrestled it free, cursing. 'Ow. Who the fuck do you think you are? Now get out or I'll call the police.'

Kicking Sabrina's phone to the side of the room, Giselle laughed out loud. 'I don't really think you want the police involved do you, Polly Malone? I know it's true.'

Sabrina remained silent.

'The pair of you were a little stupid really. Or my dick of a partner was. Saying that, if you hadn't come into the salon – and why in god's name you did that beggars belief – I never would have known who you were or anything about it.'

'I don't know what you're on about.'

'Oh, come now, Sabrina, with that stunning and distinctive tattoo on your shoulder.'

Sabrina cringed inwardly. It had taken her a long time to pluck up the courage to get that tattoo and it outing her for having an affair, definitely had not been cited as one of the cons.

'OK, so you know who I am, big deal but that doesn't mean I've been sleeping with your partner.'

Sabrina suddenly felt fearful. Giselle seemed more of a pistols-at-dawn kind of woman than one who would just bash her with her handbag.

'No, but the very distinguishable and expensive perfume that you wear, plus stray blonde hairs I found on his suit jacket are a very good indicator, don't you think?'

In the vague hope of not having a huge press story escaping via this woman, who was clearly on the edge, Sabrina realised that there was only way she could go with this.

'I'm so sorry.' Sabrina's tone was low and sincere. Giselle, clearly not expecting this response, looked taken aback. 'Let's sit down, shall we and talk about this like adults.' Sabrina rubbed her sore hand as she sat on the sofa.

Like a moody teenager, Giselle plonked herself down on a dining room chair. 'I knew it! I saw the signs. He's such a sleaze ball.' Tears starting to form in the tall woman's eyes.

'I honestly didn't know he had a partner or there is no way I would have let anything happen.' Sabrina tried to keep her voice level. 'There is nothing going on, now. It was sex, meaningless sex. And I know that doesn't help, but I'd rather you knew that.'

'How many times?' Giselle snarled. Sabrina shuffled

in her seat as the angry woman repeated herself. 'I said, how many times?'

'Three,' Sabrina whispered.

'Where did you do it?'

'Look, does any of this really matter now.' Sabrina took a huge breath in.

'Where did you do it!' Giselle screeched.

'A holiday cottage I was staying at, my shop and here,' Sabrina blurted at one hundred miles an hour.

'Meaningless, you say?'

'Yes. If you know so much about me, you will clearly have read that I was jilted at the altar. Lowen happened to be in the wrong place at the right time for some payback sex for me. I am truly sorry, and I know it doesn't make it right, but I honestly knew nothing about you. And I certainly don't care if I never see him again.'

There was a long, tense silence. Sabrina held her breath.

'I can't believe Polly Malone has shagged my boyfriend.' Giselle suddenly laughed manically. 'I fucking love you. You're my favourite character.'

Sabrina shut her eyes for a second. Being down here, she had gradually begun to realise that she liked being just herself. And in this moment, the reality of people believing she was someone else and loving that fake character had suddenly lost every single ounce of its appeal.

'And that's just it: I play a character. Polly Malone isn't me. I'm human, I clearly err like most people do but again, I am genuinely sorry for what happened.'

Giselle's face turned again. 'He's such a lying wanker.'

'Yes, he is. What are you going to do?'

'Well, I can't leave him just yet, can I? With him lying in a bloody hospital bed.'

Now that the woman had started to calm down, Sabrina stood up in the hope Giselle would stand up too and leave without her having to ask her to. She did.

'How is he?' Sabrina asked casually.

'On the mend.' Giselle then started to sob.

Sabrina's empathy gene came running to the fore. She put her arm on Giselle's shoulder. 'Well, that's a good thing, isn't it?'

'Yes. It really is. I'm sorry you had to be dragged over the coals, too. Now I know what really happened, you didn't deserve that.'

Sabrina's face then lit up in realisation. 'He didn't say it was me, did he, Giselle?'

Giselle shook her head. 'It was only a little bit of weedkiller. I just wanted to hurt him so badly, like he hurt me. I didn't realise he'd end up in hospital. I'm so sorry, because I wanted to hurt you, too.'

'Have you been to the press with this? Giselle, please be honest with me.'

'No. I sent Helen to look for you the other day, but I think it'll only be a matter of time, now, that someone will find out that the legend that is Polly Malone is running a stall in a market town.'

'Yes, aided by you lying to the police – thanks for that. Do they know it's you who poisoned him?'

'No. Lowen made up some cock and bull story that he'd remembered not being able to get the lid off some weed killer in our shed, so he'd opened it with his mouth. The things people believe.'

'Yes, Giselle. The things people believe.

'Will you grass me up, now?' Giselle looked slightly broken.

Feeling like she was on the set as Polly Malone again, Sabrina smiled. 'I've got enough of my own shit to worry about, Giselle. That's your and Lowen's business, not mine.'

At that moment, Conor bounded through the front door.

'So, what colour did you go for then...Jilly.'

'Poison Apple Red,' Sabrina said abruptly. 'And Giselle is leaving now, aren't you Giselle.'

Sabrina slammed the door shut behind her and grabbed herself a beer from the fridge.

'Call yourself a Brady!'

'What the fuck?' Conor looked perplexed.

'That was Lowen's bloody girlfriend! She grassed me for poisoning him and it was her who did it, all along!'

'Shit, I didn't think for one moment that...'

'What is it with men? Do you ever think?!'

'I also think I'm on borrowed time for a huge scoop in one of the papers. She's not going to keep her gob shut, especially if money is concerned.'

'Come on, calm down. It will be OK – we can deal with it,' Conor soothed.

'And as for keeping a promise to me about not mentioning the market until I tried to sort it, everyone knows don't they! God, Conor! Who can I trust anymore, not one person, it seems.'

'I think you are misdirecting your anger here, calm down. It's going to be OK.'

'What are you, a bloody clairvoyant, now, too?' The pressure of everything that had gone before, caused Sabrina to let out a massive sob. 'Why is everything so hard. Dom hurt me so badly and now he wants me back and I try and sort my life out but basically I'm proof that you can run, but you can't hide. And I shouldn't care if the press start going on about me, but I do. And all I want is for people to stop lying to me. It's such a bloody mess!'

'I haven't lied to you, precious girl. I would never hurt you. I think the world of you, so I do – I told you that already.' Conor went to put his arms around her, and she pushed him away. 'OK, OK, I did mention it to Frank, who told Charlie and luckily nothing happened because Giselle thankfully got to the eejit first.'

'See. I can't even trust *you*!' She let out an odd sounding wail. 'You promised me, Conor.'

'I don't believe I said the word promise.' He grimaced. 'And no harm was done. I couldn't let you deal with all this yourself, it's too big.'

'I said give me a week,' Sabrina growled.

'This is ridiculous.' Conor's face was pained.

'It's ridiculous to you! But I want to trust you Conor, I really do but... I need to sort things out by myself.' She ran to the bedroom and started throwing clothes into a case. 'I need to sort *myself* out. Where the fuck am I going with my life?'

Conor strode in after her. 'What are you doing?'

'I know exactly what I'm doing.' A look of fear spread over Conor's face. 'I'm going back to London.'

He stared at her blankly. 'But what about Frank's Halloween party for the kids?'

'Jesus, I don't give a crap about Frank's fucking party.' Sabrina was struggling to close her case.

'And the Victorian Market? It's so much fun.'

'It'll all be just as hilarious without me, I'm sure,' Sabrina seethed. Conor went to help her. She lifted her arm to push him off.

'And the rent for here?' Conor was grasping at straws now.

'I paid Kara up front, now get out of my way please, I'm going and nothing will stop me.'

'Dominic doesn't love you, Sabrina.'

'I know, but maybe it's easier that way, eh?'

'Why are you being like this?'

Conor held her by the shoulders and started to spell out his words. 'He doesn't love you, and he will never love you or care about you like I do. I know it sounds crazy because I've known you for literally minutes, but I fecking love you. I knew you were the one for me the minute you streaked across this lounge half naked, and I've said it before and will keep on saying it that I don't care who you are or what you do, I just love YOU. That's it. YOU, Jillian Swift, every glorious piece of YOU.' He was shouting now.

Raw with emotion, Sabrina was in floods of tears. 'I want to love you, Conor, and I should love you, but I can't just now.'

Conor punched the sofa hard. He was breathing deeply. She went over to him and lifted his chin.

'I have to do this. Let me do this.' She looked into his eyes and felt a pull as strong as the tide. Her voice lowered. 'There was never any resolution and I need something, anything.' Her voice cracked.

Conor turned away from her. 'And that's life, sometimes. Not everything can be wrapped up perfectly in a tight little ball. Bad things happen to good people, that's a fact.'

'You don't understand.'

'That's the thing: I really do. What was it your mammy said? "Follow your heart and you won't get lost." If you do this, you will lose not only someone who would lay a golden pathway of love and trust below your feet if only you'd let him, but you will lose yourself, too.'

At the mention of her mum, Sabrina let out another almighty sob. Conor moved to her side again. 'You can't drive in this state.'

'Watch me! You can't stop me. And if you do say you love me like you do, then you'd want me to be happy and let me go!'

Conor stood in front of the door.

'Let me go.' Her eyes were wild.

The handsome Irishman silently moved aside to let her go past. Sabrina, slightly wrong-footed by his sudden change of mood, looked back up the stairs to see him still standing in the doorway watching her go. She felt her heart do a little leap.

'I'll be waiting.' He said softly.

Chapter Thirty-Six

'Mummy said that if you cry inside and don't let your feelings out, then you drown inside. Is that right, Auntie Rini?' Sabrina lay on her bed at the Dickinsons' Essex home with her friend's insightful eight-year-old sitting on the unicorn-printed bean bag she had dragged in from her bedroom.

Sabrina propped herself up in bed, her face streaked with tears. 'Well, there's no drowning going on here, I promise you that, Thea.'

'Der, that's what I mean. You've been crying for hours and hours, I heard you. You nearly drowned my Barbie already, look. I put her close to your face to look after you.' With that, she picked up her dolly by its damp hair and headed off downstairs to her dad, who was loudly calling her for breakfast.

Dee walked in with a mug of tea and put it on the mirrored bedside table.

'I've upset Thea, now. Sorry.'

'Don't worry. She'll get over it.' Dee smiled. 'It's quite a drive up here, and most of it was in the dark. You must be so knackered.'

'I'm exhausted. Thanks for letting me stay, matey.'

'You're always welcome, you know that. Do you want some breakfast? Stu is doing his legendary smoked salmon and poached eggs on bagels. I daren't get anywhere near him. He thinks he's bleeding Gordon

Ramsey the minute his Chelsea Football Club apron goes on.'

Sabrina laughed. 'Posh grub on a Sunday, sounds good, but I need to get going and resolve this properly with Dom. He wouldn't have come all the way to Cornwall twice if he didn't care and I think I owe it to him – to us – to see where his heart really does lie.'

Dee nodded, looking sad but determined. 'You have to go your own way with this, Rini. And I may not agree with what you are doing, but I'm here for you, you know that.'

Sabrina rubbed her hands over her face. 'Conor said he loved me. He's known me for five minutes, that's ridiculous.'

'Conor is so lovely, Rini. He's a solid man.'

'I know. I know. But that doesn't discount the fact he did tell half the bloody market about the closure and I asked him not to.

Dee sighed. 'Is that the worst things he's done?'

'Er, yes. But...'

'Let's stop this stupid fault finding when something good is clearly in front of your face, shall we, Rini? He did what he thought was best for you. I mean, could you really have taken it on yourself?'

'I hate you, Delilah Dickinson.'

'Let's not start that again. You know I'm always right.'

The women laughed.

'I don't get why don't you want to be with him, though? He *is* Action Man personified. He hasn't really let you down ever and he has told you to your face that he loves you. He is also bloody hot! Come on Rini, let's stop this fear, shall we?'

'What fear?' Sabrina screwed her face up.

'That this might be the real thing, that this could be what you've been waiting for your whole life. Stop running away from it. He loves you mate, warts and all.'

Sabrina sighed. 'Despite everything, I need to find some kind of closure with Dom. I think I still do love him. Granted, I don't like him very much, but...God, this is doing my head in now.'

'You love the *idea* of you and Dom.' Dee tutted. 'What else has that man got to do for you to realise that he's not right for you.'

Sabrina shot out of bed. 'I need to get going.'

Didn't Dom say in his grandiose way that November the fifth was the day that you would start living happily ever after? You might ruin his grand plan if you arrive early.'

'Yes, because love runs in that programmed way, doesn't it?' Sabrina started throwing clothes out of her large case. And I think it's time I sorted my life out. And... if I go when he's not expecting me, I can see if he's been telling me the truth or not, can't I?'

'And what about your birthday? The girls are set on making you a cake.'

'Aw. I'm sorry, I forgot about my birthday. We shall celebrate it soon, I promise. I will make this up to you and the girls, but I have to do this.'

'Do you think this really is a wise move?' Dee's voice had softened.

'Maybe not. But when did sagacity or sanity ever feature in affairs of the heart?' Sabrina kissed her friend on the forehead and headed to the shower.

Chapter Thirty-Seven

There was something about a busy central London Street at rush hour that couldn't be replicated anywhere else in the world. The red buses, the black cabs, the multi-coloured theatre signs and constant streams of agitated car and van drivers. Rickshaws, the battalions of cyclists and jay walking pedestrians. Beeps, toots, sirens, and the woosh of air brakes all filling the gloaming. A cacophony of city life, of London's rich tapestry of transport and human existence.

It was a freezing evening on November the fourth when Sabrina Swift clicked the door to her Kensington hotel shut and wearing a little black dress, covered by a smart black Dior coat and D&G patent heels, pulled her black Panama hat down over her face and got the concierge to go outside and hail her a taxi.

Wanting to settle herself before she faced Dom, she sat in the window seat of the café, overlooking the grand front door to her old home in Bloomsbury Gardens. With hot chocolate in hand, she began to feel slightly nervous. She was just about to ask for the bill, when a car from Dom's chauffeur company pulled up outside and she could see the driver on his mobile phone. Next the main door opened and in the light of the grand lobby there was the French Stick, made up beautifully, wearing a Chanel coat and Louboutin heels, with her growing bump now showing, perfectly round. And then there was Dom, looking tired in joggers and in his favourite Nike sweatshirt giving her a huge hug and passionate kiss, before waving her off into the London night with an "au revoir" and "see you next Monday, Mon Cherie".

Unexpectedly devoid of all feeling and congratulating herself at her perfect timing, she murmured, 'The cheating bastard.'

Taking a deep breath, she checked her phone to see a text come in from Conor – the first he had sent since she had gone! Her heart jolted. She chose not to read it yet. She couldn't muddy the water, not now – she had to do this first. She'd waited patiently and come this far.

She paid her bill and with her empty suitcase in tow, walked slowly and deliberately towards the flat. Pressing in the external code, she took the lift and when outside the door, took a huge breath before turning the key in the lock.

'Ma Chérie, did you forget something?' Dom shouted.

He was lying on the sofa with a large whisky in hand, and nearly jumped out of his skin when he looked up to see Sabrina standing there, looking the epitome of chic and beauty.

'No, Mon Chéri but you clearly did.'

'Sabrina? It's the fourth today.' He smiled nervously. 'I was planning to meet you tomorrow at the airport – you're early.'

'Oh, silly me, is it?' Sabrina put her handbag down on the edge of the sofa. 'Are you ready for me tonight? I was hoping maybe so. Let me just put my case in the bedroom, shall I?'

Dom jumped up. 'Let me, let me – it's so messy in there. Mrs Batty bloody resigned last week with no notice.'

'Oh, did she? I wonder why.' Sabrina kept her face straight.

But Sabrina wasn't waiting for anybody. She pushed her way in to their old room to find a dressing table full of make-up and expensive French perfumes and rows of shoes. She then went to the bathroom cabinet and threw its glass doors open to find cleansers, toners, moisturisers and a plethora of girly shower products.

'Oh, she – I mean, Françoise – hasn't moved her stuff out yet?'

'Er, not – I'm so sorry, she was erm going to come and do it whilst we were in St Lucia.'

'Oh, I see.' Sabrina's voice remained level. 'You assumed I would just go there on a whim, did you? I'm not your puppet, Dominic.'

'I said I was going to surprise you.'

'And I said don't book anything.' Sabrina went to the bed and pulled back the covers.

'She was going to move her silk nightdress out of the bed too, was she? When exactly were you going to tell me. Dominic?'

'Tell you what?'

'Oh, Dom, don't treat me like a fool. You were in Cannes with her too, weren't you? What was it, a nice little holiday before she was too far gone to fly during her pregnancy? The pregnancy that you are supporting, with the woman who you are not only supporting but are planning to keep on having a relationship with alongside me.'

'You've got it all wrong? Don't be silly, Sabrina.'

Sabrina put on a mocking voice. '"Oh, we're in separate beds, oh Sabrina, we don't sleep together anymore. She is too young, just a pretty face with my baby inside of her". BULLSHIT! ALL... BULLSHIT... DOMINIC!'

'The more I've got to know her, then…'

'Great, then fucking be with HER!'

'But I don't want to lose you. I love you, too, Swifty, I really do.' Dominic's face was a picture of tragic distress.

Sabrina started to laugh.

'So, what were you going to do?'

He looked away from her. 'I sorted her a flat in Islington.'

'And you expected me to live here and then pop and see her when you could? How deluded are you?'

'You brought a case?'

'The case is empty Dominic. I can now finally fill it with my stuff and get out of your life.'

Sabrina threw the case open on the bed and started throwing the few clothes she wanted to take with her into it.

'And what exactly did Little Miss French Stick think you were going to be doing whilst *we* were in the Caribbean?'

'She's just happy to have a flat and be looked after.' Dominic's face looked pained.

'I bet she is.' Sabrina nodded. 'Well, it looks like everyone would have been happy then, doesn't it.' Sabrina's voice cracked. She slammed the case shut. 'Except me!'

Dominic went towards her and held her arms. 'I'm so sorry for being so weak.'

Sabrina pulled away. She looked up to the ceiling in an attempt to push her tears down. 'I can't even fucking divorce you as we didn't even get married.'

'If you need money – if you need anything, Sabrina. I'm not going anywhere. You still mean the world to me.'

'It's just sad.' Tears started to run down Sabrina's cheeks. 'I'd have done anything for you.'

'I know that.' Dom looked broken. 'I've fucked it properly now, haven't I?'

Sabrina nodded and dragged her case off the bed. She turned at the door. 'Goodbye Dominic. Oh, yeah and just to make you extra happy, a journalist from your paper called Caroline earlier. Thanks to the poison story, they know everything, now.'

'I honestly hadn't heard. So, if that is the case, you must get an exclusive organised. Do it all in your own words.'

'That's what Caroline said.'

The door slammed to Dom shouting. 'If you're not going to listen to me, then listen to your agent!'

Chapter Thirty-Eight

S abrina was sat in Caroline's Putney town house in
her dressing gown. Plonking a couple of expressos
down in front of them, the feisty agent threw a
newspaper towards her and joined her on a high stool
at the kitchen island. The headline of POISON MALONE
HEADS TO *TINSEL TOWN* screamed back at them.
Underneath the headline were three mug shot type
photos of Sabrina in character, Sabrina out of character
with long hair and Sabrina with her new pixie cut and
glasses.

'At least by having your say all the photos of you
are hot.' Caroline took a drag of her vape. 'And they've
got most of the facts right. It was bloody decent of you
not to grass Giselle up for poisoning Lowen.'

'Dom got away lightly, of course.' Sabrina took a
sip of her scalding coffee.

'Dom got away lightly because he orchestrated this
for you.'

'What?' Sabrina's brow furrowed.

'He called the editor and—'

'Of his rival newspaper?'

'Yes, he knew it was happening and he wanted you
to get the most money possible.'

Sabrina sat back in her chair and sighed. 'Shit! All
those papers he could have sold.'

'Yep!'

'He always was a fair man.' Sabrina sounded slight-ly wistful but gave herself a mental shake. *Don't be getting soft on the twat, he was hardly fair in love and war, now, was he? Come on, Sabrina.*

'One hundred and fifty grand in the hand.' Caroline rubbed her hands together. 'Don't say I'm not the best agent in the world, either. I negotiated that for you, you know.'

'How could I forget.' Sabrina laughed. 'And I want you to have half of it.'

'Don't be silly. Twenty per cent on everything as it always has been.' Caroline downed her coffee in one.

'No, I mean it. It'll soften the blow for what's com-ing.' Sabrina screwed up her face.

'Oh my god, you're not going to tell me what I think you are going to tell me.' Caroline reached for her vape.

'I'm so sorry, Caroline but I need to get out of Lon-don, especially now.' She picked up the newspaper and waved it in the air.

'This will all die down again, like it always does.'

'Until the next best scandal, it will.' Sabrina ran her hand through her hair. 'I don't want this life anymore.'

'So, what are you doing? Where are you going. Is Dee putting you up for a while? You surely can't be going to down to the depths of Cornwall to be a cashier again?'

Sabrina laughed.

'I'd rather not say just yet and jinx everything, but I promise to send you a postcard.'

'You'll send me a fucking invite to the opening of that acting school you've been harping on about for so long.'

'You're so bloody blunt.'

'I mean it Sabrina, you're so incredibly talented. Use that talent to your own advantage.'

'Aw, that's one of the nicest thing you've ever said to me.'

'Maybe I should have said it sooner.' The women laughed. 'You've got this. And I don't want a cut of the newspaper money, just make sure you send all the best little prima donnas you create, my way.'

'You strike a hard bargain, Caroline Smart.'

They then looked at each and through laugher, chanted, 'Who wants a soft agent anyway.'

Chapter Thirty-Nine

'Have you seen the article?' Linda Harris greeted Charlie Dillon as he came in for his morning coffee. 'She did a proper interview with the *Hartmouth Echo*, in her own words, it says here. Who'd have thought it.'

'Yes, we appeared to have had an actress in our midst. Let's hope she's happy eh. Looks like she's been through a lot, poor cow and I always liked the girl.'

'You talking about Jilly?' Kara pushed the door open and immediately sat down her hand to her back.

'Yes.' Linda stressed. 'She had us all fooled.'

'Well… maybe just some of us.' Charlie winked.

'You knew and didn't say anything?' Linda's eyes were alive with disbelief. Charlie nudged Kara. 'Erm. Yes, I knew too, Mrs H.'

'Anyway, funny that's the lead story in the *Echo* and not our livelihoods going down the pan.' Charlie sighed. 'Big Frank's started the petition so if you could put your energies into getting as many signatures as possible, rather than sullying everyone's good name, that would be most useful, Linda. Have a good day.'

Kara placed her order from her seat. 'It just can't happen.'

Nigel had joined her at the counter. 'Yes. It will be a sad day if the outdoor market is shut, it really will but we are not going to let this *happen*. It must be stopped.

It will be stopped.'

Gideon appeared behind him. 'Well, it's Victorian Market Day tomorrow and we shall embrace the opportunity. Glanna's made some banners up and we are all going to be protesting. The locals are behind us, and Alicia has got the *Echo* and *South West Today* radio and TV involved too.'

'Ooh that should cause quite a stir, I best put my best blouse on.' Linda Harris pushed her hands under her ample bosoms and waddled back over to the coffee machine.

Kara went back out to her market stall with a bag full of pastries, one of which she shoved into her mouth immediately. Star came and joined her. 'Anyone would think you are eating for three.'

'I just want them out now, Star.'

'Not long now, sis. Was just reading about Jilly. I knew there was something about her. Good on her, I say. Wanting to escape the madness.'

Conor was walking up the hill, his body language showing a man who really didn't care about anything much anymore. 'Hey. Conor.' Star waved him over. 'Look at you, sharing your space with a famous actress. It must be quiet in that flat without her. She was good fun.'

She then clocked his face. 'Oh, God, I know that look... I didn't realise that...'

She put her hand on his, then pulled it away in a strange, exaggerated movement. 'She'll be back. I know she will. She will.'

'Steren, don't come your hocus-pocus with me.' Star was slightly taken aback; it was usually only her mother and her dear aunt who called her by her christened name. 'I'm not stupid. It's been nearly a month now and not a word.'

'Oh, Conor.'

'And I don't want your sympathy either.'

He stormed over to talk to Charlie, leaving Kara and Star making a sympathetic face towards each other.

'Shit, poor bloke.' Kara started to shove her second pastry in.

Star looked to her sister. 'After what happened with me and him, he deserves happiness. He truly does.'

'Conor! You got a sec.' The voice came from behind the Tinsel Town market stall.

'Biff lad, what's up? You got all you need float wise, etcetera for the day?'

'Yeah, but something odd just happened. A woman came in. She was wearing huge dark glasses and one of the beanie hats that we sell in here. She questioned me as to what I was doing here. I just said I was helping you out. She took a box of crackers off the shelf, pulled one out, disappeared for a sec, then gave me this one cracker. I was like, shit, she's nicking the crackers but before I could say anything, and I will repeat her exact words, she said. "When you see Conor Brady, tell him to pull this." Sorry mate, the box can't be sold now.'

With a look of delight on his face, Conor waggled the cracker in the bemused boy's face. 'Pull it, Biff. Quick, pull it.'

A red hat, a *Fickle Fish* and a handwritten note fell to the floor. Conor picked everything up and read the note hungrily.

"*I hope I haven't been too long*", Conor's smile lit up his whole face. 'She bloody read the text I sent her. Good old Oscar Wilde and his musings.'

NICOLA MAY

'What you going on about?' Biff was looking even more bemused as Conor turned the note over and read aloud.

'Meet me at the flat rocks at ten a.m. And bring the fish.'

'The fish?'

'Yeah, the fish.' Biff pointed to the cracker prize.

Conor ran down to the *Happy Hart*.

'Billy mate, I am so sorry doing this to you on a market day, but Jilly's back and I've got to go to her.'

'Well, what are you bloody waiting for, I'll manage.'

Frank was out sweeping his outside area when his grinning nephew shouted across to him.

'She's back! She's on the head.'

'Then, take my motorbike, lad, and ride like the wind.'

Chapter Forty

Conor parked up the motorbike and likening a dragon as his warm breath hit the cold air, he began to run up the cliff path as fast as his legs would carry him. Feeling an exhilaration, the like of which he had never experienced in his life before, he reached the top of Penrigan Head. Sabrina was already there, sitting on one of the flat rocks, swinging her legs like a little girl on a fairground ride. Her hat was pulled down over her ears, her scarf wrapped around her face. She suddenly felt his presence and turned around to face him. He could tell she was smiling just from her beautiful periwinkle blue eyes.

'Hi.' He said casually, putting his helmet down on the floor.

'Hi.' She said as casually back.

And then she jumped down and Conor was swinging her around and hugging her and kissing her nose. He pulled her scarf down. 'If you tell me I can't kiss you now, I'll tickle you into submission, so I will.'

Their kiss was deep and passionate, a whole month's worth of turmoil and missing and wondering, and now realising that all of that was now forgotten, because her heart hadn't let her get lost. It had led her here, to Conor Brady, to someone who truly loved her and to a place where she would always have something to do, something to love and something to hope for.

When they eventually broke free, Conor grabbed her back to him and hugged her tightly. 'Please tell me you are staying down here now and it's not just another holiday.'

'Just a holiday.' Sabrina smirked.

Conor broke free and held her at arm's length. 'Jillian Swift?'

She smiled coyly. 'Well, I told you I had my first holiday romance down here, so I kind of was hoping that this one may be my last.'

'You little…'

Conor brushed her lips with his.

'I have to say that text you sent when I was away in London was bloody hilarious.'

'The "If you're not too long I will wait for you all my life", one you mean?' Conor grinned.

'That's the one.' Sabrina laughed with happiness and anticipation.

'That was our man Oscar Wilde, not me.' Conor kissed her again.

'Damn! He ate the Blarney Stone too, didn't he?'

'He created it.'

They both laughed.

'But now – drum roll, please. We have to see what the *Fickle Fish* says.' Sabrina held her hand out for the cracker prize.

'You're crazy.'

'I'm an actress, I'm allowed to be. Or correction I was an actress.'

'I don't want you to not be happy down here though, my darling girl.'

She removed her gloves and rubbed her hands together to warm them. 'Give me the fish.' She sheltered herself between the rocks and placed the small red thin fish shape on her palm.

'I think you've lost it, so you have.' Conor was now

watching intently.

'It's moving.' Sabrina shrieked. 'Oh no.' Her voice lowered.

'What?'

'Curling sides means I'm fickle.'

'Poco loco, you were right there.' Conor shook his head.

'Phew. Curling sides and heads means passionate.'

'Yes, phew indeed. So can we please get off this fecking freezing cliff and play out what your fish mate is telling you, so.'

They had kissed for so long in the warmth of her car in the cliff car park that the windows and windscreen had completely steamed up. When they eventually broke free, Conor looked over to her and took her hand.

'I can't actually believe you're here.'

'Well believe it, honey. I'm here to stay.'

'I'm so worried I won't be enough for you. I don't have a fancy job or car. I could take you to the VISTA again, though, if you fancied.'

'Stop, those words.' She brushed his lips with hers. 'I love you, Conor Brady. Everything about you. That material world is behind me, now. I want the sea and the sky and the birdsong but most of all, I just want you. You are everything I want and need in human form. And I'm sorry I left you hanging, but being away for this time allowed me to think. I had to go through all the emotions surrounding Dom, surrounding my future career, and of course about my feelings towards you. But whatever I was thinking, or surmising or trying to work out what would be the right thing to do, all of my thoughts kept coming back to you and to Hartmouth. My heart lies here with you and this beautiful setting.' She took one of his hands. 'From the minute I met you, Conor Brady, I felt an inexplicable safety around you. You made me laugh and more importantly you made me lovely dinners. Shit, sorry... I promise to be serious about my emotions from now on.'

'You eejit,' Conor laughed and kissed her forehead.

Sabrina lifted his hand and kissed it. 'You are very different to anyone else I've ever dated and that's a good thing, as I've never felt the way I feel about you about anyone else.' Conor had tears in her eyes as he held Sabrina's hand tighter. 'You really are my Action Man and we all know that actions always speak louder than words. You have literally held me through thick and thin and not given up on me with all my dramatics and uncertainty. And for that I am truly grateful.'

'Aw, you softy. I told you I'd wait. Maybe only for a couple more weeks, though.'

'Oi.' Sabrina laughed and poked him in the ribs.

'I love you, too.' Conor kissed her forehead. 'And I'm so happy you are here. That feeling when I pulled that cracker in Tinsel Town – honestly, I thought my heart was going to burst when I knew you'd come home.'

Releasing his hand, Sabrina blew out a big breath. 'It's been a lot.' She bit her lip.

'It really has.' Conor kissed her nose. 'But I've got your back... and your front... and those tits...' He gently squeezed her right breast. 'Oh Dickens, those glorious tits!'

'Oi, mister.'

'Quick, change the subject.' He put his hand over his groin. 'I read all the newspaper stuff.' Conor blew out a huge breath. 'Well done you.'

'I didn't have a choice, and it wasn't as bad as I thought it would be. My social media is cancelled forever as "Sabrina Swift, actress" from now on. And I didn't ever explain about my name, did I? My mum was Gillian Swift, too. God knows why she wanted us to have the same name. She's Gillian with a G, I'm with a J, as you know – she thought changing the letters would make it easier. I was a born actress and a character called Sabrina was in a TV show I watched as a child. From ten years old I was adamant that everyone called me by that name, and amazingly it just stuck with my friends and family, too.

'Bless mum.' Sabrina sighed. 'She'd love it that I'm so happy now and that I'm using the name, she chose for me.'

'Aw.' Conor softly kissed her on her forehead. 'Jilly Swift is a cool name. I like it.'

'I'm glad. So, when I do set up the acting school down here for kids I can have a whole new persona – but it will be my right and actual one.'

'So, you really are going to do it? That is such amazing news.'

'I need to find premises and work out how to legally set it up, but yes, that's my dream and I'm going to follow it.'

'You don't think you'll be sad or frustrated not acting again?' Conor enquired.

'Well, if that Tinseltown role comes rolling in, then who knows.' They laughed. 'But the joy of teaching my craft and seeing other people go up through the ranks will make me happy, I'm sure. I also don't want to be going off anywhere and leaving you for long lengths of time. A month was long enough.'

'Talking of Tinsel Town?'

'Oh, I definitely want to keep that going until

Christmas, as planned.' Sabrina sniffed. 'Maybe with that young lad's help? He seems such a good bloke.'

'Yes, that's Biff, Nigel's son, straight as a die, that one. I guess you will need finances to back you, for your new venture, so every little helps.' Conor wound the car window down a crack.

'Indeed, but I already have the bulk of those.'

'Oh.'

'Yes, I had some savings already and I was also paid to spill my guts to the papers. To give Dom his due, he gave the story to a rival newspaper, so the fee was amazing. Also, my incredible agent, waived any kind of fee, to give me a leg up.'

'Shit, Dom wasn't all bad then.' Conor sniffed. 'And nice one from your agent, too.'

'I think it was his way of making amends for being such a tosser, and he probably was relieved we didn't get married, or I could have taken him for a fortune. But yes, let's err on the positive that something good came out of it, at least.'

'Grand, grand.'

'That doesn't take away that I'm so grateful you sorted keeping the market stall running. Dee said actions, not words are what really counted. You have done nothing but treat me right, Conor Brady and show me how much you cared. I was blind to your actions initially but that's because I've been blind to real love all my life, I think.'

'Well, thank God you got yourself matched with an Irish angel, now.' They both laughed. Conor put his hand on the car door. 'Now, I must away on that motorbike and when we get home you can show me all of those perfect breasts of yours and not just half of them, like last time.'

'Are you always going to be this cheeky?'

'Oh, yeah.' He got out of the car and pushed his

face through her now open window. 'I won't ever let you regret this.'

Sabrina felt her eyes wash with tears. She nodded. 'I know, you won't.'

Chapter Forty-One

December the twentieth, and the Ferry Lane Market Stallholders Monthly Meeting was in full swing. Frank tapped his coffee mug to stop the noisy chitter chatter that was flying around a festively decorated Monique's. Sabrina was pleased to see her expensive baubles hanging from the ornate light fittings and a holly garland adorning the front window.

'Good morning, everybody.'

A united "Good Morning" flew around the café.

'As this is our last meeting before Christmas, please accept the mince pies with Monique's compliments. I know it's early in the day, but Linda will be bringing out some sherry and mulled wine shortly.'

'Hardly anything to celebrate is there really though, mate,' Charlie Dillon piped up.

'We'll get to that most important issue on the agenda in a minute, old fella, but firstly, I want to read out a message from Brian Todd. 'He says,' Frank reached in his pocket for his reading glasses. 'A big thank you to Jilly.'

Sabrina did a little wave to the table.

Frank looked over his glasses at her like a headmaster. 'A big thank you for taking on his stall and for also sending him the money that Lowen never paid him.' An audible gasp from the table. 'And he looks forward to seeing us all again in the new year.'

'I knew Lowen wouldn't pay up.' Sabrina chipped in.

'So that cost you double?' The butcher sounded shocked.

'Lowen Kellow is one of life's losers, and thankfully I could afford to pay Brian so...'

'Good for you.' Nigel the fishmonger shouted across at her. 'And thanks for employing my lad. He loves working your stall, he does.'

'That was down to Conor, but he's going a great job.' Sabrina stood up. She looked to Frank. 'Can I?' Frank nodded and ushered Mrs Harris to bring out the alcohol. 'I'm sorry I deceived all of you, but I hope you can understand why. Life in the public eye may look like something everyone would like to have, but from my experience, it's not. And by living and working amongst you, I hope I've earnt my Ferry Lane Market stripes without taking anything from you in return.' Frank went to butt in, but it was her turn to quieten him. 'Thank you all, for accepting me for who I was – correction, who I am.' Her voice cracked. 'For liking me as plain old Jilly Dickens. I'm no different to anyone else. It's just everyone else thought I was.' She did a funny little nervous laugh. 'I will be sad to say goodbye to Tinsel Town, but it will be good to meet Brian, he sounds like a decent man. And as for Biff, Nigel,' She nodded towards the fishmonger. 'I'm going to be setting up an acting school for kids, wherever I can find some premises and I'd happily have him help me there, if he still wants a job.'

'Wow, an acting school.' Star smiled. 'My two will be there as soon as they are old enough.'

'So will my four,' Kara piped up. 'Anything to take them off my hands.'

'Grand.' Sabrina grinned.

Frank smiled to himself at his nephew's girl catching on to the Irish lingo. 'And that's not all. I'll do my best to run some shows for charity and make sure that the funds are pumped back into the community.' Everyone was then on their feet, clapping. 'Stop.' Sabrina's face was bright red. 'I don't deserve that. I'm just so happy to be able to call this place my home. I feel so loved and accepted.'

Once everyone had settled down, Frank tapped his sherry glass. 'Now are all your glasses charged?'

'All except mine.' Kara held up her glass of water.

'Because I have actually saved the best until last.' You could have heard a pin drop. Frank held a brown A4 envelope up in the air. 'In this envelope is the result of the council meeting following all of our opposition, the petition and the TV coverage, so beautifully orchestrated by Alicia – thanks, Alicia.' A "here, here", went around the room as Alicia smiled sweetly.

He lifted the envelope higher and began to tear it into little pieces. 'But we don't need this this anymore.'

There was a mumbling and many confused faces around the room. 'Because the outdoor market is here to stay.'

Sabrina didn't think she'd seen so many grown men cry with joy in one space. Even Big Frank had a tear in his eye.

'So, what happened?' Glanna was the first to ask once the hollering and shouting had calmed down.

Sabrina couldn't wait to hear everybody's reaction.

'A company called Gilmon Developments evidently trumped Lowen's company with a huge offer and proposed that the land be used for a Go Cart Track, Cinema and Theatre. All facilities will be tailored for disabled children's needs and have their own self-contained car parks leading directly from the coast road, so there will be no need to disrupt the outdoor market at all. There will be a couple of spare units for rent, so maybe one of those would suit your new venture, Jilly?'

Sabrina put her thumb up, delighted.

'Great for holidaymaker business, so will impact us all positively, too,' Charlie piped up.

'I'm made up.' Nigel downed his sweet sherry.

Ben Clarke slammed his hand down on the table. 'Bloody brilliant!'

On registering the company name and what Frank had just announced, Sabrina suddenly couldn't stop her tears from flowing. Gilmon – Gillian and Simon. Of course! Bless her dad. When she had gone to see him just weeks before, he had promised that he would help her if he could, and help he had. And yes, she had kept so many secrets from these beautiful people already, but this one could just remain hers. For knowing that the results of all her workaholic father's endeavours had led to this, was the biggest gift of love he could ever have given her. Simon would be able to come down with him too and use the facilities, so it really was a win-win situation.

Linda Harris, already two sheets to the wind, lifted her glass and shouted. 'I feel like Ferry Lane hearts are no longer breaking.'

Kara stood up, suddenly looking white. 'Shit! Someone needs to go and get my Billy, because my waters are!'

Epilogue

'Christmas Day tomorrow, I can't believe it.' Sabrina snuggled into Conor's arms as they lay on the sofa in their apartment, a blanket over them. Christmas tunes playing in the background. Lights twinkling from their little tree balanced on the dining room table.

'I wonder how Billy and Kara are getting on.' Conor kissed Sabrina's nose.

'I know, so sweet. Three boys and one girl, now – he's nearly got his five-a-side.

'Maybe we should provide the extra player?' Conor raised his eyebrows questionably.

'I've never loved anyone quite like I love you, so the thought of producing a mini Brady isn't the worst idea in the world.' Sabrina put her finger on his nose. 'But for now, let's just enjoy each other, eh?'

They snuggled closer together.

'I think I prefer Christmas Eve night to Christmas Day, to be honest.' Sabrina sighed contentedly and kissed Conor's neck.

'I love *every* day now that I get to spend it with you.'

'Aw, Conor Brady, I knew you'd eaten that Blarney Stone whole.'

'Oi. You said you were going to be serious.' Conor laughed and kissed her lovingly on the forehead.

'As it's Christmas, yes I am, actually.' Sabrina wiggled herself free and went over to the tree. She handed Conor a small square shaped present from the colourful pile of gifts at its base. 'You can open this one tonight.'

Conor sat up and ripped open the reindeer wrapping paper. Inside was a framed print of a poem in old fashioned writing. The already emotional Irishman put his hand to his heart as he read aloud,

Home is where the heart is
It's where we go to rest
Home is where the heart is
It's where we're loved the best

Tears began to fall down Sabrina's cheeks.
'Welcome home, Conor Brady.'
He jumped up and squeezed her tightly to him.
'Welcome home, Jilly Swift.'

THE END

AUTHORS LOVE FEEDBACK

If you enjoyed your visit down to Ferry Lane Market, it would mean such a lot if you could pop a review up on Amazon for me.

Now go follow YOUR dreams and have a great day.

Love
Nicola
Xx

Also by Nicola May

Welcome to Ferry Lane Market
Starry Skies in Ferry Lane Market
Rainbows End in Ferry Lane Market

The Corner Shop in Cockleberry Bay
Meet Me in Cockleberry Bay
The Gift of Cockleberry Bay
Christmas in Cockleberry Bay

Working it out
Let Love Win

The Hub
Love Me Tinder
The Women of Wimbledon Common
The School Gates
Better Together
Star Fish
Christmas Evie

For more information on Nicola May and her books, please visit
her website at www.nicolamay.com

Printed in Great Britain
by Amazon

38236947R00172